Seed
of
Doubt

by

Robert Milton

ATHANATOS
PUBLISHING GROUP

Seed
of
Doubt

by

Robert Milton

ATHANATOS
PUBLISHING GROUP

Seed of Doubt
  by Robert Milton

ISBN: 978-1-936830-56-5

E-Book ISBN: 978-1-936830-57-2

Book Website: www.seedofdoubt.us

Published by Athanatos Publishing Group
  www.athanatosministries.org

PART ONE

1

Connor Bryce stood immobilized outside of Jansen's doors for a split second. A bead of sweat trickled from his shoulders down his back.

The moment of truth.

Connor gave a slight knock as he pushed the door open and stepped inside. Jansen wasn't alone. His office wasn't huge, but the large windows and bright lighting made it look spacious. He sat behind his desk, a dark ash wood with a cherry red polish. Another man sat in front of the desk, facing Jansen with his back to the double doors. The stranger didn't turn around when Connor entered.

Jansen waved Connor into the office the way he would wave a waiter over to his table. Connor took a seat facing Jansen's desk beside Guy Number Two, who still didn't look his way.

"Bryce, I'll make this brief." Jansen paused as if waiting for a response. He got none and went on. "You've been slacking, Bryce. You're unprepared, unfocused, and what skill you *did* have has vanished. You bring me idiotic ideas targeted toward half of one percent of the population, and you can't even write a decent proposal for that." For months now, Connor had been carefully working on a proposal to develop and manufacture new lines of hiking and camping equipment designed for people with physical handicaps, having been inspired by his paraplegic father-in-law.

Blood flushed Connor's cheeks, "Do we have to do this with others in the room?"

"I will speak to who I want to when I want to; I don't care if there are a million people in the room! Besides, I figured you might want to meet your replacement before you left. Bryce, this is Trace Lasser."

Trace looked at Connor and extended a hand. If Lasser knew how close he'd come to losing that hand, he wouldn't have done it. Connor wanted to rip his arm off and beat both men into oblivion. He was being replaced by a guy named Trace? Humiliating.

"I can rewrite the proposal, and the hiking equipment idea was solid. You said so yourself months ago."

"I said that to get you out of my hair for a few months while I looked for someone else. Don't you see? This has been in the works

1

for a while. You don't fit in with this team, Bryce. This company cannot continue to tread water in these tough times with you dangling from our leg like a ball on a chain." The other gentleman, Trace Lasser, smiled at that comment, watching both men like a long volley in tennis.

"Sir, I have a wife...I haven't had time to look for other opportunities. You can't give me a week to wrap things up? What am I supposed to do?"

"Not. My. Problem."

The words stung.

"Trace will be starting in the morning. Your old desk is now his new one."

"You can leave the picture of your wife though," Lasser said. "She brightens up the place."

Connor stood and took a step toward Lasser's chair, "If you ever say something like that to me again, I'll—"

"You'll what?" said Jansen. "You'll do nothing. As of now, you don't work here anymore, so I'll say this one last time. Get out."

"This isn't right. It can't happen like this," Connor pleaded.

Jansen picked up the phone, "Yes....get me security please."

"Forget it," Connor snapped, "I'm leaving, but this isn't over."

With those words, Connor walked out of the office and quickly down the hall to the restroom, his shirt now sticking to the moisture on his back and chest. He splashed cold water on his face as he tried to catch his breath, all the while replaying the last few minutes of conversation. Just like that, his life had changed. It's amazing how quick a man can go from success to failure.

Moment of truth....no thanks.

* * *

The drive home was long, as rush hour in Baltimore was unforgiving. Connor looked at the small box of belongings in the passenger seat. The honeymoon picture of him and Kelly lay on the top of the pile, staring back at him as he drove. Tears quickly filled his eyes. Years of deadlines and overtime and he had nothing to show for it but a call to security and a box of memories. Finally he turned into the driveway.

He tried to pull himself together before he went inside. He had to be strong, or at least give the impression that he was strong. A husband needs his family to know that they'll be provided for; showing weakness and panic in troublesome times would have the opposite effect. Kelly Bryce met him in the kitchen. The smell of roast and herbs filled the two-storied house. He'd told her the events of his day on his drive home, but she wasn't aware of how exhausted he was until she saw his face. His eyes wore defeat; his skin looked haggard. This would take some time to recover from.

He hugged her tight and then pulled up a chair at the kitchen table.

"I just don't understand where things went wrong. If he hates the idea...then fine. If he hates my proposal...fine. But something tells me it's more than that. He had this planned for a while. It had to have taken him a month or two to find someone else; all the while I'm busting my butt to write one heck of a good proposal. Then today he drops me like a rock. This is not the way a fortune-500 company does business. It doesn't add up."

Kelly hesitated a moment as she pushed back a few rebellious strands of hair dangling over her forehead. She was intent on letting her broken husband vent for as long as needed before she spoke. She was crushed for him; her knight in rusty armor.

Connor had been the definition of a hard-working man and honest husband. He deserved better than this. It'd been in both of their minds that he might have Jansen's job one day, and though they had spoke about it once a year or so ago, they'd mutually decided not to talk about it until after the outdoor equipment idea was pitched. Now flames danced around that dream like so many others.

Kelly searched her mind for a cure that didn't exist. She walked behind him and began to rub his shoulders, kneading the knots in his muscles.

"I'm so sorry. I don't know what to say. Maybe the board of directors will overrule him. Doesn't he need approval before firing you just like that? Maybe he will come back with some left-field explanation of what went wrong. Maybe Jansen will admit his mistake and apologize for exaggerating everything."

He wasn't exaggerating of course. Men like Jansen didn't exaggerate. They were precise. Exact. If he said he wanted an outline of a project in five thousand words, it better be five thousand words on the dot, even if the author had to go back and add or subtract "and's" and "if's" to ensure an accurate word count. Connor knew this, but to not dishearten his supportive wife, he agreed with her.

Only after a hot meal and a hotter shower did he finally begin to unwind, though more for Kelly's sake than his own. She was crushed

3

for him; he had to remain composed...as if he would simply bounce back tomorrow with another great job. They lay in bed, side by side, both staring deeply into the pages of their individual books. Kelly, avid plant lover and owner of her own greenhouse and flower shop, was learning the correct way to grow healthy bonsai trees in different humidity's. She decided it was best not to keep talking on the subject unless Connor brought it up. He hadn't in about an hour.

Connor preferred to escape reality, and most nights would lose himself in the latest Ken Follett spy novel. Tonight however, he stared at the open page in front of him, not reading a word, fighting feelings of anger and despair as he reflected upon his most recent turn of events. Jansen was an idiot. What in the world did he know about camping or hiking equipment? This was a multi-million dollar idea; no other competitor that Connor knew of had even thought to reach out to a large population of people with physical handicaps and develop equipment that made their hobbies easier to enjoy.

The phone rang by the nightstand. Connor picked up the receiver quickly, not wanting to disturb his bride who had already fallen asleep.

It was one of Connor's co-workers. Former co-workers.

"Connor, its Brantley. Hope I didn't wake you?"

"You didn't. Can't sleep much right now anyway."

"Yeah I heard. I'm sorry about that. That's kind of the reason I'm calling. I heard how things went down, and I don't like it. But there's more. I had to work late tonight to finish some corrections on a few design flaws from our last recall. Anyway, I just overheard a conversation going on down the hall. That new guy...Trace Lasser...it was him and Jansen. I heard Jansen tell him to start production in the morning. Production of a new line of outdoor equipment for the physically challenged."

"That's my idea!"

"Exactly. I don't know what's going on, but I know what I heard. Jansen and Lasser just stole your plans."

"And my career." Connor flushed with rage, then calmed. "I'm going to rip him apart. Brantley, thanks for the call. I'll deal with this in the morning."

"No problem buddy. Hey, don't do anything stupid. Maybe you should call your lawyer first?"

"Oh I won't do anything stupid. I just want to talk to Jansen man-to-man for a few seconds before I slap a lawsuit on him."

Connor lay in bed an hour after that phone call as anger surged through his veins. Anger birthed its vile cousin rage, and rage bred

4

hatred. *I just want to punch that man right in his crooked eyes. I could run this company backwards better than he can forwards,* Connor thought. He turned his lamp off and continued to rant in his head. Soon the thought of blackening Jansen's eye wasn't enough.

Connor's hatred craved more gruesome scenarios; shredded tendons as horses pulled Jansen in opposite directions, bones popping as he screamed in pain. Fiery crashes with the evil boss stuck inside, pinned against the steering wheel, flesh slowly dripping like wax off a candle. Bank vaults falling randomly out of the sky onto Jansen's car as a crowd gathers around to laugh at the old man laying flat as a pancake inside.

But even that would be too unjust...too swift of a punishment. Men like Jansen deserved much worse. Connor began to relish the thought of his boss dying in pain due to a slow-moving, incurable cancer. He smiled as he pictured cancer cells overtaking healthy ones in Jansen's body; muscles weak, organs failing...loss of bladder control. Or better yet a parasitic infection that caused Tourette's or dementia or leprosy. These were the only forms of punishment that would be suitable for men like Gregory Jansen.

Then another thought hit Connor, and the corners of his lips twitched into a treacherous smirk. A perfect punishment.

Jansen should burn in Hell.

2

Connor woke lazily from his coma the next morning. It'd been a while since he'd slept that well. The events of the previous day seemed surreal, and he quickly decided not to pour over every painful detail. He staggered down stairs and joined Kelly at the table for breakfast. Her hair was messy and she wore a pale green robe lightly cinched around her waist. These were the moments when she looked her best, Connor thought. Since their son Sammy had left for college, Connor and Kelly had a little more time to themselves; time to study each other more, pay attention with greater detail, the way they had when they'd first met.

"How you feeling this morning?" Kelly asked.

"Better. I slept like a baby."

"Good, I was hoping you would."

They ate grapefruit and toast, then Kelly said, "You know, I was thinking, maybe we should go on a vacation...you and I, take advantage of our empty nest. I can leave the shop to Hazel for a few days. We could go down to the Florida Keys, get away in the Smokies, head north to Maine, west to Cali...anywhere you want to go. Let's just rest and relax, get away from all this work chaos. What do you think?"

Work? Chaos?

The fog quickly lifted—the phone call from Brantley last night. Jansen and Lasser stole his idea and his job in one fell swoop. He'd completely forgotten about that, even now the conversation bordered between real and fake. Kelly had no idea, but she knew the look on his face.

"What? What is it? What did I say?"

Connor told her the conversation he'd had with Brantley. The snake Jansen stole his idea, fired him, hired some other chucklehead for less money, and there was nothing Connor could do about it. Well, almost nothing. He told Kelly he was going to handle it today. He'd hire a lawyer to get back what was rightfully his—either his job or compensation.

But first, Connor decided to go to the office and talk to Jansen face to face. He knew he wouldn't punch the guy...not on company property. Connor just wanted some answers. Why the deceit, why the shadiness? Kelly opposed her husband going back to the office without a lawyer; she would have barricaded the door had she guessed his true intentions. Thankfully she had no clue. Connor told her he was going back to talk to the Human Resources manager, Gwenda, because he needed his personnel file and 401k information. She finally agreed that was a good idea.

He showered, dressed, and was soon out the door and on his way. Connor parked his car in his usual spot, turned it off, and sat there silently trying to collect his thoughts. Moment of truth. The only wish he offered skyward was to not break Jansen's nose. He got out of his car and shut the door. A cool breeze hit him in the face, carrying with it the aroma of the Baltimore sewer system. Sirens blared in the background from miles away, a typical soundtrack to city life. Connor took a deep breath and entered the building.

The first person he saw was Trace Lasser, the new Connor. Lasser had terror in his eyes as the real Connor walked up to him. "Where's Jansen?" were the only words Connor Bryce spoke. His beef wasn't entirely with Lasser, and he certainly didn't want to break *his* nose.

Lasser tried to make his voice deeper, "Hasn't shown up yet. Is there something I can do for you?"

Connor looked the man up and down, "Doubt it."

He walked past Lasser and continued down the hall, Lasser quickly on his heels. "Bryce, I don't want any trouble. You're not even supposed to be here. This is restricted to employees only."

Connor spun around quickly. "First, don't call me Bryce. You had your chance yesterday to introduce yourself like a man, but you sat and smiled while I got kicked in the gut. Second, my employment here might not be officially over, and third, I'm not going anywhere until I talk to Mr. Jansen. So you can either go start production on *my* project or you can get me some coffee. I like it black."

The men stared at each other for a few seconds, the taller Connor looking down at Trace. Lasser showed no sign of emotion at being called out about stealing Connor's work. No surprise there; Trace had waved good-bye to ethics years ago.

Lasser backed down; men like him usually did. "I have work to do," he said. Connor held his gaze. Lasser turned around and walked back down the hall. Connor needed to find Brantley, his only apparent ally. He walked directly to Brantley's office and poked his head in to find an empty room. At the end of the hallway to the left was a walkway that led to the production and assembly warehouse. Connor walked down the hall, across the walkway, and into the warehouse.

Then he saw it with his own eyes.

Men and women stationed every twenty feet apart putting pieces together from an electric conveyor belt that divided the room. Smaller countertops around the perimeter of the room were full of employees making sketches, comparing notes, and processing data on numerous laptops. Production was fully underway.

A closer look revealed what Connor had dubbed the EasyLimb. This was a mechanical set of canes that strapped to a person's forearm, meant to aid and give support to hikers that couldn't put a lot of weight on their feet. Made from spring-loaded titanium poles with rubber-tread bottoms, this device would make the casual hike for many physically challenged outdoor lovers much easier and enjoyable. It was Connor's first idea in the equipment line many moons ago. And now it was being built behind his back. He felt rage build inside again, then turned and began a march directly to Jansen's office. Connor would wait for the old snake right there in his lair. Imagine

7

the look on Jansen's face when he walked into his own office and Connor was sitting in *his* chair.

Halfway down the hall he heard crying, high-pitched and hysterical. That had to be the Myra, the receptionist, in another one of her dramatic fits. She hung up the phone and put her hands in her face. Connor cleared his throat to get her attention. She looked up, surprised to see him, and sobbed some more, making no attempt to clear her face of the snot running down onto the ledge of her upper lip. Finally she dried up enough to speak.

"What are you doing here? Did you come here to laugh?"

"Laugh at what? I came here to meet Mr. Jansen. I want to speak with him for a few minutes before I proceed with other actions."

Myra began to cry again, as the sound of her blowing her nose echoed through the small hallway. She looked up with red, judgmental eyes.

"I just got off the phone with his wife. Mr. Jansen is dead."

* * *

The taller one struck a match and brought it to the end of his cigar, puffed the cigar to life, then waved the match to its death. His name was Presley. Presley had been a cop since the Carter administration, maybe before; he'd lost track. He couldn't remember *not* being a cop. Presley stood six-foot-seven, had sideburns down to his chin, and was, in his younger days, a hunk of burnin' love with the ladies. However, Presley was also African-American, and if the King of Rock-n-Roll was anything, he wasn't black. Presley took some photographs, then handed the camera back to Suarez.

"What do you make of it, Pres?"

Presley stared at the wall, as if he were counting the blue flowers in the faded yellow wallpaper. "Not much. Suicide to me, but we'll see. There's a bottle of sleeping pills there on his nightstand. I'm guessing his blood work will come back full of meds. Get Lisa to dust the bottle for prints all the same. You interview the wife?"

"Yes, she's pretty distraught. Told me everything was going fine; been married thirty-nine years. No secrets at this point. I'll wait till she calms down a little more and then try again. Meanwhile I'll review the bank records and recent phone calls. Standard operating procedure."

Presley took his gaze off the wallpaper and shifted it to Suarez. "I've seen a hundred suicide's...nothing's standard. There's a reason this guy wanted out."

Tyrone Presley had seen his share of overdoses. He'd worked the acid-tripping 70's, the cocaine-snorting 80's, the heroine-crazed 90's, and the meth-addicted 2000's. He'd been scared to see what fancy drug awaited each new decade. With each chemical invention came new deaths, either by accident or on purpose—the drugs didn't care. They would fly down, tingle the senses, offer new life, fast rides, immortal living; they would steal sons and daughters, rich and poor, black and white, old and young. And in Presley's experience, the end was almost always the same—some poor son, some poor daughter, zipped up in a black bag with a tag on their big toe. Nothing standard about that.

One time in '83, he worked a case down in Miami where a nine year-old boy was found dead behind a seafood restaurant. Turns out, his father was the ring leader of a service that sold children to Columbian and Argentinean drug lords for extra shipments of Devil's Dandruff, or "C," a new cocaine that had recently hit the market. The man was supposed to make the exchange of children-for-drugs every other month at a specified marina in the Florida Keys. The users who were sold on the stuff would sell life and limb for an extra taste of "C," and as necessity breeds invention, it soon seemed a wise idea to barter with the dealers, children for drugs. The kids would then be sold by the dealers into some Russian or Turkish slave trade, whoever paid more at the time. The original parents had no idea what was happening to their children, but at that point they didn't care. Out of sight, out of mind—into ecstasy.

Apparently, one day the boy's father and ringleader of the scheme decided he wanted to bid the Argentinean drug lords against the Columbian drug lords. He tried to auction between both sides back and forth in an attempt to drive the price up so he could take a larger cut of the "C" shipment. The man hadn't learned rule number one, and that was to never manipulate drug lords. In return for his greed and dishonesty, either the Argentineans or Columbians (no one ever figured out who) put a bullet through the head of his nine year-old son, execution style. The father was never seen or heard from again, and it was assumed that after learning about the death of his son, the dealers finished the job and sent him to the bottom of the Atlantic.

That's what drugs do to people. Ugly. It was enough to make Presley leave Miami and almost enough to make him turn in his badge. This case seemed to be completely opposite. An older businessman, married, rich, comfortable, healthy…an empty bottle of pills by the nightstand. No note to his wife. It didn't make sense, but again, suicide rarely did.

Another officer came into the room. Presley sized him up in a split second. He wore a freshly pressed black uniform, neatly shaven, shiny gold badge, .38 on his side...he was even wearing his hat. Couldn't have been more than 21, probably straight out of the academy.

"Sir, there's something you need to see outside."

Presley raised an eyebrow, "Is there now? Well then, I'm right behind you, officer." He admired fresh enthusiasm, even envied it. Soon the toils and troubles and ugliness of the human race would zap that poor man's spirit and turn his pretty gold badge a dark, rusty brown.

He followed the young officer out of the bedroom and down the stairs, then outside to the back porch. The officer guided Presley between the flower garden and the porch rail, then without speaking, pointed between two rose bushes. There they were, plain as day, shoe prints.

Pres spoke up, "How fresh are these prints, son?"

"I talked to Mrs. Jansen, she just put a new layer of top soil down yesterday afternoon, so it seems it's been walked on since then."

"So it does seem. And what size shoe did Mr. Jansen wear?"

"Ten, sir."

"And these prints?"

"Appear to be a twelve, sir."

"What's your name Sergeant?"

"Hudson sir, Eli Hudson."

"Good work, Hudson. Write this up in your report, take pictures, and collect every pair of shoes on this block. We have to match that tread pattern."

"Yes sir."

Presley's partner Suarez came around the corner. Now Suarez was an interesting sort. He was from somewhere in California...San Francisco, San Diego, San Bernardino, San Juan; Presley never remembered details like that. Unimportant. But what was important was Suarez's instinct. In Presley's experience, most Californians, whether by stereotype or reality, seemed a little too relaxed, impervious to anything out of the ordinary. However, Miguel Rodrigo Suarez had the instinct of a fighter pilot and could sniff out a trail if it led underwater.

He was somewhat short, although most men were short compared to Presley, but unlike Pres, Suarez was stout. No family, no pets, he spent what little free time he had playing soccer with kids at the Boys and Girls Club and lifting weights in his two bedroom apartment. The two were opposites, but most good partners were.

"I tried to talk to Mrs. Jansen again. She's a little calmer now but is going to stay with her sister until after the funeral. I told her we're going to need her at the station for an hour or two, but then she could go wherever she wanted."

"Fine by me," Presley said. "Hey, have you seen these prints?"

"I just heard someone talking about them a minute ago, came to see them for myself. Could it be our deceased?"

"Unlikely. The shoe size is at least two sizes larger than any shoe in that house."

"I talked to Lisa and she said we can expect fingerprints back from that pill bottle within twenty-four hours. Until then I'll keep this away from Mrs. Jansen."

"Good idea."

"So...it might not be suicide?"

Pres took a drag from his stubbed cigar, and then slowly exhaled into the stifling summer air. He looked down at the prints in the soil.

"Doesn't look like it."

3

Dinner that night was special; seared tuna with mango salsa over a bed of steamed rice, boiled asparagus, and buttered rolls, washed down with a white wine Chardonnay. Annika Mims, gourmet chef, brought her talents home and surprised her husband for their fourth wedding anniversary. Just yesterday it seemed they were walking down the aisle, tonight they sat side-by-side sipping bubbles and feeding each other red velvet cupcakes. Their relationship read like a fairy tale from the very beginning.

John Mims earned his engineering degree from New Mexico State University, home of the Aggies. Four months and a thousand applications later, he'd landed a well paying job in Ahwatukee, a nice suburb southeast of downtown Phoenix. One rainy night after working late on some civil drawings, he'd witnessed a horrible accident on his commute home.

11

Just before John crossed the bridge over the Salt River, an 18-wheeler on the opposite side of the road had hit a nasty puddle, which caused him to hydroplane. The truck's tires lost contact with the road, and began to move sideways instead of forward. The driver over compensated, causing the truck to jack-knife, overturn and skid across the median into oncoming traffic, sending its steel pipe cargo barreling down the road like rolling pins.

John saw it all unfold a half-mile in front of him in what seemed like slow motion. Cars and trucks swerved left and right, some braking, others accelerating, all with the hope of dodging the big rig and its pipes. One car in particular, a white Saab, was directly in the path of the skidding truck. The Saab driver cut hard right and punched the gas at the last possible moment, but the truck still barely clipped its end, pushing it into a tailspin. The car hit the shoulder at an awkward angle, flew high onto two wheels, then rolled numerous times down the bank and splashed into the river.

The rain poured down.

Suddenly everything was still. The big rig had come to a halt. Most of the pipes had barreled into the woods, taking down trees with them. The other vehicles had come to a complete stop. The smell of burnt rubber hung in the air. Everyone simply froze, unsure of what to do next. Without much thought, John threw his car into gear and quickly zigzagged his way through the chaos and confusion toward the bank of the river. The top of the submerged car was barely visible now, as water poured in through the smashed rear window.

John rushed out of his car and within seconds found himself waist deep in the muddy water. What in the world was he doing? Without thinking, he took as much air as he could into his chest, then sunk down into the water. He was blind in the belly of the brown river and had to rely on his sense of touch as he frantically grasped for anything that resembled a door handle. Within moments, he found the handle and pulled up while his lungs burned in his chest. The door opened slowly against the pressure of the water, but John wasted no time in finding the seatbelt. He detached the seatbelt from its lock, wrapped his arms around a lifeless form, and pulled the driver from the car. John burst to the surface of the water and relished an immediate breath of fresh air.

He pulled the driver onto the bank and laid her on her back. It was a young woman. Her eyes were closed and she sported a nasty gash from her left temple down to her bloodied ear. At that point, others had arrived on the muddy bank. John shouted orders to different people; call 911, don't overcrowd her, start CPR. He had to go back in the water. He didn't know how many people were in the white Saab; for all he knew there could have been three kids in the back seat. Perhaps he should have checked there first.

His second dive found the rest of the car empty; even so he dove a third time just to make sure. Nothing there. As he exited the water the final time he was informed that the woman had revived. He'd found her sitting against a tree with a rag to her head, shivering under some dry blankets. Within minutes paramedics arrived, and John asked if it would be okay for him to follow them to the hospital. Permission was granted.

Her name was Annika, and he had saved her. And so began his fairytale. The accident had happened almost six and a half years ago; now they sat in front of their fireplace and reflected on four wonderful years of marriage. Annika owned one of the highest reviewed catering businesses in all of Phoenix, preparing meals for everyone from the governor to star athletes. John was a senior civil engineer for a large contracting company, and worked mostly from his studio in the lower level of their three-storied house.

Life was good, dinner grand, and Annika gorgeous. She had a certain twinkle in her eye that John had only seen on a few prior occasions. With their bellies full, they took their champagne glasses to the mini-pool on the back deck and cooled off from the hot Phoenix night. John had planned this in advance, and earlier that day had hid Annika's present under the skirt of their gas grill. He got out and retrieved the present, which was shaped like a box of crayons. He slowly waded back in the pool and smiled. The setting was perfect; the stars were bright and the full moon acted as a spotlight on Annika's face.

"I hope you like it," was all John said as he handed her the gift.

She unwrapped it slowly and tugged at the corners of the box. Finally she opened it and pulled out a sapphire necklace outlined in small diamonds. The stunning blue rocks reflected on the water and caused a rich, azure glow to dance lightly on the surface. Her lips curved, almost touching her teardrop eyes.

"It's...beautiful. Thank you so much. I love you."

"I love you too."

"Now I have something for you."

John smiled.

Annika walked up the pool steps and into the bathhouse, moving slowly, knowing her husband was watching her walk. He was. She moved gracefully in and out of the moonbeams as drops of water slid to the ground around her. When she walked out of the bathhouse, she had a golf bag full of clubs slung over her shoulder. John stared at his wife, who now stood in front of him wearing a bikini and holding golf clubs.

"No way," John mustered.

"Yes way, and there's more." She threw him a set of keys, which he snatched out of the air. "These are for your new golf cart. It'll be delivered tomorrow."

"No way! Annika I don't know what to say? Thank you so much. Say you'll play a round with me this Saturday, help me break 'em in?"

She smiled, "Done."

"I can't believe you got me clubs and a cart...this is too much."

"Not enough for the man of my dreams. Now I suggest we go inside, I'm not done with your present yet."

He smiled, "Done."

Annika played some Sinatra in the bathhouse as they showered off and toweled dry. She had been nervous about this particular moment for the last few weeks. She blocked all potential negative responses from her mind and tried to remain halfway confident. She walked over to John, who sat in a large deck chair built for two, and snuggled up next to him.

"You're very sweet for that, babe, thanks so much. You always seem to know what's on my wish list."

"Just don't drive your cart into a pond, sound good?"

"Fair enough. Now, about my other present," John said with a wink.

Annika smiled and remained calm.

"Well, I have something I want to tell you. It's a present for you, but also a present for me, if you'll accept?"

He looked perplexed. She continued.

"We're both successful with our careers, have put a little money back into savings, and are in very comfortable and stable positions right now."

John took her hand, "Annika, just tell me what's on your mind. No need to talk in abstract generalities."

She squeezed his hand, "I want to have a baby."

A heavy knot formed in John's stomach, and he sat back without a response.

* * *

The next morning, Presley and Suarez wasted little time. The first place to get answers was the one place Jansen spent most of his time: his office. They were there waiting patiently in the parking lot when Myra the receptionist arrived and unlocked the doors. Trace Lasser made the decision the day before to continue work, noting that Jansen would have wanted production to continue.

Presley had stayed up late into the night reflecting on the details of the case. Something wasn't right. It was those shoe prints. He called Suarez at two in the morning. He was awake as well. Pres brought over some late night tacos and the two discussed different theories until the sun came up. Why would a successful man with tons of money and a loving wife kill himself? If he didn't commit suicide, who killed him and why? What about the shoe prints? Were they old prints and perhaps the wife had been mistaken? Did they belong to the neighbor, or the termite guy; did a kid throw a shoe into the garden and then retrieve it? Suarez had no clue; Pres didn't either.

To make things even more interesting, the fingerprints on the pill bottle weren't Jansen's. No records of the prints were in the police database, meaning the murderer, if there was one, didn't have prior convictions. Earlier the night before, Presley had all employee personnel files sent to the lab, which included pre-employment drug tests and all employee fingerprints on file; which they'd kept in case of an emergency. The results were expected soon.

Myra might have some answers; Presley doubted it.

Presley and Suarez talked to Myra in the foyer while other employees slowly trickled in. Actually, it was Pres and Suarez listening to Myra for what seemed like an eternity as she worked herself up into tears at every mere thought of Mr. Jansen. Soon they realized they should give up on her for now and talk to someone less dramatic. They asked to speak to Trace Lasser, as he was the one that seemed to be calling the shots now. Myra obliged and led them to wait for Lasser in Jansen's old office. Just the sight of his desk had her in tears again.

While waiting for Trace, the two cops took a mental inventory of everything in the office; the computer on Jansen's desk—that might be useful; the 55-gallon saltwater aquarium—probably not. A putter and a few golf balls along the wall in the corner, the fern plant by the window, the shelves of books which had probably never been read;

15

some of these might be useful, some not. It was always some miniscule detail in cases like this.

Trace Lasser came in the room moments later. After a few short minutes of questions, it was clear to Presley that Lasser would be of little help. For starters, he had only been working there for two or three days. He barely even knew the names of any other employees. Secondly, he wouldn't shut up about his new line of outdoor equipment being manufactured right down the hall. And finally, the man showed little remorse that Jansen had lost his life, almost like he hadn't even found out yet.

The three men left the office and walked down the hall towards the production warehouse. Lasser was eager to show off his latest technology. Brantley, manager of the Recall Division, called Lasser from down the hall.

"Mr. Lasser," Brantley caught up with the group and handed Lasser a folder.

"Sorry to interrupt, but here are the updated consumer reports you wanted this morning. I've been looking over the returns due to defects, and I believe we can change some things based on our current prototype..."

Lasser held up a hand to cut him off, tired of the babble.

"Sorry, I don't really have time for this. These are detectives, and I was just showing them around, so if you don't mind...just come back later." Brantley looked embarrassed; he had no idea he'd interrupted police work. He turned to go.

Suarez spoke up, "Actually, we'd like for him to join us. Probably need to ask him some questions too."

The men gave a round of introductions as they walked.

Presley said, "So, Mr. Brantley, how long have you worked here?"

"Thirteen years this November. Thought it would be good to move closer to my family, they live up in Philly."

"I'm not sure moving closer to family is ever a good idea."

"I think my wife might agree with you."

Brantley let out a small, awkward chuckle that he tried to cover up with a fake cough when no one else smiled. The men continued to walk down the hall, asking routine questions about Jansen and the nature of his work and who was responsible for what and blah, blah, blah. Suddenly Presley stopped.

Footprints on the carpet. Dried dirt. He turned toward Lasser. "How often is this office cleaned?" Lasser, being new, had no clue.

16

Brantley piped in, "Every Tuesday. Late at night we have a crew that comes in and cleans."

"So these prints are fresh?"

Lasser seized control again, "Yes sir, I imagine so."

Presley looked at Suarez. He was onto something. "Call forensics and tell them to get down here. No one allowed in this hallway the rest of the day." He looked at Lasser, "Understood?"

"Yes sir."

Before Suarez could call forensics his phone rang; he stepped out of earshot. Presley studied the prints. From the naked eye, they looked like the same prints from Mrs. Jansen's garden yesterday. Of course it was impossible to tell until soil tests were run and the treads were matched. If that happened, it would be Christmas. One gift-wrapped murderer. The suspect was sloppy…maybe he wanted to get caught. A question popped into Presley's mind as he looked at Lasser's feet.

"Mr. Lasser, what size shoe do you wear?"

Lasser looked uncomfortable. "Twelve."

Same as the garden.

"And you Mr. Brantley?"

"Eleven and half in tennis shoes, eleven in dress shoes."

"I'm going to have police officers meet you at your homes in thirty minutes. You are to give them every pair of shoes both of you own; everything from cowboy boots to flip-flops. Is that understood? I can get a warrant if needed."

"Are we in trouble?" Lasser asked.

"You won't be if you do what I ask. No one is in trouble. I'm just trying to cover all my bases, I expect your cooperation."

"Yes sir," said Brantley.

"Yes sir," said Lasser.

Suarez came back into the fold, looking excited. He pulled Presley a few steps to the side. "Lab just called, they have a partial thumbprint match from one of those employee files you sent over last night. Matches the pill bottle 97%. Connor Bryce. Worked here up until yesterday, then he was let go."

"Let go by who?" Presley said.

"Jansen."

"Looks like we need to pay Mr. Bryce a visit. You gotta address?"

"Right here."

The men excused themselves, and then left the building in a hurry.

Brantley overheard the whole conversation.

So did Lasser.

4

John Mims had not been entirely truthful with his wife Annika. There had never been any need to. When they'd begun dating, it didn't take long for him to figure out that she was the girl for him. As is usually the case, the couple had a million things in common, and the few differences they did have were cause for laughter and playful disagreements. Something he found incredibly attractive about Annika at the time was her drive to succeed in her profession. She was career-oriented, ambitious, and highly self-motivated. He was the same way; a true go-getter that would not stop until he had captured the horizon. Looking back now, he was proud of the fact that they had both accomplished their dreams and were barely in their mid-thirties.

But Annika told him something else when they were dating that sealed the deal in his mind; she did not want to have children. An important topic such as this is usually discussed in serious relationships, and many couples choose not to have children. No problem there. John didn't want children either, and one of his "future wife" requirements was to find a woman that shared his desire. Obviously problems would arise if he fell in love with a girl that was dead set on having children. Yet secretly, it's not that John didn't *want* to have kids…he couldn't.

When John was 16, he was diagnosed with a Rhabdomyosarcoma, a form of prostate cancer that, in extreme cases, is found in teenagers. The cancer was caught at an early stage, and with the help of radiation and chemotherapy, John was cancer free less than a year later. The problem came with the radiation. In killing the cancer cells, it also killed his ability to reproduce. The prostate gland is in close proximity to the male sex organs. In a rare event, the radiation permanently damaged John's testicular glands and its ability to produce sperm. At the age of 17, doctor's told John he would never have children.

It's hard for teenagers to understand the full magnitude of news like that. John's reaction was typical. At first, he was indifferent. Having a family seemed decades in the future, a million miles away from the present. But as he matured, he felt the full weight of his loss. Soon his apathy turned into depression. It became difficult to

18

watch fathers with their children at ball games. It was heart breaking in college to get involved in serious dating relationships, knowing at some point he would have to tell his girlfriend that he was unable to make all of their future dreams come true.

Slowly he turned bitter towards family all together and decided to throw all of his effort into his career. He would become an engineer, earn an incredible living, and cherish the bachelor life. Any woman he would ever settle down with, if he ever settled down, would have to be on his same page—the no-kids page.

Then there was the accident and Annika. She hadn't wanted kids either. She'd told John she simply didn't have the desire to ever be called "mommy." She liked kids, as long as they belonged to other people. John told her about his cancer as a teenager, but he didn't tell her he could not reproduce. Since she'd never wanted to have children, why bring the humiliation upon himself? And so they made an agreement—they would not have children.

Now it seemed he was in quite the pickle. A pickle he couldn't win. He could stick to his guns and tell Annika flat out that he didn't want children. He could remind her of their decision together many years ago to not start a family. He could tell her it wasn't fair that she changed her mind now. This would save him shame and self-emasculation. But it's not what he wanted. He wanted to tell Annika yes, of course—he would love to start a family with her. Boys, girls, twins, triplets…it didn't matter. He yearned to make her dreams come true, to give her a daughter to dress in pinks and yellows and flowers and lace; a boy to bandage scraped knees and build cardboard forts with. But he couldn't. He never would. He had no choice but to tell her the truth—the truth that was sure to break her heart.

She took the news…gracefully. After their dinner and gift exchange the previous night, Annika had told John that she'd wanted to have a baby. He sat back in his chair and felt ill. He'd always known deep down that she might change her mind some day. And she was allowed to; people can change their minds. He'd just never known how he would react to it. He'd quickly gone over the options in his mind as she waited for a response. Her eyes held optimism and hope.

When he told her the truth about his past, she was crushed—for him. She'd never known the pain and hurt his secret had caused; the emotional toll it had taken on him all these years. Although the dishonesty was rightfully hurtful, she'd understood why he had never told her the truth. Now she'd forced him to relive the humiliation of baring his secret. They'd cried in each other's arm for almost half an hour. Finally, when they could both manage to speak, they had mutually agreed to go visit a fertility clinic first thing the next morning.

That morning was now. They drove to the clinic holding hands, both thinking optimistically about the outcome. Who knew what the human body was capable of? Medical science had improved by leaps and bounds in the last decade. Perhaps there was a way now to make things work. In truth, he was simply happy to have Annika there with him. His entire life he'd faced this challenge without a single person to talk to. There were his parents, who were great and loving and kind and supportive…but who wanted to discuss that kind of problem with their parents?

The waiting, of course, was the hardest part. Annika planted herself in the lobby while John was in the exam room. Half an hour, later he exited the side door and took a seat next to his wife.

"Nothing to it," he said.

"What now?"

"Now we wait another half hour while they read the test results. Doctor said he would call me back when they're done. Told me to try to come out here and relax. Why am I so nervous?"

She took his hand. "I am too. But remember what he told us over the phone. If the news isn't good today, there are still a lot of options for us. This is just step one, just a baseline to see where we're at. I love you either way. Not the end of the world, agreed?"

"Agreed," John said, trying to convince himself he meant it.

He took a deep breath and looked around the crowded room. He studied the faces of the other men waiting in the lobby, most sitting by their spouse. Their faces wore failure, shame, embarrassment, defeat, and worst of all…pessimism. He'd known those feelings.

It used to be a largely held belief that all problems of infertility were due to issues with the female. This stance was widely accepted for many reasons. One, it was the females who gave birth, and if they couldn't get pregnant, surely they must be the problem. Two, for the longest time only males were doctors. There is nothing more fragile than the male ego. Male doctors had never heard of a man not being able to reproduce. Scientifically and egotistically, in their minds it simply wasn't possible. Third, in olden times, a man's family said everything about him. There was no greater shame for a man, especially hundreds of years ago, to not have the ability to reproduce.

It showed weakness. A man with no children was a man that had no help to work his fields, no help to thatch roofs, no help to hunt for food. A poor man.

In doing research the night before, John discovered that 15% of all couples face problems of infertility, and 40% of those problems lie with the male. He now sat in the same room with a large percentage of those men. Friends, in a way, bound together by one common goal: to overcome and procreate. It was a Braveheart moment.

Every time the nurse opened the door to call another couple to the back, Annika's head popped up like a whack-a-mole game. Invariably, minutes later that same couple would be seen coming back out the door, looking even more dejected than before, surely befallen by negative news.

The door opened.

"Mims."

John and Annika stood and looked at each other. This was the moment of truth. They grasped hands and walked to the back. The nurse showed them to a room where they waited anxiously. When the doctor came in a few minutes later, they looked to him for an answer, trying to read his face for any sign of an outcome: a smile, a frown, a twinkle of the eye, a furrow of the brow. They got nothing.

The doctor recognized their anticipation and began to talk. His glasses slipped down the bridge of his nose and he pushed them up again.

"Well, I know you two have been waiting patiently so I'll get right to it. The test results came back negative. I'm sorry Mr. and Mrs. Mims, you still cannot have children."

Annika's heart sank. John's cracked.

The doctor went on. "Now like I said earlier, there are still some things we might be able to do. There are certainly some options. First off...I want you to see a friend of mine in Glendale. He's a specialist in fertility enhancement for men. If there's anything that can be done, he will know. Now, another option for you two might be adoption. I know it's not the traditional way, and it's a very personal decision, but adoption is a beautiful thing, and there are thousands of children out there waiting to find loving parents. Just something to think about."

John and Annika were filled with disappointment; Annika more than John. He'd figured this would be the outcome. He'd expected to hear bad news. Now his hurt stemmed from having the hopes of

21

his wife inflate only to be blasted from the sky. He was used to that pain after all these years. She was not.

They thanked the doctor for his time, told him they would think about all the things he'd said, and made their way back to the car in silence. John began the drive home, and after a few minutes broke the quiet.

He grabbed his wife's hand as she stared out her window. "Everything will be alright. I want you to know that. Just a few minutes ago you told me that you'd love me either way. You also said that it wasn't the end of the world. Remember? Well, it's not the end of the world. We will be okay, I promise. I love you."

"I love you too," she whispered.

Annika continued to stare out of her window as a single tear escaped the right side of her cheek, out of view of her husband.

* * *

Connor Bryce was in the living room when his cell phone rang. It had been a crazy last couple of days, and he had half a mind not to answer the incessant ringing. The caller ID showed that it was David Brantley; anyone else and he would have ignored the call.

"Brantley, any news today?"

"Yes, and it's not good."

"What's the problem?"

"The police have been here all day."

"Good, did you tell them Lasser stole my idea and then had me fired?"

"It's way more serious than that, Connor. They don't think Jansen committed suicide, they think he was murdered."

"What? Why would they think that?" Connor stood up and paced the living room.

"They've just been here asking some weird questions, even asked me about my shoe size. And some dirty footprints on the floor in the hallway intrigued them. Connor, listen to me, they think you did it."

Connor stopped pacing. "Did what?"

"Killed Jansen. Listen, I'll probably get in serious trouble for even telling you this, but I overheard the two detectives talking. They matched your fingerprints to the bottle of pills Jansen overdosed on. Connor, how is that possible?"

"It's not possible. It's gotta be a mistake."

"I believe you, and I agree. But the cops don't. They're on their way to your house now and they're probably going to question you until you puke. Just be prepared and watch your back. Oh, and they're going to check your shoes."

Even as Brantley spoke Connor made his way up the stairs and into his master bedroom. "Ok, thanks Brantley."

"Let me know how things turn out, and good luck buddy."

"Will do."

Connor put his cell phone in his pocket and hurried into his closet. There were so many questions that he didn't know where to begin. Brantley said the cops had asked him about his shoe size and something about dirty footprints on the office floor. For some reason, Connor felt compelled to check his shoes. He knew he hadn't left his house the night Jansen was murdered. He'd slept soundly all night long. And what was that about his fingerprints on the pill bottle? Even if that were true, the obvious explanation was that he was being framed. Prints can be lifted and easily put other places with clear tape. Everyone knows that. And Jansen had so many political connections he was sure to have a list of enemies a mile long.

The repercussions of the Brantley conversation swallowed Connor's mind in confusion and doubt. Reasons, more than one, had led police officers to believe he was somehow involved in the death of Jansen. And now those same officers were headed to his house, making him suspect number one.

If only Kelly were at the house, she would come up with a clear-minded approach to the current situation. She always seemed relaxed in the face of pressure; even when she freaked a little, her eyes still held a calming promise. Maybe he should call her, or better yet go to the flower shop and see her face to face. She'd wanted to be home with him anyway but he'd encouraged her to go to work, reassuring her that he'd be fine. But he wasn't fine. His head was spinning.

Connor now stood in his closet looking at his twenty-something pairs of shoes lined up in a single file across his floorboard. Flip-flops, sandals, gym shoes, yard shoes, hiking boots, multiple colors and styles of dress shoes—all neatly aligned, toes pointing at the wall. Connor sat on the floor and began to examine each shoe. If one of his were dirty, he would find it in no time. His name was being drug through the mu...mud. Connor stopped, dumbfounded. There...on the bottom of his black wingtip dress shoes, was dried dirt. The same shoes he'd worn the day he was fired.

The doorbell rang as muffled voices shouted.

Police.

Panic set in. He had to get rid of his shoes. If, somehow, the police did have Connor's prints on a pill bottle, they would now also have his pair of dirty shoes, which, for reason's Connor didn't know, were important to the case. All this, plus the fact that he was recently fired by the deceased Jansen...things were not looking good for him.

If only Kelly were there.

Another knock at the door, this time louder and harder. Connor walked to the bedroom window and looked outside from the second story. Three police cars were in his driveway; six officers were at his door. He watched them talk amongst themselves, probably discussing their next course of action. There was no scenario in which Connor would not leave in handcuffs.

Unless he made his own scenario. Quickly an idea formed in his mind. Right or wrong, Connor knew he would live by this one decision for the rest of his life. He had to get out of town. He couldn't let the cops find him sitting by himself in his closet with a pair of dirty shoes in his hand. He might as well flip the switch on his own electric chair.

Without thinking, Connor grabbed a backpack from the hallway closet. He ran into his bedroom and filled the bag with clothing. Then he shoved in his dress shoes, having to pull the canvas material tightly together just to zip it shut. His cell phone was in his pocket, as was his wallet. Lastly he grabbed a pocketknife, a lighter, and his cell phone charger from his nightstand and quickly zipped those into side pockets. He would call Kelly from the road.

The road. Just the thought of living on the road for next few weeks was enough to make him sick. Where would he go? North, South, large city, small town? And what about money, food, a bed at night, computer access? The details could be worked out later. Right now his main concern was the six pistols outside waiting for a chance to spit fire.

He hurried down the stairs and into the kitchen. The police outside had stopped knocking; their quietness made Connor uneasy. He grabbed two apples and some granola bars and stuffed them into his hoodie pouch he'd slipped on minutes earlier. He grabbed his keys off the counter and tiptoed downstairs into the basement, then silently opened the side door that led to the backyard.

As he left, he heard his front door crash in and footsteps pound the floor above him. Connor shut the door, and walked casually into the Baltimore heat. Once the house was out of sight, he ran.

5

Presley and Suarez were the first to enter after the door had been rammed down. All indications were that Connor was home; his car was in the driveway, lights were on in various rooms, and a neighbor mentioned seeing him only an hour ago. Still, Presley felt eeriness in the quiet house, a dull electricity; he knew they'd been given the slip. Call it a sixth sense, but Pres could *feel* the warmth of the presence that had just been there. It was in the air. And he was right, the house was empty.

It would have to be searched, of course, top to bottom. With any luck, they could still find and question Connor's wife, Kelly. She would be picked up at her flower shop soon. Maybe she could answer questions regarding her husband's whereabouts, as well as the night of the murder. It was doubtful she was aware of her husband's intentions; most wives of murderers weren't.

Presley stood lost in thought in Connor's study, staring at a potted white lily on his desk. The highly perfumed flower cast an intoxicating smell throughout the room. White lilies were known to have sweet aromas. To the Chinese, the word Lily means "forever in love." Some hold the flower as a symbol of summer and abundance.

The rest of the office was very organized. Not a thing was out of place on his desk. Presley was careful not to touch anything until the forensic unit arrived, but a lot could be judged by the naked eye. A trained detective could tell a lot about a man simply by how he kept his desk. Connor appeared to be organized, in control. No surprise there; the few people they'd interviewed about him stated as much. But Presley wasn't interested in Connor's ability to keep his desk clean; he wanted to get inside his mind. Why would he kill? Why would any man kill for that matter? Presley fought back the temptation of answering such meaningless questions. Not meaningless in that they didn't matter; meaningless in that there were no answers for some questions. There was no "one reason" people killed. There was no "textbook murderer." There never would be.

Suarez interrupted Presley's thoughts with a slight knock on the office door. Pres regained his thoughts and turned around.

"You need to see this, upstairs."

Pres nodded and followed his partner up the stairs and down a long hallway, into the master bedroom. The closet was their final destination, where Suarez pointed down.

"Right here. There's a pair of shoes missing," Suarez said. He pointed along the floor where all of Connor's shoes were lined up neatly. "Looks like a pair of business shoes too, since he keeps all his nice shoes together."

Presley thought it over. "Maybe it's the pair he's wearing right now."

"Perhaps, except there's another space over here by his tennis shoes; looks like there are two pairs of shoes unaccounted for. And since we know he's not at work, I would assume he's not wearing dress shoes."

"You check the size of all these?"

Suarez smiled. "Yep. Most are 12's...same size as our print in Mrs. Jansen's flowerbed. And there's more."

Suarez got down on all fours and motioned for Presley to do the same. Pres suddenly felt he was getting too old for this. Once on the ground, two grown men on knees and elbows inside a closet, Suarez showed Presley what he'd found. Dirt particles—right in the middle of the empty floor space where the dress shoes should have been. The specks of dirt were hard to see standing up, yet on hands and knees were plainly visible.

Both men stood up and exited the closet into the bedroom. "Good work Suarez, we'll let forensics take it from here. They'll match that dirt, plus both of our shoe sizes are the same. And we have fingerprints and a motive. This is our guy."

Presley walked out of the house and into the front yard while dialing his cell phone.

"Yes...yes. Hey it's Presley. Listen, I need an APB put out on a Connor Bryce. White male, 41 years old, six foot one, brown hair, brown eyes. Believed to be on foot. Considered armed and dangerous."

As Pres closed his cell phone, the forensics team arrived and started to unpack their gear. He approached the unit leader, Eddie Stillman. The two men didn't get along, and rightly so. They'd met decades ago when they were roommates for their three-month stay at the police academy. Presley had had no interest in his roommate until he saw a family photograph, which included Stillman's delectable younger sister, Lacy. Stillman was against the relationship from the beginning, citing that he knew what kind of guy Presley was and how his sister could do better. He, of course, was right. The relationship ended...ugly. Presley graduated the academy and then transferred to Miami to work narcotics. Stillman went into forensics, and the two men parted ways amicably.

That seemed like a thousand years ago. Presley was a changed man, different from that cocky jerk of years past. Looking back as he had many times, it became easy to see why Stillman didn't like him. Presley even admitted that, had the roles been reversed, he probably would have knocked himself into next week. And the sister, Lacy...she'd ended up marrying an oncologist and was living in Austin, Texas. Stillman had been right all those years ago...his sister *could* do better. She had. Now they tolerated each other when needed, opting for avoidance whenever possible.

Today, it wasn't possible. Pres had his suspect, Connor Bryce, in his crosshairs. The priority now was for the crime scene to stay intact. Forensics had to a lot of work to do, and if sloppy police work was their song, Presley wasn't singing it. Too many times he'd seen criminals go free because police had botched their evidence collection or had tainted the crime scene. Not today. Not with Bryce.

Stillman stood silent and waited for Pres to talk.

"His name is Bryce, Connor Bryce. Just put out an APB on him. We think he's on foot. Listen, I need specific care taken in the master closet. There's some dirt on the carpet where a pair of shoes should be. I need to see if you can match that to topsoil already on file in the lab. Let me know when you find out. I need everything to go right today."

Stillman lit a cigarette and savored the first taste before he exhaled. "That it?"

Presley was not in the mood for games today.

"No, that's not it."

He plucked the cigarette from Stillman's mouth, dropped it on the driveway, and then stepped on it with the heel of his boot. "No smoking in the house." Presley turned and walked away. Maybe he hadn't changed that much.

* * *

The stifling Baltimore heat was working wonders for Kelly's greenhouse. Of course, it was always hot in the summertime, but this summer was different. Heat indexes soared into the 120's on a regular basis. The blurry lines of heat escaping the pavement could be seen on the interstate. The ground itself was so desperate for water that it began to crack and split in some places. In turn, flowers and plants took an absolute beating. It seemed like every green thumb in Maryland was in a state of panic. Kelly couldn't keep mulch or soil in stock, at least not the expensive stuff. Some types of mulch could retain water better than others. Typically, people would buy the cheapest mulch and then spend all their money on high-priced plants and flowers. Now that they were in the middle of a heat wave, all the expensive plants were beginning to die, making mulch that could hold water longer a luxury.

Despite the distractions of being busy, Kelly found it hard to focus. Her husband had just been swindled out of his high paying job, and the boss that fired him had committed suicide. She'd tried to talk Connor into taking a vacation, and maybe after things settled down they still would. For now, he'd thought it would be best if he started the dreaded job search again while she continued to focus on her shop. Connor had looked deeply into her eyes and promised her that he would be okay; that they as a couple would be fine. Still, she didn't feel reassured when she realized she might have to support the family for a while. Thankfully because of the drought, business was booming, though that would not last forever.

As Kelly was helping an elderly man load bird seed into a cart, one of her employees, a high school girl named Leigh, mimed the you-have-a-phone-call sign to her from across the shop. When Kelly was finished, she went into her office and picked up the receiver.

"This is Kelly."

"Hey babe, it's me." He seemed out of breath.

"Connor, I was wondering when you'd call. I haven't stopped thinking about you all day. How are you?"

"Not good." His voice quavered…she knew he was frantic.

"Connor, what's wrong? Talk to me."

"Babe, I don't have long. I need you to listen to me. Listen to everything I say. Save your questions for the end. Can you do that?"

"Connor you're scaring me."

"Please babe, listen. Can you just trust me?"

"Yes. Yes of course I trust you."

"Ok good. I called you at your shop from a pay phone so there'll be no record on either one of our cell phones of this call. Do you understand me? The police cannot know that you and I talked now, okay?"

She was lost, but answered "Okay."

28

"Babe, I don't have long. Kelly…" he paused, "they think I killed Jansen. The cops think I killed Jansen."

She seemed calm. "Well that's ridiculous. We both know you didn't kill him. He committed suicide. Very tragic, but what does that have to with you?"

"He didn't commit suicide. Brantley called me, told me cops showed up and were snooping around. He heard them say my fingerprints were on the bottle of pills that Jansen overdosed on. My prints! He also told me to check my shoes because of some dirty footprints in the office hallway at work. I checked my shoes Kelly…" his voice began to strain, "My dress shoes were dirty."

The full weight of the situation slowly dawned on Kelly, and instantly the air turned heavy and stale in the room. "Connor, where are you now?"

No answer. "Connor?"

"I ran."

With those two words Kelly's world stopped. From that point on, her life would be different. Running crossed the line. Perhaps things could have been explained, but once someone runs, all rules were gone. Her vision became clouded as she noticed a bead of sweat run from her temple all the way down to her neck.

"What do you mean you ran?"

"I packed a bag and went out the back door in the basement. It was a dumb, I know. I panicked and I ran. But someone is framing me. They have to be. Right now every finger points to me, and I couldn't stand the thought of being behind bars. They might never let me see you again. I didn't know what to do, Kelly. It was a mistake, but I can't turn myself in now."

"Wrong. Yes you can. You have to."

"Kelly I can't. I can't trust the police; their minds are already made up. I can find the answers I'm looking for. I just need time and space."

She fought back despair.

"Where are you going to go, when will I hear from you again?" Just those words escaping her mouth caused tears to fall.

"I've turned my cell off so I can't be tracked; I'm not sure where I'm going, somewhere far from here. You have enough money for a while. I'm sorry babe. I'm so, so sorry; I promise I will make this right. Don't lose faith in me. Forgive me for being stupid. I'll find ways to get in touch with you. The less you know, the better. The police are about to ask you a million questions, plus you'll probably be followed and watched for a long time. Assume every conversation you have is being listened to. Just get used to it. It's all my fault, but I will fix it. Please, Kelly, please don't stop loving me."

Kelly was catatonic. Her brain, dead. All she could do was moan.

"Kelly? Kelly? I know this isn't easy. I know I've screwed up. All I need is for you to believe me. If you tell me, right now, that you don't believe me…that you think I killed Jansen, I'll turn myself in. There will be no reason for me to live if you don't believe me. But if you believe me, that I didn't do it, then I have to fight to clear my name. So, the question is, do you believe me?"

Kelly tried to focus, tried to make her brain form complete thoughts, tried to make her mouth utter a sound other than a groan. Finally she managed, "Yes, yes I believe you." And she truly did.

"Good. Okay, I have to go now. Please be patient. Don't believe everything you're about to hear about me. You know in your heart it's not true. I'll talk to you soon. I love you."

Kelly regained her composure, "I love you too."

The phone went silent. She held the receiver to her ear for a moment, listening to the dial tone on the other end.

What had just happened? Thirty minutes ago her husband was without a job. Manageable. Now, he was being accused of murder and on the run from the law. Was there even a word for that? What was she supposed to do…go on living life like normal?

She sat at her desk for a few minutes in a feeble attempt to compose herself. One thing was for sure, she couldn't stay at work any longer. Then again, she didn't feel like going home either. The house would be an alien wasteland without her husband—dark, empty, alone…cold. She would go on a drive, maybe visit her parents for a few days.

A knock on the door got her attention. It was young Leigh, her employee. "Mrs. Bryce, sorry to interrupt. There are some men here to see you. They say they're police. I asked them to wait up front."

Wow.

That was fast. Would she ever have another free second to compose her thoughts without bad news raining down on her parade?

"Thanks, Leigh, I'll be right there."

A few minutes later and Kelly was walking up front to meet the officers. She had to pretend she hadn't talked to Connor. She needed to act shocked at the news she was about to receive. In truth, her mind was already warped with despair and confusion. Kelly took a deep breath and introduced herself to the two men.

"Mrs. Bryce, we need you to come down to the station for some questions. You can ride with us; we'll bring you back when we're through."

"Okay, what's this about?"

Presley answered her, "You're husband, ma'am. I think its best we talk at the station, we're going to need some privacy for a few hours."

"My husband? Is he hurt?"

"Please ma'am, the sooner we can get to the station, the sooner we can answer your questions and the sooner you can answer ours."

Without speaking, Kelly gathered her things, put one of her managers in charge of the store, and followed Presley to the back of the police car. She sunk low in the seat, feeling like a hardened criminal.

Kelly gazed out the side window as they pulled away from the greenhouse. Her gaze was unfocused, her mind in another galaxy. Something, however, pulled her attention back to earth. From her peripheral vision, an outline tugged at her memory. As they drove past the gas station across the street and diagonal to the flower shop, the shadowy figure of a man wearing a hoodie stood by a pay phone outside. Kelly knew that shadow.

As the police car passed the gas station, the officers up front were oblivious to any bystanders in the parking lot. Everything happened in a split second. Kelly focused her eyes toward the man as they drove by. The face was too dark to make out any details as the hood was pulled down well over the eyes, but the man had his right arm across his chest with his hand on his heart, as if he were giving the pledge of allegiance. His white fingers stood out clearly against the background of his navy blue hoodie. His thumb, index and pinky finger stood outstretched, while his middle and ring finger stayed in his palm.

As the cop car drove by with Kelly in the back, Connor discreetly flashed his wife sign language for *I Love You*. She saw the sign, closed her eyes, and knew everything would be alright.

31

6

"So tell me, Mrs. Bryce, where do you think your husband is going?"

"I told you this already. I have no idea where he is now or where he could be going. I woke up this morning and came to work, as usual. Connor was asleep when I left, and I was careful not to wake him. He'd had a rough few days, so I wanted him to get some rest."

"And you're sticking to your story that he was with you in your house on the night Mr. Jansen died?" Suarez was doing the questioning while Presley stood outside the window and watched Kelly Bryce's body language as she answered.

"There is no "sticking to my story," it's the truth. We slept all night long. Neither of us left the house."

"Is there anyone else that can attest to Connor being home all night other than you?"

"No, but I'm not a liar. Don't you think I would tell you if I knew my husband snuck out and killed his boss? You think I want to live with a murderer? But he's not a murderer! Connor Bryce is the most gentle, hardworking man I have ever known."

Suarez walked around the table and slid some pictures in front of Kelly.

"Mrs. Bryce, is this your bedroom closet?"

She looked at the picture. "Yes."

"Well Mrs. Bryce, it's in this bedroom closet that we found dirt particles that just so happen to have come from Mrs. Jansen's flower garden. Same topsoil. Same dirt. How do you explain that?"

"It has to be a mistake."

"It's not a mistake, Mrs. Bryce. Connor was there."

Kelly raised her voice for the first time. "He wasn't there! He was with me all night. Have you ever thought that someone might be setting him up? Has that ever happened? Don't you find it odd that he was just fired the day before, with some new guy coming in taking credit for all of his hard work? I've explained this to you. Why don't you look into that?"

Suarez remained calm. He'd seen people break before.

"Mrs. Bryce, we have his prints on a pill bottle that was on Gregory Jansen's nightstand. Is that also a set up?"

"Does it matter to you what I say?"

"Yes ma'am, it does. Listen, Mrs. Bryce, we're all on the same team. You're not in trouble. Not at all. We all just want to find Connor as quickly as possible, and any insight you have as to his whereabouts could prove very beneficial. But you won't help us, and that's because you refuse to step back and look at the evidence. Now let me tell you what I think happened. I think Connor was peeved at getting fired the way he did, and in my opinion, rightly so. But he didn't stop at getting angry. He snuck out while you were asleep, broke into Jansen's house in the middle of the night, and force fed him enough pills to knock out an elephant. Then he came back home and slept the rest of the night right beside you. Please Mrs. Bryce, take a big step back, look at the evidence, and help us find Connor."

Kelly sat there motionless for a short span; her mind still trying to comprehend this stormy chaos. Was it possible? Could Connor kill? No, he could not. Not her Connor. She looked Detective Suarez squarely in the eye, "I have no idea where he is or where he's going. But if I hear from him, you'll be the first person I contact."

"Thank you. And we are exploring all options, even the possibility of your husband being framed. If Connor didn't do it, you might be in trouble also. We'll have some officers watch your house around the clock, and with your permission we would like to record all of your phone calls."

"You probably already are."

Suarez left the room and immediately looked at Presley.

"She seems honest. Passionate at least." Presley stood in front of the window, still looking at Kelly Bryce sitting in the empty room. "Yeah, I think she's telling the truth—at least how she believes it. She either has no idea Connor left the house that night, or he truly didn't leave the house that night. Either way, she'll always believe her husband is innocent. Have a couple of our finest trail her for a few weeks, and get those taps on her phone. One thing's for sure, if she hears from him in any way, she isn't telling us."

"Anything else?" Suarez asked.

"Yeah, get his picture out to the media; every state east of the Mississippi River. Connor Bryce is about to be famous."

* * *

The old Ford F-150 slowed down and pulled onto the shoulder. Connor trotted to catch up to it as the driver leaned over and manually rolled down the window. "Where you headed, partner?"

Connor looked into the face of the man that was to be his ticket out west; his ticket had a mustache and a cowboy hat. Connor smiled politely, trying to look as normal as possible, "Arizona."

The driver smiled back, "I can take you as far west as Louisville. Picking up my drummer there, then we're headed down to Nashville. My name's Hal. And you are?"

"Hey, I'm Steve." The two men shook hands. Steve was a good "non-fugitive" name, wasn't it?

"Well Steve, if Louisville is okay with you, I say we get moving."

"Sounds good."

The road was long and lonely, but the two men made decent traveling companions. Hal was just a good ol' boy from Southern Maryland headed to Nashville where he had a few connections in the Country music industry. It just so happened that Hal had sent his contacts one of his band's latest songs, and they loved it enough to ask the band down to cut a single. Hal had loaded up his bags, his guitar case and hit the road. He would swing by Louisville to pick up his drummer (who was there visiting his girlfriend), and the rest of the band members would meet them in Nashville.

"Yes sir. One day you'll be hearing our songs on the radio."

Connor...Steve...sat back and relaxed. "I hope so. What's your band's name?"

"Deep River. Kind of corny I know, but..."

"No I like it. Should fit in well at the Grand Ole' Opry."

"So what's your story? You on the run or something?"

The joke missed its mark, but Connor tried to laugh it off. He had to act as normal as possible as he delivered his cover story ready. "Headed to see my family in Phoenix. My wife and I got laid off from our jobs. I worked in construction and she was a teacher. Anyway, I had an interview in Baltimore and spent my last two hundred dollars on a one way flight. Figured I'd think of some way to get back. This is a lot better than a bus."

"That it is, partner. That it is."

They rode on making small talk for a few more hours. Hal wanted to share his band's country music with his new friend Steve, who obliged. The road trip was therapeutic to the soul, and for a brief moment, listening to lonely country music tunes took Connor's mind to another place. His mind went back to the first time he'd met Kelly.

They were both juniors in college, where Connor's roommate Alan had set them up on a double date with a pair of biology majors. Alan had met the ladies before, Connor had not. Connor was paired with

Florence, a gal with the looks of a koala bear and the personality of a marble; perfect for another guy, no doubt, but not Connor's type.

Alan, having known the girls before hand, paired himself up with Kelly, a long-legged brunette that loved to smile. Connor couldn't keep his eyes off of Kelly the entire night, and though he tried as hard as possible not be rude to his own date, Florence the koala, whenever Kelly spoke she captured the attention of anyone within earshot. It wasn't long before the night ended, and Connor faced a common college predicament; he was in love with his roommate's date. This wasn't just some hot, new freshman face; this girl owned him. He had to talk to Alan about it and was unsure of how he would react. Luckily, the problem worked itself out.

Alan had learned that Kelly wanted to go into Botany after school, perhaps do research on plant genetics or work with conservation groups. Florence on the other hand, wanted to go on to med school after undergrad and become a cardiologist just like both of her parents. As fate would have it, Alan liked the thought of being in a relationship with an aspiring doctor, and if Connor's hunch was correct, Alan also liked the fact that her parents were absolutely loaded financially.

It was Alan who came to Connor to inquire about his thoughts on Florence, and when Connor told his roommate that she was very nice, yet not his type, Alan immediately inquired if it would be okay to ask Florence out on a second date. Connor acted supportive, as any good buddy would. One week later he was on his first date with Kelly.

Only now it wasn't his history he was concerned over, it was his future. The latest Deep River song ended, something about a farm and some turnip greens, and it zapped Connor back to his current dilemma. His life had changed in a few short days. He questioned his own sanity at certain points, and knew he was flat-out crazy at others. How in the world was he in such a predicament? Was it possible…at all possible…that he'd blacked out for a period of time, committed this heinous crime, and then woke up like nothing happened? He'd heard of episodes like that before, even seen a few cases on those Detectives Files shows on television. If he didn't kill Jansen, which he was sure that he didn't, then who did? The questions in his mind never stopped, the answers never came. What he needed was time— time to think, time to clear his head, time to slow down.

"You hungry, partner?"

Connor smiled at his new best friend Hal, who called him Steve. "I could go for a bite." He couldn't remember the last time he'd had anything to eat, and at the sudden realization he became desperate for food.

"There's a Denny's about twenty miles up the road, not much more on this stretch of blacktop after that."

"Denny's it is then."

Hal got the Grand Slam, Connor the French toast. The two sat and talked like old buddies. It was almost an answer to prayer, or luck, in Connor's case, that Hal was the one who pulled over to give him a lift. The man with the mustache that played country music, a true cowboy, and a nerdy equipment designer—surely the unlikeliest of pairs, enjoying a meal fit for a king at Denny's.

"Alright Hal, tell me a little bit about yourself."

"What do you want to know?"

"Just the basics I guess. Don't get too sappy on me." Connor said with a smile. "I don't know. What else do you do beside country music? How is it that a guy like you, from Maryland, is on the verge of making it big in Nashville?"

Hal sat back and smiled. "Attitude."

Connor willingly took the bait. "Do explain."

"My attitude. I refuse to be negative. Nothing that's worth having comes easily. And I'm okay with that. I pay my dues, work hard, keep a good attitude, and when my opportunity comes, I'll be ready. My life is too short to complain, to be…mundane. Now don't get me wrong, sometimes things don't work out my way, and sometimes I'm flat out in some deep weeds, but I never stop singing. And that's how I know I'll make it in Nashville…because an attitude like mine can't lose."

Connor sat back, "Spoken like someone who hasn't faced many problems."

Hal's face turned serious and his smile faded. He paused for the briefest of moments as he composed his thoughts. He broke eye contact with Connor and looked down at the table.

"I wish you were right. I wish I could tell you that my dad didn't have a stroke a few years ago, that my sister and I didn't have to take turns feeding and bathing him every day for three and half years until he passed away. I wish I could tell you that my mom knew my name; that she isn't suffering from Alzheimer's. I wish I could tell you she smiles when she sees me instead of thinking that I'm there to deliver the mail. I wish I could tell you that I didn't get divorced last year

36

because I got caught cheating on my wife. I wish I could tell you that her and my little girl are safe at home right now, playing with toys and wondering when their daddy will be home. I wish I could tell you those things, but I can't. That's me. Those are the problems I've been through recently. Some of them I've brought upon myself, other's I didn't. But it doesn't matter, I'm not proud of them either way. I've tried to right most of those wrongs, and the endings are still unclear. All I control now is my attitude. I believe in the power of the mind. If the mind wants something bad enough, it will find a way to make it happen."

"Wow...listen, I'm sorry, I had no idea...I was ju..."

"Hey buddy, no need to apologize. Everyone has their story. I'm guessing you do too. But that's between you and your maker, none of my business. I have an ear or two if you ever want to talk. No better place to cry it out than at a Denny's," Hal said smiling.

Connor smiled back, "Well noted."

"Just remember, your thoughts can be your best friend or your worst enemy. Let'em work good for you instead of bad. But enough about me for crying out loud, how'd your interview go?"

"What?"

"Your interview...the one you flew out here for, how'd it go?"

Connor recalled his cover story about interviewing for a construction job. His lies would have to grow thicker and thicker. "It went well. Said they'd let me know within a week. Who knows, I might have a surprise waiting for me when I pull into Phoenix."

Hal paid the tab for both of them, said it was the least he could do for a man trying to get back home across country. As the pair headed out the door and back to Hal's truck, a news bulletin came across the television screwed into the wall above the cash register. It informed people to be on the lookout for a man wanted in connection with a homicide. The man, whose pictured they showed for a full minute, was to be considered armed and dangerous. Any and all tips would be greatly appreciated.

Ruth, the nice waitress who had served Hal and Connor, thought the man in the picture looked a lot like the guy that had just left, and even though she'd heard the other gentleman call him "Steve," she decided to call the hotline just to be safe.

7

The call that came in was their first true lead. A waitress at a Denny's in West Virginia said the guy she saw on the news was the same man that she'd served French toast and coffee. Apparently he was seen leaving with a guy wearing a cowboy hat. The two drove away in an old Ford pickup truck. No one got the plate number.

Presley and Suarez had to get special permission from their Captain to pursue Connor Bryce across state lines. A few strings were pulled, favors called in, and the men were granted access to track down their killer. Other officers would continue to work the investigation locally and all information would be shared as needed.

Presley drove a white Chevy Malibu; not his dream car, but it got good gas mileage.

A half day's drive down the interstate and they pulled into the Denny's. Waitress Ruth was through with her shift by that point, but came back to be interviewed after a phone invitation from the police. She'd been watching the news the last few hours and was even surer now that she had served Connor Bryce. She was also helpful by informing Presley and Suarez that she'd heard the other gentleman (whose name she had not picked up), call the man she thought was Connor, Steve. It all sounded confusing to her, and most assuredly was, but Presley and Suarez had it figured out. Connor Bryce had simply hitched a ride with an unsuspecting Good Samaritan and had given him a false name. Another admission of guilt.

"Miss Ruth, you have any good hotels around here?"

"Yes sir, The Gateway Motel is a half mile up the road in the other direction; forty-five bucks a night."

"Thanks ma'am."

Back out in the parking lot, Suarez said, "So what's the plan now?"

"Well, it's getting late. I say we crash here for the night. In the morning, if we haven't gotten another decent tip, we head west. That's the direction he's going now, just not sure how far. We'll drive till we hit the Mississippi. If our trail dries up then we'll turn around and come back. But something tells me our trail won't dry. He'll make a mistake somewhere. And his picture is on every news station from here to Lousiana. By this time tomorrow he'll be in handcuffs."

The two checked into The Gateway Hotel, which as far as Presley was concerned was a gateway to a staph infection. The rooms were disgusting. Cigarette butts were on the floor, the air was thick and foggy, the hot water heater was broken and the television received one channel.

No matter. Presley didn't want to watch television anyway. He spent most of the night going over personnel files and background information on Connor Bryce. The man seemed brilliant, and up until his recent termination from the company, was the model for success and innovation. His wife's claim seemed to be true—that Connor did in fact create the idea for outdoor handicap equipment, and that the production of that equipment had started the day after he was fired...one day after Jansen had died.

None of this made sense, but one thing was for sure, the truth would come out in the end. It always did. Presley got up from his small table and examined the bed. A gold comforter lay on top, no telling what kind of hideous stories it would tell if it could speak. He threw the comforter back and revealed dark blue sheets. Places like this didn't have classic white sheets; white would easily give away every spot of dirt, food or any other kind of stain that called the sheet its home. Dark blue sheets were safe because they always looked clean. Disgusting. Presley would sleep sitting in the desk chair that night, wondering if there was any way in which things would end well.

* * *

Connor and Hal parted ways at some point in the middle of the night; Connor wasn't sure, he'd lost track of time. Hal pulled into Louisville, and though he insisted Connor spend the night with him and his friends, Connor decided it best to push on toward Arizona to get to his family quicker. He talked Hal into dropping him off at the bus station, where Connor paid cash for a one-way ticket to Phoenix. The two men shook hands and said good-bye.

Connor was in for a long ride. The bus ride would be a two-day trip. But what kind of hurry was he in? The more time the trip took the better. He wanted to call Kelly so bad, yet resisted the temptation to use his cell phone, knowing that his call could be traced. If, at some point along the ride he came across a pay phone, maybe he would call her collect. Instead, as the bus pulled away in the darkness, he got a pen and piece of paper out of his backpack and wrote the following words:

My Dearest Bride,

Please know that I'm alright. I miss you terribly. I haven't stopped thinking about you since I left. If only you were here with me, holding my hand, all my fears would be erased. I'm not sure how long I will be gone. A few weeks...maybe a few months. I have some things to work through; my thoughts, my feelings, how this could have happened, and any outcome in this scenario that can put me back together with you as quickly as possible. Thank you so much for believing me and staying by my side. Thank you for loving me. I'm going to call you soon. Never stop thinking my name.

Always and Forever,

-C-

His eyes welled to tears as he signed off. His poor wife was sitting back home, waiting for her fugitive husband to give her some kind of a sign that he was still alive. If he...when he made it through this, he would spend the rest of his life thanking her for her love. Then there was Sammy at Virginia Tech. Sammy had probably seen the news reports, and was possibly even now questioning the actions of his father. Hopefully at the end of this, if it ever ended, his son wouldn't hate him for the rest of their lives. Connor put his head back and dozed off for a few short hours.

The sunlight beaming through the windows woke him up; that and the jerk of the bus as it came to a stop. He had no idea how long he'd been sleeping, but it was a much welcomed rest. The bus paused to fuel up, and the driver told Connor they'd be stopped for about thirty minutes to give everyone enough time to eat, drink, use the restroom, etc. Connor walked into the gas station and asked the elderly man behind the counter if they had a post office nearby. No luck.

"If you give me the letter, I'll mail it."

Connor didn't like that proposition, but he didn't have a lot of choices. Not because he didn't trust the guy, but because he'd just rather do it himself...make sure it got done. "I'd hate to ask you to do that. This is a very important letter. It's going back to my wife in Baltimore. Plus I don't even have a stamp for you."

The old man smiled warmly. He was missing his entire top row of teeth. "Well, sonny, you buy a drink and a candy bar from me and I'll put a stamp on the note for you and put it with the rest of my outgoing mail. No trouble at all. Name's Theodore," the old man said as he extended a wrinkled hand.

Connor smiled. Theodore was genuinely nice. What bad would it do to tell him his real name, all the way out here? No one outside of Baltimore even knew he existed. It occurred to Connor he didn't know what state they were in.

"Hi Theodore, I'm Connor."

"Pleased to meet you. Anything else I can do for you just let me know."

"Well, honestly, I've been traveling through the night and am embarrassed to admit it, but I don't even know what state we're in."

"Missouri." The man said warmly, though he pronounced it Mi-zur-ah.

"Well then, I would love an ice cold drink and a candy bar from the state of Missouri." Connor said as he handed the gentleman his letter. "You've got yourself a deal."

Connor went back to the bus, soda and candy in hand, feeling somewhat relieved. In two or three days Kelly would get his letter, and at least to some extent, her mind would be a little more at peace. The brilliant part was, even if the cops found it, it would be postmarked from some obscure little town in Missouri, and in two days time he would be a thousand miles away from the Show-Me-State. And something told him he could trust the inviting little man behind the counter. Just good old country folk…can't beat 'em.

As the bus pulled out, Connor put his head back and began to think. Some people would call it praying, Connor called it self-consultation. Please help me through this…please find strength…please give me an answer. His mind went blank as he listened to his thoughts.

Nothing.

He finished his drink and candy bar, shut his eyes, and went back to sleep.

Old man Theodore went in a back room, handed the letter to his wife, and asked her to mail it. She didn't ask any questions, just said that she would when she went out for groceries. On the other side of the store, stocking snack cakes behind a shelf, a teenager named Sawyer had watched the man at the counter, trying to place where he'd see that face recently. Then it hit him…the news! The guy that had just left the store was a criminal! Sawyer pulled out his cell phone to call his mother. She would know what to do.

* * *

The second lead in as many days. Things were looking up for Presley and Suarez. This one came from a small gas station in Missouri. Looks like Bryce was bussing west. Presley was on the phone with the Vice President of Buffalo Bus Travel, and Suarez was on his laptop cross-referencing major interstate state routes with large cities. Between the two of them, they should be able to pinpoint Connor Bryce's next stop. Presley hung up the phone and half-smiled at Suarez.

"Got him."

"Where?"

"Next scheduled stop is Oklahoma City."

"We'll have to step on it to beat them there."

"I can do better than that," Presley said. "We got a chopper."

They quickly packed up their things and checked out of The Gateway Cesspool. The police station was a twenty minute drive, but the helicopter was supposed to be fueled up with a pilot already in the seat waiting on them.

And waiting on them it was. The chopper looked like it had flown a thousand missions during World War II, and the pilot fit the part as well. The man was surely pushing ninety. Presley and Suarez exchanged glances, then without a word hopped in their seats. The space was crowded and the smell of gasoline hung in the air. An orange warning light continually beeped on the dashboard of the cockpit. Before they took off, the pilot turned around and said, "Don't pay that light any attention, it never shuts off. Bad fuse or something." Suarez sat back and shut his eyes. He hated helicopters, and this in some way, resembled one.

A few minutes after liftoff, when Suarez's stomach had settled down, he asked, "How much does the bus driver know?"

"Nothing. I could have had him pull over to the side of the road until we got there, but Bryce would be long gone by then. It's best right now if no one knows what's going to happen. The bus stops for fuel and food, Bryce gets off like no one is on his tail, and boom, we cuff him and fly him back to Baltimore. Should be as easy as that. I won't mess it up, you won't mess it up. We gotta get this guy off the streets; find out what happened. He's scared, and you never know what a person will do when they're scared."

"10-4. What's the plan when we touch down?"

"After we land, I have an unmarked waiting on us. Then we find the place where our bus driver usually stops, according to the V.P. I talked to, it's some truck stop diner called Tookies."

"Tookies?"

"Yeah, said the driver likes their chicken pot pie and cheap gas."

"Sounds like a heck of a place."

"We get there before the bus, confirm the man that gets off is Connor Bryce, let him get back on the bus, then we take him."

"Sounds good."

The flight was choppy in some places, but all in all, the war bird flew beautifully. The minute they touched down Suarez was able to breathe again as the color slowly returned to his face. Just like Pres had said, an unmarked police car was waiting for them. A few minutes later and they were in the parking lot of Tookies, a rough-and-tumble joint that, according to their sign out front, specialized in great wine and boiled peanuts.

Pres and Suarez got out and surveyed the area. The Oklahoma heat was stifling; much different than the heat they were used to in Baltimore. Midwest heat will make you sweat just thinking about it. At least Baltimore had a breeze coming off the water most of the time. No breeze here. Just staunch misery. The surrounding landscape was blurry as the heat escaped the surface of the land, cooking anything lying on top of it.

If everything was on schedule then the bus was about thirty miles out. This was the perfect place. No escape routes around. No trees to run into. No city. Just a truck stop out in the middle of nowhere. Pres and Suarez went inside and ordered some lunch. Nothing to do now but sit and wait. Pres ordered the club sandwich, and that wasn't the only thing he got. On the bill he received from his waitress he found her phone number at the bottom. Good grief. Suarez ordered a house salad with Italian, but failed to get any digits.

Right on cue, the Buffalo Bus pulled into the parking lot. On the side of the bus their slogan read, *Save a Horse, Ride a Buffalo*. The bus stopped and the passengers disembarked. The last one off the bus was Connor Bryce; that told Presley that Connor was probably sitting in the back. Connor strode across the parking lot and into the diner. This was the first time Presley and Suarez had a chance to look at the man they had been pursuing.

Connor looked tired, ragged, and weary. Presley noticed his hair was badly disheveled and his eyes screamed from lack of sleep. But more than tired, his face looked worried. He was a man on the run, fighting for his life, like an animal that sneaks through woods, knowing he's being hunted; that at any moment he would feel a bullet rip through his flesh well before he even heard the shot.

But as Presley watched him, he reminded himself that Bryce was also a killer. He tried to picture Connor sneaking around Jansen's house in the middle of the night, silently slipping through the window on the porch, tiptoeing up the stairs, then quietly yet violently feeding Jansen pills that would knock him out in a matter of seconds, never again to wake up.

Only a monster would do that.

* * *

Connor sat at the counter and ordered a BLT and fries. The journey had been long, but much needed; and he was almost to his destination. As much as his wife Kelly consumed his thoughts, he had to try and stay focused on the current mess he was in. He had to sort through the chaos and find answers.

The first way to find answers was to keep from getting arrested. This meant watching and reading the news reports about the manhunt that was sure to be going on back in Maryland and its surrounding states. If he could stay free, he could figure things out. If he could talk to Kelly, maybe she could tell him how things were going in Baltimore. The more he thought of talking to his wife, the more sense it made. Plus if he talked to her, perhaps then it would be easier to get on with things. He simply couldn't stand the thought of not hearing her voice any longer. As he finished his meal, he asked the waitress behind the counter if there was a payphone close by. She pointed outside as she poured another customer some coffee.

Connor paid and walked out into the parking lot. The payphone was along the far wall. He quickly found that it was occupied, yet recognized the man that held the receiver as the Buffalo Bus driver. The two knew of each other only because they'd spent their last day in a half on the same bus. However, the bus was fairly crowded with travelers, and neither man had spoken to the other. But as Connor made eye contact with the driver on the phone, he noticed the man's eyes grew slightly larger, and thought he saw his lips move and form the words *"I see him."* The driver looked panicked and quickly turned his back to Connor.

Connor froze.

Who was the driver talking to? Was it possible someone was on his trail? Suddenly he took inventory of everything around him. Thirteen tractor trailers were parked in the side-by-side manner typical of truck stops. Seven vehicles in the parking lot: four were pickup trucks, three were cars. Of the three cars, one was a beat up Buick, one a jazzed up Mustang, and the other a Chevy Impala. The Impala stood out; tinted windows, two antennas on top of the trunk, one on top of the roof—unmarked police car. It's funny how police cars are supposed to be unmarked but everyone can still tell them apart.

Dang! How had they found him? Connor kicked himself mentally for not being more careful, for not seeing that car when the bus first pulled up. He turned around and walked casually back into the restaurant, picking up a newspaper as he walked in. He deduced that the police were probably going to wait until he boarded the bus again; if they had wanted to arrest him earlier, then they would have done it by now. Additionally, arresting him on the bus would extinguish any chance he had to escape; he would be trapped on there. Plus the police wouldn't want to put the people in the restaurant in harm's way. It was a beautiful plan now that he thought about; which would mean that the police were watching him right now as he sat at the bar top pretending to read a newspaper.

Connor, acting calm and collected, laid the paper flat on the counter and quietly read; every few minutes he turned the page and quickly surveyed the faces in the diner. In the corner booth were two elderly gentlemen sipping on coffee, both wore USS Intrepid hats high atop their heads; they probably accounted for one of the pickup trucks, possibly two. Another man dressed in mechanics coveralls sat alone in a single booth and was inhaling his tomato soup and grilled cheese. Another pickup truck. Then there was the muscle-headed twenty something year old guy that sat a few seats down from Connor at the bar. The music blaring through his earphones could be heard throughout the diner. His keys sat upon the countertop, and Connor could easily pick out a key to the fast and furious Mustang sitting outside.

That left the beat up Buick, the Impala, and one, possibly two more pickup trucks. There were a few more people in the diner, but he recognized their faces as fellow passengers from the bus. Connor, between changing pages, spotted a pair sitting at another booth along the far side wall. The booth was set up so that neither of the people sitting there would have their backs to the rest of the diner, and with a simple turn of the head could view the entire inner room. If I were a police officer, I'd sit there, Connor thought. Both men in the booth looked like cops, and though that was a stereotype, so far in his game of matching people to their vehicles, Connor's stereotypes had held true. Yes, this was them, the pair that was hunting him. As long as he continued to act normal, they would continue on with whatever plan they had, presumably to arrest him once back on the bus. That of course, could not happen.

The bus driver poked his head in the door, "Rolling out in ten minutes."

At this announcement, the other recognizable faces from the bus gathered their things and began to pay their bills. The two gentlemen Connor guessed were police also seemed to be getting ready to leave, confirming his initial suspicions. One way or another, something was about to go down. Connor got up and casually walked to the restroom, which proved to be a small, sticky closet with a single fluorescent light bulb that flickered to no particular pattern. What was he going to do? Right now the police officers were waiting for him to come out and board the bus just so they could take him down.

He had to find another way to leave. Undetected.

An idea popped into his head— risky, but it was all he had. He had to get to the tractor trailers parked on the other side of the parking lot. It was the only way. Quickly, he cracked the bathroom door and looked down the hallway. No movement. Back at the other end of the hallway stood and emergency exit with a red bar across it that read ALARM WILL SOUND. The door looked a hundred years old, but Connor noticed recent scuff marks on the floor as well as a dolly in the corner, giving him the impression that the door was in semi-frequent use. If the alarm were to go off, he was as good as arrested, but at this point he had to chance it.

Moment of truth.

In a split second, he made his decision. He walked toward the door, pushed it open, and walked into the toasty Oklahoma air. No alarm. No buzzer. The door shut soundly behind him. Now seconds were precious. He ran across the backside of the parking lot toward the lineup of eighteen wheelers. Now, which one would he choose, and how could he get in without getting punched in the face by an angry truck driver? The lunch crowd was leaving, and as if someone were looking out for him, he heard a few of the big rigs crank up within a span of thirty seconds. One of the rigs was carrying cars, Jeeps to be exact, another stroke of luck. Connor hurried toward the truck as it shifted into first and released the parking break, making a hideous noise. Staying out of view of the driver's side mirror, he quickly crept up the back of the truck and found a Jeep with a soft

46

top. The truck was picking up speed now as it pulled back onto the main road. After a minute of finagling, Connor got the Jeep's top off and squeezed into the backseat, completely out of breath and thankful to be alive.

As the truck moved on, Connor looked back toward the diner for any sign of his pursuers making chase. The diner was barely visible now; the bus still out in the parking lot. It would have one less passenger.

8

Some people say that everything happens for a reason; that somehow there is meaning behind every move. Turn right or turn left, two possibilities with two different outcomes—one is meant to be, the other isn't. Kelly Bryce was not this type of person. To her, some things just happen. No right or wrong, black or white...not everything had to have a purpose. This was the approach she took to most of life, and certainly the view she took as the wife of a current fugitive wanted for murder. There was no cosmic, underlying moral to what was happening to her and her husband; no deep hidden meaning of life in this awful time. This situation just happened, and now she had to adjust.

It had been days now since she'd last seen her husband. She had been in the back of a cop car; her world turned upside down. He was standing by a pay phone outside of a gas station near her shop. He'd told her that he loved her. The memory seemed like a lifetime ago.

Since then, she had tried as hard as possible to focus on her flower shop and spend as little time as possible all alone in their cold, empty house. She'd talked to Sammy on the phone and had done her best in explaining things as well as she could. Thankfully, at 19, he was mature enough to grasp the situation. He didn't believe his father was a murderer; instead he'd simply chalked it up to a horrible misunderstanding. So far, he'd been left out of the media frenzy. Reporters were all over Kelly whenever they got the chance, and she was thankful her son hadn't gone through that yet. They were like hyena's on a fresh kill—giddy and relentless.

Hopefully things would die down in a short amount of time, or better yet, the police would solve the case and clear her husband's name. She hadn't seen or heard from the two detectives in a few days, but she was fully aware of the unmarked police car that sat down the road from her house, trying to look as inconspicuous as possible. She was also quick to recognize that same car as it followed her casually to her shop and back. The detectives, Presley and Suarez, told her it was for her own safety, so that if the "real" killer were out there, he or she wouldn't come back to finish her off. That was a lie. They believed Connor was the real killer, and simply wanted to make sure he didn't try to come back home. Her phone conversations were also being recorded, but at this point it didn't matter.

So no, things didn't happen for a reason. They just happened. Kelly decided she could either cry over it or find a way to conquer it, and though she had lost a few tears in the last day or two, now was the time to toughen up and come up with a plan. What could she do on her end? Her husband was out there, somewhere, running for his life. What could she be doing back home to put the pieces of this cruel puzzle together? If she didn't believe that her husband was a killer—which she didn't—then who was? The million dollar question.

First, she would do some research on one Trace Lasser. The mystery man had swooped in from out of nowhere and stole her husband's job, took credit for his genius idea, and then just like that, Jansen was found dead. And who was there to take his place…Lasser. There were so many red flags in that scenario that Kelly didn't know where to begin.

While doing her homework on Lasser, she would also try to find out how Connor's shoeprints could have been found at the Jansen home and at Connor's office, when Kelly knew beyond a shadow of a doubt that he was home with her the entire night. The fingerprints on the pill bottle could be explained a hundred different ways, but the shoeprints were a question mark. Who else had access to their shoes?

A thousand questions, twice as many scenarios. Now it was lunchtime and she wasn't hungry, but the growing pain in her stomach forced her to eat some peanut butter crackers. The knock on her office door startled her, causing her mind to jump back into reality and out of the daydream she was in. It was Leigh, one of her young employees. Leigh had heard the stories about Connor Bryce all over the news, everyone had, but she'd never said anything to Kelly about it. Instead, Leigh talked sweeter and kinder to the customers than she ever had before; not that she was rude, but recently her work ethic and mannerisms proved to be that of a model employee. This was Leigh's own way of showing support to her boss.

"Sorry to interrupt, you have a call on line two."

48

"Okay thanks. It's not someone from the news is it?" Leigh and the rest of the staff had been asked to screen calls as best as possible before they reached Kelly.

"No ma'am, the guy said he worked with your husband. Last name is Lasser. I figured it was okay."

Kelly felt nauseous. Trace Lasser was calling her at work, today? This was the man that was possibly framing her husband for murder and potentially ruining the rest of their lives. But she had to be strong, act confident. If she were going to find out about his past and who this guy really was, as she planned to, she would have to attempt to gain his trust, at least on some level.

"Thanks Leigh, I'll take it." Leigh left and shut the door.

Kelly picked up the phone. "Kelly Bryce speaking."

"Mrs. Bryce, this is Trace Lasser."

Her voice held no reflection of emotion. "Hello Mr. Lasser."

"Listen, I know we never met, and I understand now is probably not the best time, but I just wanted to call and tell you how awfully sorry I am about Connor and how things have played out. I'm not sure what he told you about me, but we didn't get off on the right foot. From everything I've heard he was one heck of a worker and even a better man. If there is anything I can do to help you and your family out in any way, please feel free to let me know."

Kelly fought hard to keep the crackers down as the thought of heaving appeared near in her future. Stay focused. Don't get too emotional. Stick to the plan. Gain his trust.

"Thanks Mr. Lasser. I…"

"Trace, call me Trace."

"Alright Trace. Yes, it's a very difficult time, thanks for your kind words. I know I have to keep myself strong and stay positive. I believe everything will work itself out, and that in time Connor will be home with me where he belongs."

"That sounds like a great place to be."

The comment caught her off guard. She paused, then, "Well, thanks again."

"Sure, and remember, if you need anything, don't hesitate."

"Will do." Kelly quickly hung up. She was getting short of breath and found it difficult to suck in enough air to correct the problem.

That sounds like a great place to be…What was that? Was it possible she took that the wrong way? And what way did he mean it? Was he actually coming onto her over the phone mere days after he stole her life away? Or was she overreacting? Regardless, she did not want to spend one more second of her life talking to that man.

She composed herself briefly and turned on her laptop. Still not sure where to start, she Googled the name 'Trace Lasser' and found almost twenty-two million results. A quick glance revealed that most of the results were for a Trace Laser, apparently a very popular laser sight for guns of all shapes and sizes. She would have to refine her search. She tried 'Lasser Jansen business,' and narrowed her results down to two thousand and some change. The top result, the one with the most views, had a headline that read "Jansen-Lasser: The Next Power Couple."

The next power couple? Kelly clicked the link and read the blog.

> *In one month, Sarri Jansen and Trace Lasser will be husband and wife. Sarri, the daughter of the successful entrepreneur Gregory Jansen, is an Oxford graduate with a degree in political science. Trace Lasser, son of Massachusetts Senator Charles Wellington Lasser, is currently studying economics at Syracuse University. The wedding will be held at St. Paul's Cathedral. The two will spend the next three weeks on an undisclosed island in the Mediterranean.*
>
> *Very rarely do we see couples like this tie the knot. Oh sure, there are plenty of powerful couples in Washington, but usually both parties come from the same cloth, either the political world, the law world, or the business world. This collision of business and politics will keep Washington on its toes. With the Jansen family's powerful business approach and the Lasser family's political clout, not much can happen in the nation's capital without the inner support and financial banking of Trace and Sarri. We wish the couple well, and no doubt will hear from them in the future.*

Bombshell. Trace was Jansen's son-in-law. Unbelievable. The article raised a million more questions. Like why Trace would choose business instead of politics like his father? And was he still married to Sarri, and if not, was there an ugly fall out? If there was an ugly break, then why did Jansen give ex-son-in-law Trace a job he didn't deserve in the first place? The answers to these questions and their implications could get a lot uglier before they get any prettier. Kelly shut her laptop down and pushed it gently away from her desk. It would take some time to unravel this thread. She sat back, took a deep breath, and made a mental note to pick up some coffee on her way home from work. She was about to pull an all-nighter.

* * *

Life had been tense in the Mims house the last few days, and as hard as they both tried to ignore the elephant in the room, it was time to talk about it. Annika had spent her last couple of evenings down at the food shelter where she shared her cooking expertise with about two hundred homeless people. They weren't in the habit of complaining about anything, but she'd guessed that they grew tired of the same foods every night, so she volunteered some of her free time into preparing cheap, easy dishes that happened to be incredibly tasty. Usually this was only a Thursday evening event, but in light of the stressful atmosphere at her house, she decided to spend an extra evening or two helping out.

John, on the other hand, had been incredibly busy at work, either by necessity or by design, and had hardly been home the last few days anyway. He had recently been hired to do engineer some drawings on two huge projects in the area, and was completely covered up in more work than he could handle. All of this was fine by him, as the mounds of paper seemed to take his mind off the fact that he had completely broken his wife's heart. She had a dream of children, and unfortunately married the one man on earth that could not fulfill that dream. Star-crossed lovers.

But now the couple was home together, and both knew the conversation they had been putting off was about to happen. It was lunchtime and Annika had called John at work. She'd used her best persuasion skills and finally talked him into coming home for a quick bite. They hadn't seen each other for longer than ten minutes in the last two days, and though times were tough, both missed the other in ways words cannot describe. They sat at a small table in their sunroom and ate a light meal prepared by Annika. John was the first one to acknowledge the elephant.

"So I've been thinking. We should give the doctor in Glendale a call, the one we were referred to, and make an appointment. What do you think?"

Annika took a sip of her lemon tea. "I think that's a great idea."

"I also think we should talk about adoption."

"What is there to say?"

51

"Well, how do you feel about it? For it or against it? Anything? I certainly think at this point it's our most optimistic option for having a baby. And please believe me when I say this, I desperately want to have a baby with you. But if I can't, after we've exhausted all other options, I think we should consider adoption."

Annika smiled and took her husband's hand.

"I have nothing against adoption. In fact, I think it is a splendid idea. If that's what it takes for me to start a family with you, I'm fine with that. I know my heart has changed regarding kids the last few months. I'm even surprised I worked up enough courage to tell you about it. At first I thought it might just be a phase and I would get over it, so I decided I would never bring it up. But it's not a phase, and I had to tell you. I'll do whatever it takes to have a baby with you, and whether we adopt or not, as long as we continue to trust each other, our baby will be the most loved child in the world. I'm almost crying just thinking about it."

"Well your eyes are beaming." John said as he gave his wife's hand a squeeze and stood up from the table. "Alright, I'll call doctor what's-his-name this afternoon; his card is in my wallet. We'll take his next open appointment."

He started to walk away, then, "Should we pray about it?"

"Pray about it? We've never done anything like that before. Why start now?"

"I don't know; this seems kind of supernatural. I mean, I think we need a miracle, and I haven't walked on water in a long time."

Annika smiled, "No, you sure haven't. But I've got all the supernatural you need."

She stood up from the table and walked from the sunroom into the bedroom. He followed her in and turned out the light.

9

Something wasn't right. Connor had been in the bathroom for over ten minutes, and the bus was ready to pull out. Presley and Suarez had kept an eye on him the entire meal. He was the definition of calm. The bus driver had shouted ten more minutes, Connor had got up, gone down the hall to the restroom, then what...disappeared? Presley got up from the table and walked down the hall toward the bathroom, hand on his pistol grip. He opened the door slowly and looked in the small room. Empty. They'd been given the slip.

"Suarez," Presley shouted.

Suarez ran down the hall, "Yeah."

"It's empty, he's gone." Presley looked at the side door at the other end of the hall. He ran through the door and into the side parking lot, completely ignoring the threat of an alarm. Suarez was right on his heels, gun drawn.

The parking lot was empty except for a handful of big rigs on the far side of the lot. Presley walked slowly to the first truck. "I want each of these vehicles searched. Bryce is in one of them. And get a K-9 unit here. If he ran off, we'll sniff him out."

Suarez was already on the phone taking care of it.

He clicked his phone shut and said, "K-9's will be here in fifteen minutes. County police will be here in ten to search these rigs. What about the bus?"

"You and I will search that when County gets here. If we search it now and one of these trucks hits the highway he could slip us again. That would leave us back at square one. No, we stay here and wait for County."

"Is it possible he still doesn't know we're onto him? Maybe he got by us somehow and is waiting patiently for the bus to start."

"That's why we search it when County get's here."

"I get that. What I'm saying is, we better be ready to go because if he's on that bus and a half dozen County police cars show up, that could be bad news for everyone involved."

Presley considered this. "Good point. Alright, we have to get the bus searched before then. New plan—I hang out directly behind the bus. No one can see me because there aren't any windows in the back of the bus. You run in the store real quick, grab yourself a soda and a bag of chips, and casually walk aboard and start a conversation with the driver; you know, small talk—football, movies, whatever. None of the passengers will pay you any mind. Just do a quick scan of the faces, find our man, then slowly step off of the bus and we nail him."

"And if he's not on the bus?"

"No time for that now, we have five minutes or less until County arrives, sirens blaring I'm sure. If you're game, let's do it."

Suarez smiled, "I'm on it."

He walked quickly back into the store and bought a soda and a bag of white cheddar popcorn. Presley walked around the parking lot until he was behind the bus, which was about fifty yards off. Then he walked a straight line directly behind the bus, out of view of any window. Seconds later Suarez walked out of the store like any other person, took a giant swig of soda, and walked casually up the steps of the bus, not even acknowledging Presley at the back end.

Once inside, Suarez stuck to the plan. But the plan changed. Ten seconds into his conversation with the bus driver, the driver asked, "Are you the police officer looking for that fugitive guy?"

Suarez's pulse quickened. "How do you know about that? Is he on here?"

The driver looked frightened, "No, he's not here. Never got back on."

"How did you know that's who we were looking for?"

"Well, I didn't know exactly…"

"Who told you!" Suarez shouted.

"My boss called me, gave me a quick overview and told me to be careful. He didn't want any lawsuits on his hands. I'm sorry, I didn't tell anybody. I promise."

Suarez hurried down the steps and off the bus, then turned and violently threw his drink against the side, sending soda shrapnel everywhere. Presley watched it unfold in a split second and immediately knew Bryce wasn't on the bus. He walked up to Suarez and put his gun back in its holster.

"What happened?"

"Driver knew we were looking for someone…he knew and somehow Bryce spotted it. We should arrest this guy for being an idiot."

"Well we can't go around doing that; our jails are crowded enough as it is. How'd he find out?"

"He said his boss told him the plan and to be careful; trying to cover his tail on lawsuits if anyone got hurt."

Presley was down, but not out. Five County police cars pulled into the diner parking lot.

"Okay, so we know he's not on the bus. Get half of these County officers to pull everyone off. I want them all in the store. We're going to chat with each one, see what they knew about Mr. Bryce. Find out who he was sitting by, what he said, what his mannerisms are. You talk to the driver. I'll take the other officers and start searching the big rigs. When the K-9's get here, send them my way."

Three hours later, all the bus travelers had been interviewed, including the driver, and no one knew anything about the man that had sat in the back for the last day. He didn't talk to anyone, barely got up to use the restroom, and basically just sat and stared at the highway. The big rig search proved fruitless as well. All the cargo was searched, every cubby hole in every cab was empty, and none of the drivers had seen anything suspicious. The K-9 unit had picked up a weak scent from the diner glass Connor drank from, but that trail died in the parking lot. Glass doesn't hold much of a scent, but it was the best they had to offer.

Suarez sat by himself in a booth in the diner, trying to figure out what he could have done differently that would have provided a more positive outcome. Maybe they could have got Connor right when he got off the bus, but it seemed smart at the time to wait until he got back on. One, so they could see him, study his personality, the way he carried himself; to see the look in his eye. And two, so they could corner him in the back of the bus, take him without a fight. That's how it should have gone.

Presley sat down and gave Suarez a blank stare. Presley walked a little lower to the ground now, a little more slouched over. He'd been deflated. He hated when someone had gotten the better of him, and now Bryce had done it twice. And being so close this time, when it was his own personal plan that had failed. Suarez had never seen him so down.

"I just got off the phone with headquarters." Presley said.

"And? They want to promote us?" The joke missed.

"Worse. We're going back to Baltimore. Captain's orders. Next flight out leaves in six hours."

"Back to Baltimore? They can't do that! We're so close to catching this guy!"

"We're not close at all, Suarez. We *were* close. He could be on his way to Mexico, Canada, or California. For crying out loud he could even back track to Baltimore. We certainly don't know what he'll do. We just have to go back, wait for another promising lead, and then we're back on him. But for now we have nowhere to go. He got us. I can't believe he got us."

Suarez sat motionless and took it all in. His partner was right. They'd been outsmarted this time. Both of them. "So what do we do for another six hours?"

"Hope he messes up between now and then."

* * *

Connor was fortunate that the truck he'd stowed away on was headed west. He hadn't thought of it at the time, but how awful

55

would it have been if his ride had gone back east? Of course, right now he didn't care where he was going. What had happened at the diner was as close as calls get. He now knew he had to sharpen his senses even more; maybe even change his appearance some. His facial hair was already starting to grow out, as shaving was one of the first things to go when you're running for your life. He could grow his hair out too; it would take a while, but he had time.

The last few hours had brought relief. Apparently the police had no idea which way he'd gone, and if his luck held, he might be in Phoenix by the morning. Although now Phoenix might be out of the question. The police obviously knew he was heading west, and he'd only decided on Phoenix as part of the cover story he'd told Cowboy Hal a day earlier. His plan was to go a large city, preferably one of the larger ones in America, and blend in with an endless sea of people until he could see things straight. Of the top six largest cities in the nation, four were out of the question: New York, Chicago, Houston and Philadelphia. That left two cities going his direction, Los Angeles and Phoenix. Maybe he would flip a coin. Right now, he was going wherever the jeep he was riding in would take him. That would have to change at the next truck stop.

That stop would come five hours later, just inside of New Mexico. The rig pulled off and the trucker went inside another grease factory for a quick supper. The sun had just dropped below the horizon, and already the desert air had rapidly begun to cool. Connor watched the driver walk into the restaurant and then quickly made his way out of the jeep which was on the back of the trailer. His knees and back were killing him since he'd been keeping low in the jeep for the last eight or so hours; however, he had much bigger problems to worry about.

For starters, his appearance. Apparently everyone and their grandmother's knew what Connor's face looked like. And since the cops knew he was on the western half of the Mississippi, they'd make sure he was the leading news story in every home.

This had to be the first issue he addressed. Connor glanced across the street, saw a large convenience store, and hurried in its direction. Once inside, he decided to buy a pair of sunglasses, an Arizona Diamondbacks baseball hat, and a shirt that said Yo Quiero Nuevo Mexico. Already he looked like a different man. With the hat on and two full days of stubble on his face, he was far from the clean-cut, combed-hair man they were sure to be showing on the news.

As Connor stood in line to pay for his items, a voice behind him said, "Yeah man, go D-backs...best in the west."

He turned around to find a long haired man that looked like a surfer, fully decked out in a Diamondbacks jersey and hat. The guy even had a rattlesnake tattoo on his forearm. Connor saw an opportunity, but knew nothing about baseball. He'd have to improvise.

"Been a fan since the beginning. You?"

The guy's eyes lit up, "Yeah man, die hard through and through."

"Me too," Connor said fully aware he was lying. He hated baseball. "I plan on going to some games this summer."

"Dude, you know the Dodgers are in town tomorrow night. I got seats on the first base side. You should come, bro. Plus the stadium's air conditioned, keep that Phoenix sun off of us." The guy talked like he should be out surfing a wave, hanging ten or riding a gnarly pipeline; or whatever it was that surfers did.

So the Arizona Diamondbacks were in Phoenix? Who knew? Phoenix it was. But Connor had pushed his luck with hitching rides so far; he had to make it look like it was the other guys' idea—a good way to keep from looking suspicious.

"I was actually on my way there now but my car broke down a few miles up the interstate. Looks like I'll be staying here for a while until I can fix it or get it towed back," Connor said disappointingly.

"No way bro, ride with me. I just stopped to load up on some caffeine and gummy worms. We'll be in Phoenix by morning."

"Oh man, thanks but I can't ask to bum a ride with you the rest of the way. I don't have much money to help with gas, and I don't know what to do about my car."

Connor truly did feel bad for lying to all these kind people who were trying to help him, but what was the alternative, saying he was wanted for murder? He'd been keeping a running list of people to confess to when this entire ordeal was over with: Cowboy Hal—his country music friend, Old Man Theodore—the nice elderly gentlemen from Missouri, and now this baseball loving surfer.

"Oh bro, don't worry about that. Listen, here's what you do. Let me give you a lift, we hit up Phoenix tomorrow, and you call and get a truck to tow in your ride whenever you can. And I'm going there anyway, so no need to worry about gas money. No sweat, problem solved. Plus, if you're down, we hit up a D-backs game tomorrow night."

"Are you sure?"

"Bro, us D-back fan's gotta stick together. There aren't that many of us," the surfer said with a smile.

"Well that's awfully kind of you, thanks so much."

"No problem dude. We'll pay for our things and I'll meet you in the parking lot. I drive a black jeep."

Connor winced at the irony.

Turns out, the surfer's name was Tony, and he was a full time student at Arizona State majoring in, of all things, Criminal Justice. One day he would look back at the passenger he was now carrying and want to punch himself. Connor hoped that the authorities wouldn't hold Tony's transportation of a fugitive against him in the future.

The two drove through the night, only stopping for restroom breaks and the occasional get-out-and-jump-around-stay-awake dance that Tony did every time he was about to fall asleep. Connor offered to drive, but Tony said he would never ask his guest to drive. Connor knew that was Tony's nice way of saying he didn't want anyone else driving his Jeep, so he accepted the role of passenger happily. Connor tried to stay up as long as possible and keep a fluent conversation going with his new best friend, trying desperately to fight off a pair of heavy eyelids. Eventually he succumbed to the temptation of sleep for a few short hours.

His nightmares plagued him.

It was dark outside as a slight mist fell. He saw himself all in black—shoes, pants, shirt...ski-mask. Dream Connor watched himself on a movie screen as Black-Ops Connor walked quietly up to the side of a house. A familiar house. Jansen's. He snuck silently through the small garden, then hoisted himself up and over the porch rail. What was he doing?

Black-ops jimmied a window open on the porch, then without a sound and using only his fingertips, slid the window until it was fully open. With a cat-like walk, he glided across the floor until he reached the bottom of the staircase. Dream Connor grew worried as he watched his twin counterpart sneak through his boss's home. Would he stop Black-ops if he could? Did he even want to?

Black-ops tiptoed up the stairs and walked quietly down the hall toward what Connor guessed was a bedroom door. Sure enough, Black-ops entered the master bedroom and stood motionless at the foot of a bed, watching an old man and slightly older woman breathe in and out of a hibernating sleep.

Black-ops stood, watching. Dream Connor began to shout at the movie screen, "Well go on, what are you waiting for? Do it!" But no, that couldn't be right. Why would he want Jansen dead? Why, even now, did he want Black-ops to finish the job, and why was he so curious, almost excited, to watch it take place? Suddenly Dream Connor changed his mind, and screamed, "No...no don't! Don't move!" And then at his former boss, "Mr. Jansen, Mr. Jansen wake up! Wake up!"

But no one moved. The couple lay there, dreaming their last dreams. Black-ops still stood, stoic and strong. Finally, as if waiting for a timer to go off, he crept around the left side of the bed, the side where the old man slept. Reaching on the night stand, he grabbed the man's bottle of pills, though he had no idea of what the old man suffered from. No matter, he would no longer suffer after tonight.

He quickly unscrewed the lid and dumped out the entire bottle into his palm. Pink and white pills stared back at him; just as good as a bullet. From a small backpack, he pulled out a bottle of water and a smaller bottle of chloroform. He took one last look at the old lady on the other side of the bed. Hopefully she'd loved her husband sufficiently. They'd probably been married a million years; way longer than most couples could ever dream. She was lucky, in fact, though she might disagree when she woke up.

No time better than now. Black-ops lifted the man's head ever so gently, cradling his hand behind the old man's neck. With the old man's mouth agape, Black-ops dropped the pills in until his palm was empty. The old man didn't stir.

Then, and this was where he had to be quick, Black-ops poured a large amount of water into the old man's throat. The man immediately woke up and began to squirm, but the hand around his mouth was so tight that he began to panic. Trying to grasp air, he swallowed everything in his mouth if only to rid himself of a blocked airway. Upon feeling the old man swallow, then hearing him suck in air through his mouth, Black-ops held a chloroform-soaked rag to the old man's mouth. The man fell back asleep, unconscious. By the time the chloroform wore off, the man would have already left this world only to enter another. The entire episode lasted seconds. Mrs. Jansen, the old lady, never moved a muscle. He should do her a favor and send her to sleep too. But he didn't hate her like he did the old man.

Dream Connor watched it all in disbelief, his emotions swarming like a nest full of raging hornets. He closed his eyes, somehow already knowing the rest of the story. Black-ops would turn and leave quietly, just the way he had come, and silently sneak back between the sheets in his own safe bed beside his own beautiful wife.

Connor watched the dream continue on a black screen, waiting for the credits to roll, contemplating the array of thoughts going through his erratic mind. Relief filled his veins, an icy, cold relief that coursed through his arms and across his chest. The old man was dead, at least in his dreams. But that had happened in real life, hadn't it? Wasn't that why he was on the run?

Connor suddenly felt his head on fire; a cold heat pressed against the side of his forehead. Glass. He was asleep; his head leaned heavily against the window of Tony's jeep. He groggily pulled himself out of the deepest slumber he'd ever experienced. He'd had the nightmare again, not a new one, but the same; this time...more complete. His first murder dreams started on the bus from Louisville to Oklahoma City, though they were much shorter and incomplete. This was the first one that was slower, more graphic. If his dreams grew any more intense, he'd have to see a psychiatrist.

"Morning bro."

Was it? Connor couldn't tell. He felt hung-over. "Good morning," he said lazily. "How long have I been out?"

"I don't know...four, maybe five hours."

"You mind if we stop soon? Gotta use the restroom."

"Right on man. I could use a break myself. We're about two and a half hours out now. Home stretch. We'll be in Phoenix before you know it."

"Can't wait."

The two stopped to fuel up and grab some chicken biscuits, then were back on the road in no time. Connor, donning the sunglasses and baseball hat of his new favorite team, the D-backs, went completely unnoticed to those he encountered. He still was quick to inventory his surroundings every step of the way. It was important to notice the small, typically imperceptible things, like someone's reaction when they look at you in the eyes or the change in their voice as they attempt to camouflage their nervousness. He didn't want to be too talkative, but it would've been just as bad to be the hermit who spoke to no one. Both types stood out; he had to blend in.

"So where you headed, after we go to the game tonight that is?"

The game? Ah, Connor at some point during his inconsistent lying told Tony he was going to the game tonight. What better way to blend in than at a baseball game; might be good for the soul too.

"I'll probably meet some buddies after the game; they'll give me a ride home."

"You sure dude?"

"Yeah, absolutely. Man you've done enough for me. I can't say thanks enough. Are you always this nice?"

"Listen man, you needed a ride, and I had one. Easy as that. No worries. And don't talk like we're strangers. We're bro's now. In fact, I think can score an extra ticket on our row if you want to hang with me and my family?"

"Your family? Man I really can't do that, but thanks."

"It's not my mom, bro, it's my sister and her husband. We got season tickets for four. The three of us usually make it, and someone can always bring a friend or two. I'll call them first to make sure they're not bringing anyone, but I doubt they are. It'll be crazy."

"Wow. Alright then. You talked me into it. But after that, you're going to have to quit doing me favors."

Tony laughed, "Right on."

The rest of the trip went by fast, as the two talked about their favorite Diamondback ballplayers. This, of course, meant that Tony did most of the talking and Connor chimed in with a lot of, "Oh yeah, he's awesome," or, "Man, that guy can pitch." Before they knew it, the vast Phoenix skyline owned the horizon.

After lunch at a small deli, they decided to go ahead and hit up the ballpark. Game time was a few hours off, but Surfer Tony liked to get there early for batting practice and players autographs. And if Tony liked it, Connor did too. But he didn't have to lie about liking Tony; he was an absolute joy to be around, and as sappy as Connor thought it sounded, he found himself wishing he could approach life with the same carefree passion that Tony had seemed to perfect.

In fact, most of the people he'd met during his cross-country getaway had close to the same approach on life. First there was Hal, with his kind spirit and always positive attitude. Then there was Theodore, the old man who had hopefully mailed Connor's letter, with his warming smile and kind heart. Now Tony, the go-with-the-flow surfer, just might end up being the most genuine of the bunch. And to make matters worse, all of these good-hearted folks were being nice to *him*, someone who had lied to their faces in order to keep himself out of trouble. These people would give Connor the shirt off of their backs, the last dollar bill in their wallets—and selfishly he'd take it.

Now in a matter of minutes, he would meet Tony's family. Not friends or acquaintances, but his *family*—at a baseball game, no less. The thought alone made Connor want to cry. He was here because he was wanted for murder, ran, and lied his way across the country and into an innocent man's trust. It was too much. He couldn't do it. Connor decided that he'd tell Tony he was going to get a hot dog, or soda, or anything, and just disappear. It's not like they'd ever see each other again. He'd actually be doing the poor man a favor. Tomorrow he'd be forgotten.

Tony was just coming back from the next section of seats where he'd sprinted trying to get a batting practice homerun ball.

"Any luck?"

"No man, but I was close. It's fun trying though. You should join me."

"Um maybe. Hey listen I'm going to go grab a soda real quick, cool?"

"Yeah man, I'll be here, hopefully with a ball in hand."

Connor made it a point to not ask Tony if he wanted anything; it would make it much harder to disappear if he had to return with a soda for his friend. He pivoted and headed up the stairs toward the concessions, knowing that he would never see Tony again.

Connor passed another couple coming down the stairs, and a few seconds later heard Tony's voice. "Connor, yo…Connor!"

He turned and saw Tony waving him back down the stairs. So close.

He took a deep breath and walked back down toward Tony, who now stood with who Connor guessed was Tony's sister and her husband.

No problem, he would say hello politely, then excuse himself and continue his flight toward loneliness.

"Connor, I'd like you to meet my sister Annika and her husband John. John, Annika, this is my main man Connor." Handshakes all around, a few minutes of small talk, and Connor excused himself to go get a soda. There was no stopping him now. What was he thinking getting involved with all these people? No matter, a few more steps and he'd never see them again. They would never be hurt by him.

John turned and headed up the stairs toward Connor as he yelled, "Hold on and I'll come with. I could go for a drink and some nachos."

So close.

10

There had been no further leads on their suspect, Connor Bryce, so Presley and Suarez had to fly back to Baltimore, Captain's orders. Now they sat silently in his office watching the steam escape from their coffee mugs. It was time to regroup—comb over the evidence again, do more interviews with people who knew him…maybe someone would give a hint or clue as to Connor's next move. Finding a killer meant knowing him, understanding him, thinking like him. First stop would be his wife, Kelly. Connor hadn't contacted her yet, and there was nothing out of the ordinary on her bugged phone calls. Her kid was at Virginia Tech down in Blacksburg. And the officers who'd been on surveillance duty hadn't reported anything odd either. Just normal, everyday life for Kelly Bryce; but as Presley knew, that wouldn't last forever.

"What's your plan?" asked the Captain.

Presley took a sip of coffee and sat his mug back down. "Our plan is, talk to the wife again, the son, dig around some on Lasser and see where he fits in, then follow the pieces from there. At some point Bryce will contact his wife; that I know for sure. Combine that with any solid leads we get—and we will get some—we'll have another bead on him soon. He can't run forever."

The Captain leaned over his desk and looked both men in the eyes. "Do either of you have any idea what continent this guy is even on? He could be running sled dogs in Alaska right now. He could be in Belgium trying out their waffles. He could be right across the street. Get out there and find him!" His fist pounded the tables and a few drops of coffee sloshed over the sides.

Neither Presley nor Suarez said a word as they both exited the office. Though impatient, their superior was right. Connor Bryce could be anywhere in the world. The thought was sickening.

Presley spoke first as Suarez rounded his own desk.

"Let's get a squad car down to Blacksburg, see if we can't get any info from the son. Tap his phones too if he'll let us. Connor might try to contact him before he does his wife. Have Reynolds get us all the information he can on Trace Lasser. You and I will go see Mrs. Bryce again; she can't be holding up well. Maybe we can help."

"Sure thing. Meet you in the car in a few." Suarez said as he grabbed a protein bar from the inside of his desk. He liked taking the backseat to Presley. Not taking the backseat really, they were both equal partners, but they wouldn't work so well together if they were both the dominant one. It suited Suarez's personality to sit back and let Pres call most of the shots. First off, Pres was better at it, and second, he could handle the Captain better. Suarez was a little too volatile to get into it with the Captain every other day. Presley was calm and cool; not prone to erupting when tempers got high, unlike his partner. Knowing this, Pres naturally took the lead by coming up with the different plans and running them by Suarez; any feedback was always appreciated. The two men met in the parking lot and headed off toward the Bryce residence. With any luck, Connor would be on the front porch as they pulled up.

* * *

Kelly Bryce had been up almost two straight days searching for any information she could find on Trace Lasser. The man was a child; that much she could tell with certainty. But was he dangerous? Apparently he'd been sued as many as four times for sexual harassment complaints at different companies over the last few years, each time the female in question ended up dropping all charges. Two charges of assault were also dropped due to lack of evidence; that might be something.

Also of interest, she'd learned that Trace Lasser and Sarri Jansen had permanently separated shortly after they were married. According to the divorce certificate, a public record, Sarri filed the papers two months after their wedding day citing irreconcilable differences. Kelly felt there were more to both stories—the harassment/assault charges and the divorce—that met the eye. Was it possible that Lasser was caught having an affair? He'd obviously had his problems keeping his hands to himself. Was he violent or abusive? Kelly had hundreds of questions, but none larger than this: if Trace Lasser cheated on or abused his new wife Sarri, thus causing their divorce, why did Sarri's father, Gregory Jansen, hire his ex-son-in-law to a prominent position in his multi-million dollar company?

The whole thing made no sense.

One thing seemed certain—Connor had nothing to do with any of it. He was just in the wrong place at the wrong time. Poor man. She'd been thinking about him every day, naturally, but felt like if she weren't able to hear from him soon she might have a conniption. There were only so many things she could do to keep her mind off of him; not that he ever truly escaped her thoughts. She'd shifted into overdrive at work lately, trying to busy her mind with plants and flowers. He was still there, and not just in the back of her mind either; Connor lived in the front. Now she sat on a couch in her home, lights off, trying to catch up on rest.

The light sound of a metal flap let her know her mail had just arrived in the small black box hanging by the front door. More bills no doubt; bills that would be harder to pay now that Connor had lost his job. Bills that would be difficult to pay once he was in jail for life. Bills that would be impossible to pay once the nasty Baltimore winter hit and the plant and flower business slowed down. Even still, it didn't matter; bills, money, house, cars—none of it mattered if she couldn't have Connor.

She wrestled herself off of the couch and walked to the mail box. Sure enough, as she flipped through, bill, bill, bill. Then, on the fourth envelope, she paused. No return address. A postmark from some town in Missouri she'd never heard of. This was Connor.

Kelly ripped open the letter and began to read her husbands' sloppy, beautiful handwriting:

> *My Dearest Bride,*
>
> *Please know that I'm alright. Please know that I miss you terribly. I have not stopped thinking about you since I left. If only you were here with me, holding my hand, all my fears would be erased. I'm not sure how long I will be gone. A few weeks…maybe a few months. I have some things to work through; my thoughts, my feelings, and any outcome in this scenario that can put me back together with you as quickly as possible. Thank you so much for believing me and staying by my side. Thank you for loving me. I'm going to call you soon. Never stop thinking my name.*
>
> *Always and Forever,*
> *-C-*

Relief flooded her body as a weight lifted off of her chest. Her husband was okay. His trek had taken him, at least as of a few days ago, to a small town in Missouri. Surely by now he had moved on, probably headed west. The silly thought crossed her mind of Connor settling down in a small farming community in the Midwest. Overalls, tractors, bathing down by the creek but pronouncing it *crick*.

Kelly couldn't help an audible chuckle slip out as her eyes filled with tears. The mental picture of her husband baiting his own hook was priceless. He'd hate country life, and he would stick out like the sorest of thumbs. No, Connor would be heading for a city; someplace where he would fit in more comfortably, where he could be himself and get lost in the busy-ness of city streets.

A knock on the door startled her. She looked out the side window and saw the two police officers she'd met a few days ago at her flower shop. They had taken her down to the police station for questioning. She'd seen Connor by the phone. Then nothing.

Her eyes misted again and she quickly used the envelope to fan cold air over her face. The cops were here for a reason, probably more questions, and she had to do her best to look and act normal. Connor's letter would remain a secret. She walked into the kitchen and put the note in a drawer.

Kelly quickly composed herself and opened the front door.

"Good afternoon officers, would you like to come in?"

"Yes Mrs. Bryce, thank you." Presley said.

"Would either of you like anything to drink?"

"Sweet tea if you have it."

"Sure do, and for you, sir?" Kelly asked Suarez.

"Water will be fine."

"Water it is."

She disappeared into the kitchen for a few short seconds and then reappeared with the drinks in hand. Presley noticed that her eyes looked a bit puffy.

"You'll have to forgive me," Kelly said, "but I'm awful at remembering names."

"I'm Detective Presley, this is Detective Suarez. I know the last time we met things were a bit more intense and emotional. I'm sorry about that. There's really no easy way to do some of the things we have to do."

Kelly shrugged it off, "No problem. It was a lot to take in at once. What can I help you two with today?"

"Let's talk about you first," Presley said, "How have you been?"

"Steady. Very busy at work."

"And when you're not at work?"

"I've been alright. I mean, I'm making it. It's difficult here by myself, but I'm not complaining. My husband is out there with nothing, and I'm here in this huge house as comfortable as I can be. He's the one I feel sorry for."

"With all due respect ma'am, you're husband ran from us."

"With all due respect, detective, you had him convicted before you'd even met him. Now if you came here to pick a fight I'm afraid I'll kindly ask you to leave."

"No Mrs. Bryce, I apologize," Presley said, "I didn't mean to come across that way. I understand it seems like we made a rush to judgment, but all I simply wanted to do, honestly, was ask your husband some questions. That's it. There are a few mysteries that only he can answer. I believe in the justice system, Mrs. Bryce, and I believe in people being innocent until proven guilty. That applies to your husband. But he's not doing himself any favors by running from the law."

"But he doesn't know the answer to any of your mysteries. That's my point. The shoes, the fingerprints, he's as clueless as I am. And I'll tell you again, he was with me the whole night. He never left the house. What do I have to do for you to believe me? A polygraph? Strap me up. Hand on the Bible? Give me one. Connor Bryce was with me, in our bed, the entire night."

Presley decided on a new approach, and after letting things calm down in the room a bit, asked, "Mrs. Bryce, have you heard from your husband recently?"

"I haven't talked to my husband since the day he left." That part was true.

"No contact at all?"

"None." That part wasn't. "You have my phones tapped and a cop watching me from down the street. Why don't you have someone move in with me?"

Silence. Then Kelly again, "Listen, I'm sorry for sounding rude. That's not me. I'm not dealing with this well; that much is obvious. I don't know how. It's the worst thing I've ever been through, but despite that, I can't help but think every second of every day, that my husband is out there alone. It's a scary world. You all probably know that better than me. I'm worried about him and I want him home. Until then, I'm not sure what else I can do to help you."

They talked for a few more minutes with nothing being accomplished. Presley stood up to leave as Suarez followed suit. Presley turned and handed Kelly his business card. "Mrs. Bryce, thanks for your time. I'm sorry this is so difficult, and do honestly wish for the best and quickest outcome. Here's my card. You might already have it, but in case you don't. If you can think of anything else or you just want to talk, call me. I can listen."

Kelly took the card and smiled as best as she could. The dam behind her eyes was sure to bust at any second. "Thank you."

"And one more thing Mrs. Bryce."

"Yes."

"If you're serious about a polygraph test, I can make that happen. Just make sure you're telling the truth. It could make or break you."

"Okay thanks. I'll think about it and let you know."

The officers walked off her front porch and back to their car. Kelly shut the door and broke down.

* * *

Connor and Tony were friends. There was no way, as hard as Connor tried, around it. After the shared experience of the Diamondbacks game, they'd exchanged numbers and decided to meet up again a few days later for dinner at John and Annika's house. Annika was Tony's sister. Connor had planned on making his escape at the ballpark by simply disappearing into the night. That changed when John joined him at the concession stands. The two had begun to talk, and John had learned that Connor's background was in engineering. And when John, an outdoorsman himself, learned that Connor designed outdoor equipment of all types, they instantly began exchanging design and product ideas.

The baseball game had ended and Connor said his goodbyes. They'd given him a dinner invitation for some night in the future, and he'd accepted. He really hadn't planned on keeping his promise, still believing that the further he stayed away from people, the better the chances were of him surviving. But friendship with Tony, John, and Annika meant other things that might help him—namely computer access, and if he played his cards right, a safe haven for a while. As of now they were under the assumption he lived in Phoenix and that the only reason he'd met up with Tony was because Connor's car had broken down in New Mexico; Tony had given him a lift back home. Connor wasn't ready to tell them the truth yet. He had to build up their trust first, then let little pieces of the truth come out one by one.

After they had parted ways after the game, Connor had walked to the nearest motel and checked in. This would be his new home for a while. It had been a few days since then, and though he and Tony had exchanged numbers, Connor still hadn't turned his cell phone on since he'd fled Baltimore. At some point he would have to either get a new phone number or find some other way he could call Kelly without his phone being traced. Maybe they could Skype somehow. That was untraceable right?

Now Connor sat on the edge of his bed and turned on the television in his room. After watching the news for thirty minutes, he was relieved to find no mention of his name or picture with the words WANTED under it. Perhaps his fame hadn't reached that far west yet. This was one of the few things working in his favor, though that could change any second. No slip ups this time. He had to stay in Phoenix for a while. There's no way he could get to the bottom of this mess by running coast to coast. He needed some sense of stability, and if he were careful, Phoenix could be it. He'd even checked into his dump motel room using a false name.

Feeling a little more comfortable that his face wasn't everywhere in the city, Connor called Tony from his motel room and found out that John and Annika were having a cookout that night at their home. Connor accepted Tony's invitation, and after getting the address, told him he'd meet him there.

He jumped in a quick shower and then began to dress, suddenly anticipating socializing like a normal person; plus he would finally get to eat a real meal. He was beginning to like Phoenix, and the thought crossed his mind to move there once this whole ordeal was over; with Kelly, of course.

A longer than expected cab ride later, Connor pulled up to the Mims residence, a gorgeous home in the perfect neighborhood. The lawn was perfectly manicured and somehow kept its emerald green appearance despite the cruel Arizona summer.

Connor took it all in as he walked up the stairs and rang the doorbell. After a few minutes, Annika answered. In a bathing suit.

"Hey Connor, glad you could make it."

Connor was caught off guard. Not in a shameful or erotic way, he just didn't expect it. No big deal.

"Thanks for the invite." He held out a bottle of wine. "This is for you two...least I could do." They stepped inside and moved towards the kitchen.

Annika smiled, "Aw, thanks so much. Party's in the back right now. You brought shorts for the pool, right?"

"No I'm afraid I didn't. Must have missed the memo. That's okay though, I'll help John on the grill."

"Don't be silly. We're playing volleyball and need a fourth anyway. You and John are probably the same size if you don't mind wearing some of his basketball shorts."

"No I don't mind; just don't put me in his undershorts."

Annika let out a laugh as she headed up the stairs, "Wait right here and I'll grab you some."

Connor stood at the base of the stairs for a few minutes and inventoried his environment. Pictures of the happy couple adorned the walls. Civil blueprint drawings hung under framed glass next to a laminated cover of a journal with John's picture on it. On the other side of the wall were photographs on Annika holding different food dishes and smiling elegantly for the camera; captions under each picture described the meal. These people were top notch; in every way the perfect couple.

She came back with the shorts and gave them to Connor. "There's a bathroom right down the hall. We'll be out back when you're done."

"Alright, thanks," he said, scolding himself for watching her, for the briefest of moments, as she walked away.

Connor changed and joined the party in the back. Tony, John, and Annika were all in the pool playing volleyball just as she had said. It was John and Annika against her brother, Tony.

Noticing Connor, Tony yelled, "You're with me bro. They're up by four, playing to fifteen. Watch the lady, she's a killer."

She's not the only one, Connor thought, but that was merely a joke. He hopped in the pool, gave a fist bump to Surfer Tony, said hello to John, and the game was back on. Water splashed and bodies flew for the next few minutes, and eventually the game was tied going into the last point; none of that win by two junk.

Tony served the ball across the net to John, who then bumped it up to Annika. Her set-up to John was ill-timed, and at the last second he slid a hand under the ball before it hit the water, barely hitting it back over the net. Connor had an easy bump of the ball towards Tony, who then set up Connor beautifully. The whole thing happened in slow motion. Connor jumped, cocked his arm back like the hammer on a gun, and slammed the ball with all his might. It was a Top Gun moment. Except the ball left Connor's palm and smashed directly into John's nose.

John flew back as the water around him immediately began to turn pink. His nose gushed blood as he and Annika began to retreat back toward the patio.

"Oh my goodness, John I'm so sorry," Connor said as he crossed under the net and waded towards John, who now leaned with his back against the wall of the pool. Annika got out and pulled a deck chair over and then helped John recline comfortably. Tony got out and grabbed a towel.

"John, seriously, I'm so sorry. That was a complete accident."

"Oh man, don't worry about it. Volleyball's a rough game," he said with his head tilted toward the sky. "Just watch out when we have a rematch."

"Seriously, how bad is it?"

Annika said, "I don't think it's that bad. Not broken at least."

"Wow I feel like an idiot. Not sure what happened there."

"Man, for real, don't worry about it. I'll be fine in no time. It certainly won't stop me from eating steaks and enjoying the rest of this beautiful day. We're cool man. No harm done."

"Good. What can I do to help?"

"Ask Tony."

Connor helped Tony fire up the grill, and soon four marinated T-bones were sizzling side by side. Tin-foiled corn-on-the-cob sat on the rack above.

Eventually John's nose stopped bleeding, and with cotton hanging out of both nostrils, he joined the others. The rest of the evening progressed without a hitch. They sat and ate and talked and laughed for hours.

When things were wrapping up, John said, "Let's do this again next weekend. Connor, you in?"

"Next weekend, you sure?"

"Absolutely. Give me a chance to redeem myself at volleyball."

"Yeah I'll come. Maybe we should play board games though."

"Ha, yeah right. Listen, bring your wife. You said she worked late tonight, but usually she doesn't, right? So she can come?"

"We'd love to meet her," Annika said.

"Well to be honest, things have been a little rocky recently, so if it's okay, it'll still probably just be me. Time away is probably the best thing for me right now anyway." The words came out so simple it had actually surprised him a little.

"Well," John said, "We're sorry to hear that, but you're still more than welcome to join us. And when things get better, she'll join you. How about that?"

"Sounds good. Thanks for understanding."

"No problem man. Marriages get difficult. That's no secret. But enough of that. We'll see you next weekend."

"All right, goodnight."

Connor left in a cab at the end of the night, as "his car" was still being fixed. As the taxi pulled away, he put his head back, shut his eyes, and tried to remember the last time he'd had that much fun.

11

Kelly had to find out more about Trace Lasser; the man who'd stolen her husband's life. He was brilliant, arrogant, powerful, and had connections throughout D.C. His father was in politics, his ex-father-in-law, business. When these men made decisions, the ripples were felt everywhere. Now Kelly had the "privilege" of trying to get inside his head. The last person she could imagine wanting to know more about was this weasel, yet he was also the same weasel that stood in between her husband and his freedom.

The first step at getting to know the real Trace Lasser was finding his weakness; and men like him usually had the same one: women. Kelly had already figured this out; one, because she'd seen the numerous harassment complaints against him in the past, not to mention the assault charges. And two, because he had basically come onto her over the phone the last time they'd talked. Getting his attention should be easy; her little black dress would do that. But gaining his trust would be hard.

The last time they'd talked over the phone, Kelly had done well to control her emotions as they burned inside of her. As far as she knew, Lasser had no idea what Kelly's true thoughts about him were. That would work in her favor. She could play the cold, lonely wife card. If her acting was good enough, maybe he would buy it. She had to come across as innocent and helpless as possible; give Lasser the feeling he was in control—ultimate power.

Slowly she'd begun to develop a plan. She would call Lasser to see if he'd heard anything relevant from the police. At some point in the conversation, she would break down; say she had no one to talk to…that all she wanted was a shoulder to cry on. He, predictably, would offer his shoulder. *Game.* She would accept and meet him, discreetly of course, at a restaurant or coffee shop, try to get him to open up as they shared each other's trust. *Set.* At some point, she would turn the tables on him—catch him in a lie or surprise him with a shock question about his past. *Match.*

Of course, he might be so out-of-this-world cocky that he would tell her anything just to get her black dress off. Overconfident guys with one thing on their mind were easily predictable. The entire thought of spending one second with that creep was too much to handle. But this wasn't about her, it was about Connor. Guys like Lasser could never compare to guys like Connor. One was a killer, the other one wasn't.

Kelly picked up her phone and forced her fingers to dial the number to Lasser's office. He picked up after seven rings, giving the appearance that he was busy. Typical.

"Yes," he said in an inconvenient tone.

"Mr. Lasser, this is Kelly Bryce."

Pause, then in a much gentler and slightly deeper voice, "Well, hello Mrs. Bryce. How are things?"

"Not good. Not good at all Mr. Lasser."

"Please, call me Trace. Now tell me, what's going on?"

"Alright Trace. I just, I'm just not sure where to turn. I've been trying to keep my mind busy with work, but I can't work twenty-four hours a day. And then I come home, and it's so quiet here, so cold without Connor's presence, I cry myself to sleep every night. And I don't want to burden you, but…"

"It's no burden at all Mrs. Bryce."

"Kelly."

"Okay, Kelly. It's no burden at all. I told you that I was here to help, and I can help just by listening."

"That's just the thing. I mean, I don't have a lot of girlfriends around to talk to, most have moved away, and talking over the phone isn't the same as looking into another set of eyes." She was playing this perfectly. "And I know you and I haven't even met, but I was thinking maybe I could come down to the office and talk with you or someone else that Connor worked with. If I can't open up to one of my friends, I might as well talk to one of his."

"What's your schedule like?"

"I make my own schedule. I own a flower shop, but it's in capable hands. I just need to get some things off of my chest." She began to sniffle over the phone.

"Here's what we'll do. I was going to work late tonight to push some of these papers through, but that can wait. It hurts me to hear the pain in your voice. Let's go out, get some drinks, and we can talk. I know a great little place a few miles from here, very quiet. That would be great for you."

Kelly's voice was soft on the other end. "Are you sure? I don't want your work to pile up just because of me."

"No problem at all. This is more important. Work will be waiting on me tomorrow. Let's say, seven-o-clock?"

"Okay."

"Great, it's a small place on Riverdale called Harps."

"I've heard of it. I'll see you there. And Mr. Lasser, Trace...thanks so much."

"My pleasure."

Kelly hung up the phone and immediately stopped crying. Her tears weren't real. She would never waste real emotion on Trace Lasser. But she would waste a few hours and a hundred bucks to meet him for drinks in order to understand his mind. Part one of her plan was complete; but that was the easy part. The hardest part was yet to come, and it would require reinforcements.

Kelly walked into her closet and found her little black dress. Even in her purest moments of modesty, she would quickly admit that she looked stunning in this miracle fabric. It hung softly on her shoulders, then eased and clung its way around her torso like a dream. The neckline didn't drop too low, as that wasn't Kelly's style, but it wasn't a priest's collar either. Not in the least.

She pulled the dress on over her head and let it fall down around her. In an instant she went from already attractive to shut-up gorgeous. She walked over to her jewelry box and picked out a stunning diamond necklace that Connor had given her for their tenth wedding anniversary. After clamping it around her neck, she stepped back to admire herself in the mirror. She pulled her hair up and, after a few quick turns of the wrist and some hair bands, perfected the I-was-in-a-hurry-tossy look that guys dream of. Lasser no doubt had seen his share of pretty women in the past, but in a few hours, Kelly Bryce would blow his mind.

After showering and having a light dinner, Kelly re-dressed herself in her earlier magic, then drove off towards Harps in her Volvo. She had to force herself to quit thinking about Connor and start thinking about the task currently at hand. Trace Lasser. The man was hiding something; he was as shady as a shadow. There was a reason Jansen gave him Connor's job. There was also a reason, in Kelly's mind, that Lasser felt Jansen had to be killed. It suddenly struck her how precise and careful she needed to be. Lasser was a dangerous man, a killer, and if he smelt an ambush of any kind, he could snap. At least they would be in a public place. She would never be alone with him.

She pulled up to Harps and gave the valet her keys. This place was upscale. Lasser would never choose a place frequented by the middle class; not when he was pursuing prey. She took a deep breath and walked inside.

Lasser sat at a table in the corner, dressed handsomely in a suit and tie. Upon seeing Kelly he stood up, pulled her chair out and offered her a seat. Always the gentleman.

He sat back down in his chair and looked at her, waiting for her to speak. This was a power move; to make the other person *feel* the need to talk first. Stay quiet, stay in control. He was no dummy.

There was a bottle of wine waiting patiently on ice. Kelly almost called the whole thing off. Breathing grew more difficult, the air heavier. Instead, she regained focus, forced in a lungful of oxygen, and said, "Thanks so much for meeting me. I know you're a very busy man."

Trace smiled, "No problem at all. Would you like some wine?"

"Yes please."

"Have you eaten? I took the liberty of ordering an appetizer or two; give us a little something to snack on."

"That sounds great." Kelly looked around the room and smiled, "I haven't been out like this in a long time, even when Connor was here, but especially recently; I haven't found the strength to get out of the house after work."

"Well," Trace said as he poured two glasses of wine, "You've been through a lot recently, more than any woman should ever have to go through in a lifetime. You've already proven yourself stronger than most."

Kelly took a small sip of her drink. The warmth flooded her throat. "I don't feel like it. I feel depressed and vulnerable. Weak. My whole world has been shifted upside down, and I don't know where to turn or what to believe."

"What does your gut tell you?"

"I don't know. That's the problem. My heart tells me one thing, but my brain tells me something else—it's saying what the police are telling me."

"Which is?"

"Which is that if Connor didn't do anything wrong, he sure has a lot of explaining to do. I don't know what to say about all the evidence they have against him. I feel so trapped, and I'm sure he does too."

"Well, this is a step in the right direction. For you, at least. I mean, I certainly hope everything works out for Connor too, things are obviously pretty deep. But at least on your end, you're trying to keep your mind healthy by talking with people, in this case, me. Holding things in is the worst thing you could do," Trace said as he ordered a Crown and Coke.

They talked for another hour, mostly Kelly telling him a lot about herself, trying to gain his trust and build up her own confidence. She would grade the night an A+ so far. Their dialogue was splendid, mixing funny stories with heartfelt ones, each exposing a little more of themselves as the night wore on. Maybe they were truly connecting; maybe it was the alcohol.

He hadn't taken his eyes off of her the entire night. And she'd seen that look before, it wasn't interest; it was lust. She'd taken small sips of wine all night, staying completely within her right mind. The same couldn't be said for Lasser.

Kelly leaned forward slowly, "So tell me about yourself, Trace."

"What do you want to know?"

She smiled, "Everything."

"Well, I'm successful, rich, and extremely good looking," he said with a wink.

"So how come a man with those attributes doesn't have a pretty girl on his arm or a ring around his finger."

"I tried marriage once. Didn't take. I don't think it was intended for guys like me. I'm a workaholic. My wife wasn't."

"Do you have any kids?"

"No. We we're going to wait a while at first, but then the ship sunk and I haven't talked to her since. It's obviously a good thing that things worked out the way they did though. My work comes first, and Sarri wanted me home at five every day."

"Sarri?" Kelly tried to act like she was placing the name, "Sarri Jansen?"

Lasser's punch drunk eyes gave a hint at his error, but he answered, "Yes, you know her?"

"Well no, but I know of her. I heard Connor talking about her once or twice. I think he'd met her before. Not sure really. I just remembered the name because it's a little different."

Lasser went on like he had nothing to hide, "Yes, well, Sarri was a little different too so I assume it fits," he said as he polished off his fifth C and C.

"Do you mind if I ask what happened between the two of you? I mean, it's possible I'm headed down that same road depending on how things shake out. What lawyer did you use? Was it an ugly process?"

Lasser was completely obliterated at this point. Kelly began to think she hadn't needed the black dress, but could have easily had the same success with a twelve pack.

"It wasn't an ugly process. Right from the beginning, I hated her and she hated me. But for business and politics, it would have been good if we could've made it work. By the time we filed for divorce, the only thing we could agree on was that we both wanted out as quickly as possible. We both had money and good families, so I took my junk one way and she took hers another."

"We're you lonely?"

"Oh goodness no. I had a lady friend or two that helped me cope with things, and I suspect she enjoyed the company of gentlemen as well. No one in Washington is faithful."

He was practically spilling his guts now.

Kelly went in for the kill.

"So you hated his daughter, married then divorced her, and you still got a job working under Jansen? You must be a genius!"

"Oh I'm no genius," he said in slurred speech, "But when you have damaging information on someone as successful as Jansen, you can name your price. That's what I did. So I guess you're right, maybe I am a genius."

"What kind of...oh never mind, it's none of my business," Kelly said as she pushed a strand of hair back from her eyes. "I can't ask a magician how he does his tricks, right?"

The man was completely plastered. Kelly found it surprising he could still talk.

"It's no secret, plus he's dead now anyway so it will all come out eventually. Sarri wasn't Mrs. Jansen's daughter. I found her birth certificate in our files one day. When I asked her about it, she broke down and told me some story about her real mom and how she used to work for Greg Jansen. Sarri said her mother was filing papers late one night at the request of Jansen, and, I'll say this discreetly for your benefit, forced himself upon her. Nine months later, my future ex-wife was born. He paid the lady off to shut her up; she never said a word. I thought Sarri had made it all up, for attention or something, but then when we split up I confronted Jansen about it. Rape, infidelity, extortion, there was no telling what other information would come out if I went public, so I did what everyone else in Washington does…blackmail. Needless to say, he offered me a job."

Kelly was completely shocked. This was unbelievable. Stay focused.

"But you didn't need a job right, you're already rich?"

"Come on now, sweetheart, you can never have too much money. I didn't like the idea at first either, but I saw their financial trends, and he told me about the new product line your husband had designed. Their stock was about to skyrocket. It still will. I'm going from millionaire to billionaire. Not a bad job if you can get it?"

"And what about Connor?"

Lasser developed a mournful look on his face as he looked at her through glassy eyes. "I'm very sorry about that. I didn't realize at the time all the lives that this would affect. Please accept my apology. If things work out, Connor can have his old job back, working for me."

Kelly was about to erupt. She'd done well to hold it in this long, but with Lasser three sheets to the wind, she'd forced herself to control her emotions and let him do the talking. But the night was getting late, and the time to make a move was at hand. Moment of truth.

"That's very nice of you to offer Connor his job back. But if he comes back to work for you, that would mean he's not a killer, and if he didn't kill Jansen, then the real killer is still out there."

"What are you getting at, sweetheart? If you were the cops, where would you look?"

She held his eyes, "You."

Lasser let out a laugh. Not the reaction she'd expected.

"Me? That's comical. I had no reason to. A cushy job, boatloads of money, what would've been my motive?"

"Who knows, but I'm sure you have some skeletons in your closet, and one of those skeletons is Jansen."

Suddenly Lasser was serious, "So what, I staged the evidence pointing toward your husband so I could kill an old man that was scared of me to begin with? It makes no sense. This is pathetic; look at you. You're making things up so that you can tell yourself in your head that your husband's not a killer. You want to feel better about him. Was that your intention from the beginning? Call me on the phone, sound desperate for help, get all pretty for the camera and then liquor me up? Please. I'm way smarter than that. Plus I have nothing to hide. I didn't kill anyone. Now get out of my face, you've wasted enough of my time."

Kelly stood from her chair and started to speak, but Lasser grabbed her wrist and said, "Unless you want to waste a few more minutes at my place?"

The punch surprised even Kelly. Not a slap, like most girls; a full-fisted punch to the eye. Lasser's head snapped back and to the side, and immediately blood flowed from the cut her ring had made just under his left eye.

He smiled.

"I didn't see that coming," Lasser said as he dabbed his cut with a napkin, "but I like it when they're feisty. I always get what I want, Mrs. Bryce, and something tells me we'll be seeing each other soon."

Kelly leaned down and whispered in his ear, "If you ever touch me again, I'll kill you."

She walked out of Harps as jazz music played in the background. Lasser's foot tapped to the beat.

PART TWO

12

Summer turned into fall, and fall to winter. Not that Phoenix had much of a winter, but it was December nonetheless. Connor had spent the last few months working with a dry wall crew hanging sheet rock in strip malls. It didn't pay much, but it paid cash; off the radar. He'd written to Kelly several times, usually once a week, but still hadn't talked to her on the phone. It seemed the man hunt for him was over, or at least had died down significantly. He stayed low, only made purchases in cash, and when he wasn't hanging out with the Mims, his home was the Roach Castle he'd moved into when he'd first arrived. Not the Hilton, but they didn't ask questions.

He longed to hear Kelly's voice, and sadly had to admit to himself he'd almost forgotten what it sounded like. She would be proud of him though. He'd survived, fighting hard to stay free so that he could win back his life and clear his name. It was a Hollywood story. Except that he'd made no progress. He tried to fight back and get answers, but he didn't know where to start. He had no access, obviously, to anyone from his old office; not Myra, not his friend Brantley, and certainly not Lasser. He couldn't call the cops, and the one man with answers—Jansen—was six feet under, staring blindly at the sky. Connor finally decided to stay his course, continue to hang low, and let the police do their work, which would hopefully end with Trace Lasser behind bars.

Meanwhile, he'd made quite the connection with John and Annika Mims. Most weekends, at least every other weekend, Connor was invited over to the Mims house for some random get together. Some nights, if the party wore on, he'd stay over and crash in their spare bedroom.

Specifically, he and John had become good friends; buddies, in guy-speak. They both loved the world of engineering, production, and design, and shared ideas and drawings ad nauseam. Even when they went out to dinner, Annika would continually reprimand them for spending the entire time sketching on napkins. Over the months their friendship grew, and they even toyed with the idea of going into business together.

John had confided in Connor that he and Annika were trying to have kids, but at this point it seemed impossible. In fact, John had seen every specialist in the southwest, and each came back with the same answer: no children. Now adoption was on the table, and it had become the most viable, promising avenue.

Talking was hard enough for guys as it is, but something clicked between Connor and John as both men shared their struggles. Connor shared also, informing John that, after months of separation, he and his wife had decided to divorce. Yes, it was admittedly difficult, but well needed.

It was all a lie, of course. The job partnership, the divorce, everything. Connor was beginning to fall under the pressure of keeping this up. He was on the run, trying to blend in with normal society, with the hopes that somehow, someway he would be able to live a normal life with his family. Meanwhile, he'd met a nice couple that were truly genuine, shared his interest, and opened their home to him. He didn't deserve them; they didn't deserve his lies. Connor hoped it would all end soon, yet the light at the end of the tunnel had been extinguished long ago.

He had to end this masquerade. He'd begun to come up with a story, another lie, which would put him moving onto another city. He could not continue to make the Mims a part of his lies, a part of the downward spiral that sadly was his life. He would leave; say he and Kelly were working on things and would be moving back to the east coast. Perhaps one day in the future he would write them a letter explaining everything; his actions, his deceit. They were such great people that they might actually understand.

Yes, that's exactly what he would do. But he couldn't tell them tonight; it would have to be next week. Tonight was John's birthday party, and you can't give a friend bad news on his birthday. Connor had gotten John an autographed baseball signed by the entire Arizona Diamondbacks team that he'd bought off of eBay; it would look great in John's man cave.

Party time came, thankfully the house wasn't nearly as crowded as Connor thought it would be. A few of the Mims' friends, most of whom Connor knew by now were there, but oddly there was no sign of Annika. The party was congregated on the back porch, when suddenly all the lights went out.

For a brief moment Connor had thought the police had found him, that this was a raid. A few seconds later though, the lights sprang back to life, revealing an enormous cake in the middle of their back yard.

81

Music started playing, some pop hit by the Black Eyed Peas. John walked up to the cake with a smile on his face, knowing like everyone else what was inside. As if she'd expected he was close, Annika burst out of the cake as everyone around cheered. The music cranked up, Madonna this time, and Annika led John in a ballroom waltz. Other couples joined in, and the party was in full swing.

Connor stood by himself, cup of punch in hand, and watched the fun unfold. At the next song, another Madge classic, someone cut in on Annika and began to dance with her husband. She then noticed Connor standing by himself and asked him to dance. Connor had never ballroom danced to pop music before, but quickly had to admit how much fun it was.

"This is a great party," he said to Annika, "and that cake thing was hysterical."

"Oh, thanks. Yeah I've had that planned for a while. I try to do something fun for him every year. Last year it was bungee jumping, this year, cake jumping," she said as she smiled.

Wow, she was intoxicating.

Connor had never actually studied her up close. She had tiny brown freckles at the end of nose, and her eyes glistened silver in the shadows of the night. She had small lines forming around her lips, a bi-product of years of smiling. Like an angel. Her hair was auburn, but turned red when the light hit it at certain angles. Connor suddenly realized the grace of her hips as they swayed gently under his arms. Who was she? He'd never seen this woman before, not the way he was seeing her tonight.

Connor and John had spent a lot of time together, but never he and Annika. Not alone. Not this close. They danced and continued their small talk. Connor learned quickly to keep her talking so that he could look at her even longer, not having to think or navigate himself through some pointless answer. When they turned swiftly, he would catch specific fragrances from her hair; vanilla, honey…something exotic. She'd asked him a question, something about Phoenix or baseball—who knows, and at some point during his mindless ramblings he must have said something funny, because she laughed so hard she had to pull her head into his chest to keep her cackle down.

The song ended. Thank the stars the song had ended.

Annika thanked Connor for the dance, and then floated back to her husband, the birthday boy. Connor stood speechless as he tried to make sense of what had just happened to him. He'd been struck in the heart, yet it was his lungs that had trouble functioning. He quickly found a seat and tried to maintain his composure. Just an innocent dance with his good friend's wife; at a birthday party no less. That's all it was. Certainly that's all it was to her; innocent fun. So why was he paralyzed; with fear, joy, anxiety, trepidation?

He had to leave. The party, though it raged on, was over for Connor Bryce.

He quickly found John, wished him a happy birthday, and told him he had an emergency at work. John understood.

Connor quickly went and sat behind his 1988 Chevy Celebrity he'd found online for twelve hundred dollars, uncertain as to whether he could actually drive off or not. He still had not caught his breath when he pulled out of the drive and back toward his motel room. He needed to watch a movie, or cartoons, something to take his mind off of Annika's face just inches from his, smiling and laughing and exchanging breaths with each other.

Sleep was out of the question. Connor lay in bed, staring holes through the ceiling. His mind ran rampant with thoughts and emotions, none of them pure or wholesome. He pictured himself in specific situations that should only involve a man and his wife, not a man and his good friend's wife. Guilt and shame crept into Connor's head, but not enough to make him stop the erotic waterfall of passionate thoughts involving him and Annika. Finally, he shut his eyes as they'd begun to burn. Thoughts of Annika danced across the screen in his head. At some point in the wee hours of the morning, he drifted off to sleep.

* * *

Months had passed without one solid tip on the whereabouts of one Mr. Connor Bryce. Their well was bone dry. Presley and Suarez had moved on to other cases now, many of which had already been closed; homicides, suicides, rapists…all behind bars. Well, the suicides weren't, but that should be obvious. How had this one man eluded them? No sightings, no calls to his wife, nothing. He'd simply vanished after they'd lost him in Oklahoma City. They had no choice now but to sit and wait.

As if he hadn't worked hard before, Presley was now at the station twenty-four hours a day. The Bryce case plagued him. Something wasn't right, he knew that much. But what? Their trail on Trace Lasser had grown cold months ago. Sure the guy was a male chauvinist and a true creep, and no doubt if they looked hard enough they could find some tax law that he'd broke or a stop sign he had rolled through, but so far it didn't appear he was a murderer. He had a solid alibi for the night of the murder, his shoes were free of any top soil dirt, and there was simply no motive to be found.

Suarez walked in with two cups of coffee.

"One of those better be for me," Presley said.

"Well good morning to you too, Sunshine. Regular or French Vanilla?"

"Regular." Suarez put the coffee on his partner's desk and then sat at his own. The Bryce case had taken its toll on Suarez too. He looked like he'd aged five years in the last few months. One of the main things Suarez prided himself on was his ability to find something out of nothing, to follow a trail until he had his man, to finish something once it had been started. But not this time. This time he had to sit and wait for the other person to mess up; his least favorite position to be in. Waiting. Sometimes they did mess up, sometimes they didn't; obviously there are thousands of cases that go unsolved. Yet this one was one different, wasn't it? Pres had been right about this case months ago—there was no standard operating procedure.

"What've we got today?"

"Jane Doe. Found in an alley behind the Chinese restaurant on 42nd. Her co-worker Scarlett called it in an hour ago."

"Prostitute?"

"Afraid so." Homicides were bad enough, but at least there was usually someone there that cared for the deceased; family, friends…someone. More often than not, in prostitute homicides, there's no one there to mourn. The girl, usually a runaway, is typically disowned by her family for her "worldly" choices. Or they have no idea where she is. Or no one knows her real name. Or others are too afraid to talk. Could be anything, but it usually ended the same way most of the time—no service, the casket lowered into the ground, dirt on top. No tears because there're no eyes to cry them.

Presley put his head in his hands and sighed, "I'm getting too old for this."

"Me too. Maybe we should sell insurance."

"Maybe we should go fishing."

The phone rang and Suarez picked it up. Presley sipped his coffee as his partner furiously scribbled notes. Finally he put the phone down and looked at Presley.

"Yeah?"

"Change of plans. Two confirmed sightings of Connor Bryce in Phoenix."

Presley smiled and stood up, "Get your stuff packed, I'll meet you at the airport in two hours."

"And the Captain?"

"I'll talk to him."

13

The sun reached in and touched Annika, causing her to lazily wake up from her slumber. She was lying next to her husband John. He let out a light groan as she rubbed his bare back. The two had stayed up late the night before as they'd celebrated John's birthday. The party was a success, but now, as John was one year older, it seemed harder for him to get his morning started. He got up and walked to the bathroom as Annika went down stairs to make breakfast. John came down and gave his wife a kiss a few minutes later.

"Good morning, you," Annika said.

"Good morning, babe. How'd you sleep?"

"Great. You recovered from last night?" she said while pouring him a mug of coffee.

"Yeah I think so. Although I can tell I'm not twenty anymore." He looked around the house and out the back window, "Wow, have you seen the backyard? It's a complete wreck."

"I saw it. Going to take a little cleanup, but I'll get to it today. What sounds good, pancakes or omelets?"

"Omelets."

She made them breakfast and they enjoyed each other's company as they ate.

"So what was your favorite part of your party?" Annika said coyly.

"Some girl jumped out of a cake for me. She was pretty hot too. You should meet her sometime. I think you'd get along well," John said as he winked.

"Maybe I will meet her, and then knock her out," Annika joked back.

The omelets were devoured as both John and Annika were much hungrier than they'd realized. A few minutes later, John's cell phone rang from the other room and he hurried across to answer it. He walked back in the kitchen with bad news written on his face. "I have to go to work."

"On a Sunday?" Annika said in protest.

"It shouldn't be for very long. A water pipe burst and is overflowing a retention pond into a church parking lot. I need to go see what we can do. Can't have Sister Helen's heels getting wet. Give me a few hours?"

She smiled, "Of course, just hurry back to me."

John got ready and hurried out the door. Annika cleaned up the kitchen and then started on the back yard. It really was a mess; paper plates, wrapping paper, confetti, napkins, pizza crust, plastic forks, earrings, someone's shoe—and that was all at the first table she cleaned up.

The party, though messy, was epic. Dancing, games, food, drink, presents. The cake that Annika jumped out of was still in the middle of the backyard. It was really pink paper taped tightly over a wire frame; not a real cake, but it had served its purpose. John had always joked that he wanted a girl to jump out of a cake for him, and now he had one.

Annika cleaned for two solid hours before she took her first break. The yard wasn't even close to its original state; it looked like it would be an all day thing. She went inside, grabbed an apple and a glass of water, and sat at the kitchen table. Suddenly she was aware of how hot she was. Her forehead was damp with sweat, and in an instant her stomach felt queasy. She wasn't prone to vomiting and had learned to control her breathing in order to stave off heaving. But she also remembered the feeling she'd had the few times it was unavoidable. She had that feeling now. Annika got up quickly and scurried to the restroom down the hall in just enough time to open the toilet lid and dispose of the contents in her stomach. She felt immediately better. Ten minutes later she did it again.

She tried to think about everything she had eaten the night before and earlier that morning. Annika had food poisoning.

Outside, it had begun to rain.

* * *

Presley and Suarez touched down in Phoenix after a layover in Chicago. Total flight time was eight excruciating hours. At least they had time to talk about their new lead. Suarez told Presley all the information he'd been given over the phone.

A husband and wife at a birthday party the previous night had noticed a man that looked familiar. The couple, Mr. and Mrs. Young, had recently moved to the area from Pittsburgh, and the husband thought he remembered the man from the local news back east. His appearance had changed some and he'd grown facial hair, but the features were distinct. Mr. Young picked up the man's name in random conversations throughout the night...Connor.

He then called some friends back home in Pittsburgh and asked them if they'd remembered a Connor something-or-other on the news back during the summer. The story ran everyday for two months; a giant manhunt. And yes, someone did remember. The man's name was Connor Bryce, and he was wanted for killing his boss in Baltimore. He led the cops on a wild goose chase heading west; no one had seen him in months.

Discreetly, Mr. Young snapped a picture with his Smartphone and sent it to his friends back east. They then sent it to the police. The picture had been faxed over as soon as Suarez had gotten off the phone earlier that morning. It was Connor Bryce.

Presley had stared at the picture almost the entire flight. Bryce looked tired; worse than the last time he saw him at the diner in Oklahoma. He wouldn't get away this time.

"Where to?" Suarez said as they claimed their luggage.

"Hotel first, food second. Then we meet with the Young's and the Mims. Someone knows where he's at, but they don't know who they're dealing with."

An hour later, after checking into a surprisingly nice hotel, Suarez had received directions to the Young's house and the detectives were on their way. They pulled up to a moderate house in a cookie-cutter neighborhood.

Presley rang the doorbell, and it was answered by a small blonde headed woman barely five feet tall. "Mrs. Young?"

"Yes, you must be the detectives from Baltimore. Won't you come in?"

The officers made their way in where they were offered and accepted a seat on the couch. Mr. Young appeared a few minutes later and offered them some pastries, to which Pres politely declined. After a few minutes of talking to the nice couple, it was obvious they wouldn't be much of a help. They hadn't been in Phoenix long, moved here for work, had never talked to Connor, blah, blah, blah. Mrs. Young, Hannah, had met Annika Mims in their spin class at a fitness center. They'd become friends and were invited to John's party. That's all there was to it. Soon it was clear who they'd needed to talk to, so without being rude, they kindly explained they had to be on their way. Their momentum was gaining speed, a showdown was ahead. They got back in their rented car and left in the direction of the Mims' residence.

* * *

Annika had tried to call her neighbors first, but after leaving frantic voicemails, left a note on her front door saying she was on her way to the hospital in case they came to check on her later. Then she'd called John. She was actually worried about him, thinking that he would have it too if he'd ate the same thing she had. He was over an hour away, so John called Connor and asked if he would go meet Annika at the hospital until he got there. Of course Connor would, that's what friends do.

However, Connor didn't tell John what friends *don't* do. Friends don't picture each other's spouses in the way Connor had pictured John's. Friends don't lie and cheat and take advantage of each other's hospitality. Friends don't backstab; friends don't *always* think of themselves first. But Connor had. Man, what a jerk. What compelled him to do this…to keep up this charade?

Fear. Always fear.

Connor thought about these things as he sat reading a magazine in the lobby. Annika had been in the back with the doctor for forty five minutes when John finally showed up. Connor sat patiently in the waiting room.

"Any news?" he asked Connor.

"None. She's been back a while. No updates yet."

"Man I really appreciate you waiting here with her."

"Absolutely. Now quit talking to me and go back there with her."

John gave Connor a nod and walked to Annika's room after speaking with the lady at the front desk.

Thankfully Connor hadn't seen Annika since he'd been there. He sent a message back via a nurse to say that he was waiting out in the lobby if she needed him, which so far she hadn't. He was relieved to see John walk in when he did. Connor hadn't stopped thinking about Annika since their dance the previous night. And he wasn't thinking about her like he thought about pizza either, he was thinking about her like he'd thought about Kelly. He was sickened at his own weakness and cursed himself for his rebellious mind. The last thing he needed now was to see her again. In fact, he *never* wanted to see her again. She owned his mind, through no fault of her own, but his mind was hers nonetheless.

Connor sat and remembered the last time he took Kelly out on a date. They had gone to a new Thai restaurant that had great reviews. Kelly looked marvelous in a striking red dress, satin or silk, he couldn't tell the difference, nor did he care. She'd taken his breath away. He pictured her sitting across from him at the table, eating Thai noodles in that famous peanut sauce that she loved so much. He was such a lucky man. He'd had it all. Where had it gone wrong? And how could he make it right?

Connor knew that he'd been lousy the last few months. Kelly, his reason for living, was back home patiently waiting for him. And how he'd left her—riding in the back of a cop car like *she* was the criminal—what a wretched man he was. He ought to go turn himself in right now. He deserved judgment; one way or another, he knew he'd get it.

Suddenly the doors burst open as John came stumbling out into the lobby. His face wore shock and surprise as his eyes filled with tears. He staggered closer to Connor, then hit his knees and began to cry. People stared.

Connor expected the worst, and immediately knelt beside his friend.

"John," he said as he tried to shake his buddy back into awareness, "John what is it? What happened? Is everything okay?"

John looked up at Connor and smiled through his tears, "We're pregnant."

14

Connor was stunned.

"John, John that's great news," he said as he pulled John off of his knees and up to his feet. The two men hugged and a few of the people that were staring offered their congratulations.

"So that's why she was sick, no food poisoning?"

"That's it. Pregnant. We're having a baby. Can you believe it?"

The two men sat down, fully understanding they'd just witnessed a miracle. Connor knew that the Mims had wanted children, but John confided in him that he was unable. Now, somehow, someway, they could start a family. Connor was truly happy for his friend.

"Well why are you sitting out here with me, get back there with her."

"They wanted to run a few more tests, so I told her I wanted to come tell you the good news. I'll go back in a minute. They want to retest me too. I just, I just can't believe it. We're going to have a baby," John said as he put his head in his hands.

Connor put his arm around his friend's shoulders, "I'm so excited for you. I can't even begin to tell you. Not a bad birthday present, huh?"

"The best present ever."

What a beautiful family moment. Connor realized the magnificence of it, and suddenly realized that he was out of place. He'd only come because Annika was vomiting like crazy and John couldn't be there for a while. Now things had changed, and the intimacy demanded privacy. He needed to leave.

"Well when are they retesting you?"

"Anytime I want. I guess I'll go on back."

"Call me later and let me know how things go. I'm sure we'll all celebrate sometime soon. Go be with your wife."

"No doubt about it. Hey man, thanks for coming out here. I was worried about her. You're a good man."

At that moment Connor pitied John more than he had ever pitied anyone in his entire life. John was completely blind. Anyone that would call Connor a good man had an awful sense of character judgment.

"No sweat. Talk to you later."

Connor left and John went back in to see Annika. The nurse said they were doing their last exam on her, but that he could go ahead and give another fluid sample if he wanted to. He did.

Finally he could see his wife.

Annika lay on an exam bed with a white sheet pulled tightly up against her chin. Her eyes were beaming. Radiant. John took one look at her on the bed and knew that the rest of his life, no matter what happened—he wanted this woman by his side. She had made his dreams come true, beyond anything he could have ever imagined. He only hoped he'd done the same for her. He sat on the edge of her bed and held her hand without saying a word.

He flashed back to the first time he'd touched her. She was underwater strapped in the driver's seat of her Saab—unconscious, lifeless. He'd saved her life, and now she had saved his. They were having a baby; boy, girl, it didn't matter. John began to think of the people he had to call—her parents, his parents, her brother Tony and his sister Whitney. He began to envision the exciting plans of things to come, showers and teas and parties and decorating and picking out clothes and registering for gifts. Some guys didn't want to be a part of things like that, but they hadn't experienced the miracle he just had. He wouldn't miss any of it.

Annika looked up at him and said, "What are you thinking about?"

"You. Your smile. Your eyes. Our baby."

Her eyes misted with tears.

"How happy are you, right now, at this moment?" John asked her.

"Happier than I've been my entire life. And it's because of you."

He leaned down and kissed her gently on the lips.

There was a small knock on the door and the doctor came in. He must not have been a poker player, because his face held disaster. Something was wrong.

"Mr. Mims, can I speak with you outside for moment please?"

"What is it doctor?"

"I think its best we speak in private, sir."

"Doctor this is my wife, anything you have to say, please just say it. We can accept good news or bad. Please just tell me, what's going on?"

The doctor fumbled with the file in his hand and cleared his throat, "It's your test results, Mr. Mims. I'm afraid you still can't have children."

* * *

His cell phone rang. It was Kelly Bryce, the call he'd been expecting. Kelly had decided that she wanted to do a polygraph test, and she wanted to do it as soon as possible. This proved a problem since Presley and Suarez were on her husband's trail in Arizona. No telling how long they'd be gone. One of the options on the table was to allow another detective to administer the test. Presley wouldn't have any of that nonsense. Other people screwed things up. He'd be asking the questions.

However, it was proposed and accepted that Kelly go to police station, get strapped up to the machine, and have an officer call Presley on his cell phone. He could ask her questions and still hear the inflection of her voice. Everything would be videotaped and sent to Presley as a file he could watch later on his laptop. The polygraph would record her answers and the Captain would oversee everything. Not the traditional way of doing it, but desperate times call for desperate measures.

Presley opened his cell phone, "This is Pres….ok…go ahead and put her on, I'll switch to speaker." Suarez was driving the pair in the direction of the Mims residence, but he could still listen as he drove. Presley pushed the speaker button on his phone and then set it on the dashboard as he got out a pen and notepad.

"Alright Mrs. Bryce, are we ready to begin?"

"Yes sir," she replied.

"Okay, I trust you've already been asked some basic questions such as name, birth date, eye color, etc.?"

"Yes sir."

"Good. I'll get right to it then."

"Mrs. Bryce, how long have you been married to your husband Connor?"

"It'll be twenty two years in November, so twenty one now."

"And has your husband ever been in trouble with the law?"

"No sir, not even a speeding ticket."

"Has your husband ever been violent or hostile toward you or your son?"

"No sir, not at all."

"Do you remember the specific evening your husband Connor came home from work?"

"Yes."

"And what did he tell you?"

"That he'd been laid off. Fired."

"And did he say why?"

"He said he didn't know why. He said his boss didn't like his latest proposal."

"And who was his boss?"

"Gregory Jansen."

"When Connor came home, was he visibly upset?

"Yes, of course he was."

"Did he say how he felt toward Mr. Jansen?"

"No, only that he couldn't understand why he would do such a thing."

"And what did the two of you do that night?"

"Showered and went to bed."

"Both of you?"

"I stayed up and read some, then turned my light out and fell asleep. Connor was right next to me the entire time."

"Was he awake when you turned your light out and went to sleep?"

"Yes."

"Mrs. Bryce, did Connor leave your side at all that night?"

"No, he did not."

"How can you be so sure?"

"I sleep very lightly, he never woke me up. And...I have mother ears."

"Please explain."

"When my son Sammy was smaller, I heard everything he did. I trained my ears to hear every cry, every creak in the wood, every thump in the night. Mother ears—it's a real thing. They never left me. I'm a light sleeper. I would have felt the bed move, not only if Connor would've left, but also when he rolled back in. I feel him get up out of bed most nights to use the restroom. It's not scientific, but it's true. I just know. Plus I woke up earlier than he did the next morning to make breakfast. You should have seen the look on his face as he stumbled into the kitchen. It looked like he'd been asleep for weeks."

"Mrs. Bryce, do you have any idea where your husband is?"

"No sir, none."

"Does your husband have any mental or psychological problems that we aren't aware of?"

"No sir."

"Does your husband own any firearms?"

"No sir."

"Alright Mrs. Bryce, last question, when was the last time you saw your husband?"

There was a long pause on the other end. "I saw him the first day you came to my flower shop. We rode out in your police car, I was in the back. I looked across the street toward the gas station, and I saw Connor by a pay phone. I didn't see his face, but I know it was him. I'm sorry for not telling you. I know I was in the wrong, but that's the truth."

"You understand we could have possibly ended this a long time ago?"

"I do, and I'm sorry. Please try to understand the state I was in; it all happened so fast. I didn't know what to do. Charge me if you have to."

"I don't think that will be necessary now. Just try to help us in the future if at all possible. I'm through with my questions now. Thanks so much for your cooperation. I'll get the results faxed and emailed to me."

"Detective, are you closing in on my husband?"

"We're getting closer, yes ma'am."

"Please, detective, please try to keep him safe."

"We will. Thanks again for your time. Call us if we can help. We'll be in touch."

Presley ended the call and looked out the window. "She's telling the truth. That man never left her side that night."

"How is that possible?" Suarez asked.

"I'm not sure, but hopefully the Mims will help us find him.

Suarez continued the drive until finally he pulled into John and Annika's driveway.

No sign of life at the Mims residence. Presley walked up to the front door and found a note taped over the peephole addressed to "*Neighbors…*" that said Annika was sick and on her way to the hospital. She'd signed it. Presley read the note again while Suarez located the nearest hospital; the GPS had one twelve miles away. Suarez put the car in drive and sped off through the rain as thunder clapped overhead.

* * *

Heaven and Hell.

That's the only way to describe John's range of feelings in the last few minutes. He'd went from being a potential new father on top of his world, to…what…now trying to figure out how his wife was pregnant when doctor's were telling him the baby couldn't possibly be his? Words can't describe that particular feeling.

Denial. That was the first reaction.

"I'm sorry, say that again," a barely audible John said as he sat by his wife's bed.

The doctor shook his head, "I'm telling you that your body still isn't capable of having children. I checked the results and…"

"That's impossible! You're wrong. Obviously you are because my wife is laying here pregnant with my child. So you've made a mistake. You're wrong—you, the test, it's all wrong." John was melting down.

"I'm sorry sir; I tried to speak with you in private. I oversaw the test myself and checked the results three separate times. I even shared them with another colleague. However, it's quite a simple test that's fairly black and white. We can retest you again if you like, in fact I would encourage it, but I don't know another way to say it except that you cannot have children."

John stood up and faced the doctor, his face flushed red with rage, shame, confusion, embarrassment, all of the above. "Get out. Please get out of our room. Now!"

The doctor turned and left the room without saying a word.

John sat back down next to Annika as she began to cry. Why would anybody ever come into a room of new parents-to-be only to smash their dreams with a sledge hammer? Was this a prank? Of course it wasn't, but what else could have been the doctor's motivation for such a cruel action? The thought of a lawsuit briefly crossed John's mind.

The couple sat in silence for minutes that felt like hours. Finally John took his wife's hand, kissed it, and said, "He's wrong. It's as simple as that. I love you and I always will."

Annika dried her face with a tissue, "What if he's not?"

Confusion set in on his face. "What do you mean "*what if he's not*"? Of course he is. He has to be."

"I just don't know of another way to explain it."

"Unless you're cheating on me?"

"John, this is no time to joke."

"I'm not joking, and this is the perfect time. You said it yourself— you don't know another way to explain it. I just told you another way. If that's not my child, it's obviously someone else's. If I can't— medically or physically or whatever—make a baby, then someone else has. I'm not accusing you; I'm just finding other ways to explain it.

Annika sat up quickly in bed, "Not accusing me? You're saying I had an affair! How could you ever say that to me? John I've never even thought about another man since we've been together. I think it's much simpler to believe your test results were wrong than to believe I cheated on you."

"Of course you do. Except that one of those ways is scientifically impossible. I can't believe I didn't see this coming." John said as he paced back and forth in the hospital room. Things were getting clearer; his emotions, stronger. "I've never been able to have kids, Annika. The test results *were* what the test results always *are*; what they *always* will be. I can't have kids. Period. Let's not pretend I've been healed all of the sudden. You're smart enough to know that. It's my fault. You wanted a baby and I couldn't give it to you. Maybe it was

95

a moment of weakness, maybe it was planned, but you found another way." John was in tears now.

"John, that is not..."

"It is. It's exactly what happened. Please be honest with me. Just tell me now so I can move on. Who was it?" He was unraveling.

"John, it was no one. I didn't have an affair," She said calmly. Annika reached out for his hand but grasped empty air. Things were escalating rapidly. John was acting out-of-character, and Annika wasn't sure how to respond. It all happened so quickly.

"Then what? You're the Virgin Mary all of the sudden? Tell me who it was? Brock? Daniel? Chris? You've known these guys forever. Why now? My gut tells me it wasn't just a one night stand with a stranger. You'd want a father for your child, so it would be someone you already knew."

The words stung like ice cold rain falling on bare skin. Annika sobbed as John continued to think out loud. "So did I mention him, have I said the name of the man that ruined my life? Or should I keep guessing?"

"John, please stop this," Annika said through muffled tears. He wasn't being fair...none of this was fair. He was beyond the point of control, beyond the point of being rational.

"Stop what, uncovering the truth? I'm such an idiot. I can't believe I didn't see this happening. Who was it Annika? Tell me and I'll stop it. I'll leave you alone forever, you and your family."

The words cut.

"It wasn't anyone. I promise you I have never..."

"Quit lying," John erupted. "Can't you see you're making things worse? You can't lie you're way out of an affair. You're pregnant! I didn't do it. End of story. There is no other explanation."

A sudden flashback from the previous night's party slapped John across the brain.

"Connor, was it Connor?"

"Connor? No not at all. I'm begging you to believe me. I have never cheated on you."

He heard none of it. "I saw you two dancing last night. In fact, I believe *you* asked him. Strutting across the dance floor, arm in arm, and right under my nose. How in the world could I have been so blind? We meet a stranger, you're intrigued, your handicapped husband can't have your baby, you look for other options, and Connor won. Unbelievable."

"That's why you shouldn't believe it. Because it's not true!" Annika was yelling now. "I have never cheated on you once, John Mims. Not once. I will not lay here while you hurl stones at me for something that I cannot explain. Maybe this is a miracle? A real miracle. Think John. Try to see the miracle with me! But you can't see anything while you're in this kind of mood. You can't think straight when you're drinking these lies. I have never cheated on you, and I shouldn't have to defend myself on what should be one of the happiest days of my life; of our lives."

"Not our lives anymore," John said as he left the room, "I want a divorce."

* * *

Connor left the hospital lobby so that John and Annika could be alone and enjoy their blessed day together. His mind seemed clearer now, much more so than it had been the night before. Annika had caught him off guard at the party, and through no fault of her own, left Connor with a slew of unmanageable thoughts and desires. He'd never quite been knocked off of his feet like that. He'd had no control. The experience had left him more alone and desperate than he'd ever been before. He was happy to see John at the hospital earlier, and happier when he saw that John was happy to see him. That's a lot of happy. Connor imagined somehow that John might have seen straight into his mind—where his previous thoughts on Annika would be revealed. But no, John was grateful that Connor could be there for his wife when she was sick. Connor didn't deserve their friendship.

He wanted to wrong as many rights as he could before he left the Mims forever. The family had been incredibly good to him over the last few months, accepting him like one of their own, and now in some small way, he wanted to say thanks. What better way than flowers and a card in celebration of their future new addition?

When John went back in to see his wife, Connor headed to the gift shop. He spent a few minutes reading through cards, picked out a heartfelt poem, bought some flowers, and headed back into the lobby. Just as he was about to leave the flowers and card with the nurse behind the desk, John burst through the double doors from the back. He looked as mad as a bull.

Connor rounded the nurse's station and was about to speak when John unexplainably punched him in the face. Connor dropped the gifts he'd bought and doubled over, clutching his nose. Maybe John *had* read his thoughts from the night before.

"What's your problem man?" Connor said as red drops dripped from his nose to the floor.

"You're my problem," John said as he punched Connor in the ribs.

All air left Connor's lungs, and as he hit his knees to grasp for more, John's foot met his ear, snapping Connor's head to the side. John stood over Connor and pointed his finger at the man sprawled out on the floor in front of him, "If you ever touch my wife again, if you ever look at her again, I'll rip your heart out."

The nurses were huddled together in confusion. Surely one of them had called security, Connor had hoped. This mad man had to be stopped.

He slowly tried to stand up, but his legs were weak underneath him. Breath was harder to come by with each passing second. Little lightning bugs swam in front of his eyes as he tried to regain focus and composure. Connor quickly searched his mind for an explanation as John continued to stand over him.

He found a knee, then got out the words, "John, please...tell me what you're talking about. What have I done?"

"You slept with my wife."

Connor found his feet now and stood up with his head back, still trying to stop the bleeding from his nose. "What? John, I have never slept with Annika. I promise you that. Where did that even come from? What changed in the last few minutes?"

"I can't have kids. That baby's not mine," John said as he pointed back in the direction he'd just come from.

Oh no.

The weight of that sentence hung in the room long after the words were gone. Connor stood there speechless.

"So you automatically think she cheated on you? And with me? John that doesn't make sense."

"I saw you two dancing last night. I saw how you looked at her, held her, watched her. You were like a teenager with that goofy look on your face. You think it's a coincidence that you show up on the scene, and then a few months later Annika is pregnant? You have a lot of nerve coming back in here with your flowers and your little card. You think it doesn't make sense to me now? I trusted you, I told you personal things about me, and this is how you treat me? You wreck my home?"

"John, I never intended to wreck your home, there has to be another explanation. Maybe the test was wrong, maybe your body worked the right way one time? That's all it takes. I would never do anything like that behind your back."

John stood there and tried to calm himself down. He wanted to clobber this guy into next week, but getting arrested wouldn't solve the problem. Finally he said, "Take your sorry tail and get out of here. And if you ever see me again, you'd better hope I don't see you."

Connor stood up and moved toward the front door without saying a word.

John stood and tried to hold back his tears. "Connor."

Connor turned around.

"If you and my wife are going to be together, promise me you'll make her happy."

Connor looked back at the ground, turned, and walked into the storm.

15

Presley and Suarez made it to the hospital in half an hour. The rain had slowed traffic down considerably, extending their drive. Presley pulled in a visitors parking spot, then he and Suarez walked toward the entrance. The rain was coming down harder than ever and the lightning seemed on top of them. Suarez hated lightning. Presley hated rain.

As the two men entered the lobby, they passed a gentleman walking in the opposite direction with his head tilted back, apparently holding his nose. The man walked into the rain without a care, and the detectives continued walking inside the lobby. There was something familiar about that man; his outline, his gait, his posture. Neither cop had seen the strangers face since his head was tilted toward the sky. Maybe it was nothing.

But it was everything. Connor Bryce. There was a reason good detectives spent hours studying pictures, details, mundane characteristics that might seem unimportant to others. There was a reason Presley and Suarez wanted to sit and study Bryce's personality in that Oklahoma diner nearly half a year ago. There was a reason this pair of detectives were Baltimore's best—attention to detail.

99

Presley turned and watched the man walk into the Phoenix monsoon. Just before the ghost disappeared behind the raindrops, Presley yelled, "Bryce."

The man stopped dead in his tracks as his silhouette slowly turned to face his accuser. Presley saw him then. His face, his beard, the way his eyes sat in their sockets. He noticed the bright red liquid leaking out of the right side of the man's nose. This was his fugitive. The three men stood at a face off; Presley and Suarez barely in the lobby of the hospital, Connor Bryce outside in the rain.

Suddenly Bryce spun on his heels and ran wildly into the storm. Pres and Suarez bolted from position, each taking a different flank around the parking lot. Visibility in the rain was limited, and soon both detectives had lost the other in the pursuit. They communicated by yelling back and forth.

"Pres? Pres?" Suarez had to shout over the rain.

"Yeah, you got something?"

"Nothing. Couldn't have gone far though. We need to stay vocal; I can't see a thing out here."

"That means he can't either. Probably under a car now; not many places to hide."

"Good point."

The sky opened as the two men continued to yell back and forth. The parking lot was large, as most hospital parking lots are. It would have been much easier had they noticed him at a fast food restaurant. The detectives weren't equipped to search such a vast area by themselves; the decision to split up was dangerous, but necessary. Divide and conquer.

Presley made his way up and in between another row of cars. "Bryce, Bryce?" he yelled. "I know it's you. I know you know it's me. I only want to talk. Obviously what we have here is a miscommunication. I have questions, you have answers. Let's talk it out."

A thunder clap like the fist of God vibrated the ground. Car alarms in every direction began their wail.

"Suarez, you still with me?"

Silence.

"Suarez? Suarez?" Presley was frantic now as he tried to backtrack to the last place that he'd heard his partner. "Suarez talk to me?"

Through the rain he heard, "I'm here. Still looking. I can't see enough to remember what car's I've already looked at and which ones

I haven't. I think we're spinning our wheels out here. We need more people."

"I know what we need and we don't have it." Presley yelled back. "We're almost done searching this lot. Then we'll move to the next one. That one we'll search together. This guy makes me nervous, like he's watching us; playing with us. You copy?"

"Yep. Meet you at the next lot in five."

The detectives continued to weave in and out of cars for a few more minutes, then made their way over to Lot D. The rain had let up slightly but was still a problem. They decided to stick together this time in the name of safety.

In and out of cars they walked, looking under and in every vehicle; through the bed of every pickup truck.

They were on their third row of the lot, working their way toward the north end, when they heard a car crank to life. The noise startled Presley as he spun toward it. It had to be dangerously close for him to hear it that loud in these weather conditions, but he still couldn't place which car had cut on. His eyes darted back and forth as he yelled for Suarez to help him out and pay close attention. Seconds later, right before Presley found the source of the noise, a pair of headlights popped on and the engine roared. The detectives zeroed in on the car and made a beeline toward the driver door. As they got close enough to see clearly, Connor Bryce shifted into gear and took off.

Bryce flew past the officers as the side window grazed Suarez's arm and sent him spinning to the ground. Presley went to the aid of his partner.

"How bad is it?"

"A scratch. Not bad enough to make us not chase him."

"Good, you stay put, I'll get our car."

Presley took off and was back in a few seconds with their car. Suarez hopped in the passenger seat holding his arm. "Where to? I lost the sound of the engine in the rain."

"He's probably heading back toward the interstate. Can't be but a half a mile in front of us. That's where I'm headed."

They took off in their car, driving much faster than the weather conditions allowed. Presley made his way to the interstate and hit the on ramp pushing seventy-five. He scored triple digits a few second later.

101

"There," Suarez pointed through the rain, "There he is." Bryce's car was spotted not too far ahead. Presley guessed he'd be east bound. Just a hunch, but a correct one. He saw Bryce's car just seconds after Suarez pointed it out to him.

"Get on the radio. Tell Phoenix P.D. I need a chopper and all units in the area. Let me know when that bird's up."

Suarez relayed all the information as Presley stayed on Bryce's tail.

"Can't get a bird Pres, even more lightning moving into the area. Another band of storms to hit in a few minutes. They've dispatched all nearby units to us though. We should have help soon."

Presley didn't respond. He was having a hard time staying focused on Bryce's car. Presley noticed the winds picking up as their little rent-a-car blew all over the highway. Bryce was moving at dangerous speeds. Pres was worried about his safety. Killer or not, these scenarios rarely ended well for the one being chased. It's a desperation attempt; people panic and do stupid things. There's usually a wreck, and sometimes the vehicle ends up in so many pieces…no one crawls out.

They drove on for what seemed like an eternity, both pushing breakneck speeds and hydroplaning like a rock skipping across water. Presley had no choice but to pull back a little bit. It was smarter to sit back and wait for others that were better equipped than to try to be a hero all by himself. He wanted Bryce, but it wasn't worth his life; and it certainly wasn't worth Suarez's.

Presley remained a safe distance behind Bryce, who seemed to slow down a touch as well. Then, swerving through three lanes of traffic, Bryce exited at the last possible second, causing Presley to do the same.

"What's he doing?" Suarez asked.

"He knows he can't lose us on the highway. The only thing it offers is speed, and the storm took that away. He's going to try his luck in alley's and neighborhoods. That's what I would do if I were him."

Bryce pulled off and cautiously ran through the first two red lights. Presley did the same. Their rent-a-car didn't have police lights in it, which put everyone on the same playing field. Bryce took another turn into a neighborhood, then past a high school. He took the next left a little too fast and buzzed a stop sign with the side of his car.

He's losing control, Presley thought. The detectives were slowly gaining on him. Bryce was getting crazy. It would end soon.

Presley and Suarez caught up to the car as it neared a large intersection. Bryce floored the gas; Pres did the same, losing sight of Bryce for a split second as they soared up and over small hill.

Red lights filled Presley's vision. Bryce was breaking hard, almost to a complete stop. Presley knew he'd been had.

The impact caused their airbags to go off, and both Presley and Suarez found their faces full of plastic as their necks snapped back and forth.

Bryce had played them again. He'd sped up over small hill on purpose, knowing Presley would too, drawing him in close and comfortable. Then he slammed on his brakes and held on for the crash, knowing their air bags would deploy.

By the time their heads stopped spinning, the detectives stepped out of their car to assess the damage. Bryce was long gone. The rain continued.

* * *

Connor knew the plan would work. Well, not really, but it was all he had. There was no way he'd outrun them on the freeway, and surely more cops would've joined in the hunt any second. So he got off, drove around some side streets looking for the right opportunity, then slammed on his brakes. When he looked in his rear view mirror after the crash, he saw two white bags and a cloud of dust. Perfect. Then, with the back of his car smashed in, he drove off into the sunset; in this case, the rain.

How the two detectives had found him earlier, he'd never know. But when he'd seen the taller one, the one that knew his name at the hospital, he figured it was time to check out. Connor now pulled into a quick mart to survey his ride. It wouldn't get very far now; surely every cop in the state would be looking for a car with its back end smashed in.

Couldn't happen. He'd have to change his plans.

16

John and Annika Mims sat in their home with Detectives Presley and Suarez. Annika had been cleared by doctors to go home as long as she took it easy for the next few weeks. John was in the process of packing up his things when the detectives arrived; his desire for Annika had vanished. He was moving out.

John was nervous when the detectives showed up; he was sure he was going to be arrested for beating up Connor at the hospital. The four sat in the Mims' living room. John was not sitting by Annika.

"Mr. and Mrs. Mims, how long have you known Connor Bryce?"

"Six months or so, I guess," John said.

"And how did you meet him?"

"Through my brother, Tony. He'd brought Connor to a Diamondbacks game with us in the summer." Annika said.

"And how did Tony meet him?"

"Picked him up in New Mexico I think. Connor's car had broken down and he'd needed a lift back to Phoenix. Said he lived here. What's wrong, is Tony in trouble?"

"Tony isn't. Connor is. He's wanted in questioning for a murder back in Baltimore. That's where he's actually from. He's been on the run for six months."

John and Annika were shocked. "Murder? Who?"

"His boss. Connor's boss was found dead in his home, and we have strong evidence putting Connor at the scene. Tell me," Presley said, "has he seemed dangerous to either of you? How would you describe him? Do you trust him?"

Annika looked at John, who didn't return her stare. "I did trust him, maybe a little too much." John said. "We had a lot in common; he seemed like an ordinary guy. Honestly, I really liked him; we'd become good friends. We trusted him enough to have him over all the time; he even slept in our guest room every now and then. Said he was having problems with his wife."

Pres and Suarez exchanged glances.

"So what else do you know about Connor Bryce? Why was he there visiting you two at the hospital?"

"He was there to see my wife."

"And what makes you say that?"

Without looking up John said, "Because Annika is having his baby."

Annika's voice immediately rose, "John, I've tried to tell you that that's not true. Please stop this; not here."

"Here's just as good as anywhere." He turned to the detectives, "My bags are packed upstairs; I was just leaving when you got here. Somehow, with someone, my wife has had an affair. I'm not going to stick around and play the part of a fool. I've told you everything I know about Connor. Now if there isn't anything else, I will have to ask you to leave so my life can continue to go up in flames."

Neither Presley nor Suarez moved. Then Suarez piped up, "Why did he leave the hospital with a broken nose?"

"Must have tripped and fell." John said.

"So if I ask witnesses what happened, will they say he tripped and fell?"

John stood up, "Look, I confronted him in the lobby, called him out on backstabbing me and ruining my marriage, and things got a little heated. I did what any guy would do if his 'friend' slept with his wife. He got what was coming to him. He's lucky I let him walk out on his own two feet."

"So you're leaving your wife, Mr. Mims?"

"That's none of your business, but yes, I am. I already told you that."

Annika sat there and listened to the conversation unfold as if she weren't there. Her heart was a pile of mush.

"Well sir, it is our business. At least it is now. Let's say that everything you say is correct, which I'm not sure it is, but let's pretend," Presley said.

"Ok, go on."

"Connor and your wife had an affair, either it happened once or fifty times, I don't think anyone cares at this point. Now, she's pregnant with his child. You confronted him, so obviously he knows about it. And now you've just been informed that he's wanted for murder on the east coast. So you're telling me that you're going to leave your pregnant wife all alone to fend for herself, knowing that the father of her child is probably a murderer with obvious mental problems. You're going to go off and start anew somewhere else, while your wife here is raising a killer's baby all by herself, never knowing when the man will pop back into her life, never knowing what mental state he'll be in. Could you live with yourself if something happened to your wife?"

John hadn't thought about the news they'd just received. Connor was a fugitive and, from the sound of it, extremely unstable. How could he leave Annika alone? His heart was crushed beyond repair, but she didn't deserve to be stalked by a killer; even if she had cheated on him. Still, he waged war in his head.

"It's not my job to protect her anymore. She had her chance with me. She blew it with her dumb decisions. Maybe you can put some guards at her door or something."

"Mr. Mims…John, please calm down. Look at your wife, sir." Presley said. "Now are you willing to bet everything you have on this theory of yours? Are you willing to bet your marriage, your home, your baby, your entire world, on your opinion of what you think your wife may or may not have done? Do you want her here by herself, with child, knowing that it's at least possible she did nothing wrong?"

John stood by the window and took a deep breath. He'd let his emotions get the best of him. But the pain inside burned worse than ever. Would it ever stop? "No. No I don't want that. You're right, she needs a man here."

"Not just any man, Mr. Mims. She needs her husband." Presley turned his attention to Annika, who sat by herself on a loveseat clutching a pillow to her chest. "Mrs. Mims, please tell me about the nature of your relationship with Connor Bryce."

"It was the same as everybody else's. I knew him just like John knew him. We had him over for get-togethers, went to some baseball games, out to dinner. Just normal things friends do. But I promise you, detective, that I never slept with him. I never even thought about it."

"I believe you, Mrs. Mims. But I have to ask, why doesn't your husband?"

"I'm sorry detective, it's very personal. I don't know how to answer…"

"Just tell him," John said.

Annika cleared her throat, "John can't have kids. It's a long story, but he can't. I thought I had food poisoning earlier this morning, but the doctor said I'm pregnant. I'm sure you can already see the problem, you're both smart guys. I'm pregnant, but my husband can't have kids. This child belongs to somebody."

"Something doesn't add up," Suarez said.

"No, it doesn't. But it doesn't mean I had an affair; with Connor or with anyone! Miracles happen, tests can be wrong, doctors make mistakes. But I will go to my grave knowing what I am telling you today—I have never and will never cheat on my husband. I love him more than myself. Someday the truth will come out, and I hope he still loves me when it does."

The detectives sat in silence for a few seconds. Her words were moving. Presley couldn't help but believe her. He'd seen a million people lie to his face, but she seemed to be telling the truth.

He turned and addressed John, "Mr. Mims, please sit back down."

John walked solemnly to the loveseat and sat next to his wife.

"Obviously you two still have a lot to talk about. Now I'm not a counselor or therapist, but I can tell when someone is lying. Mr. Mims, I believe you love your wife. And I also believe there are a few different ways to explain what has happened between you two in the last few hours. All I ask is this—stay here, talk to your wife. Has she made a habit out of lying to you in the past? Of cheating on you? Probably not. Listen to her, try to understand her—and if she's telling the truth, which my gut tells me she is, put yourself in her shoes. She's hurting, and so are you. Be a man; be her man."

John looked up from the floor and into his wife's eyes. She'd been crying silently the last few minutes and he hadn't even known. The detective was right. There were too many unknowns to throw away his marriage now.

"You're right," he said, "I'll stay. I don't know how either of us are supposed to go on acting normal, but it's better than being alone."

Annika lightly grabbed his hand, "There is no normal, John. Not anymore. But there isn't anything we can't face—normal or not. I believe that."

"What about Connor?" asked John.

"We're closer now than we've been before. He's starting to get sloppy. Sooner or later we'll get him, that's for certain. We'll need to ask your brother some questions, Mrs. Mims. Then we'll continue our search. I don't think he'll come back here anytime soon. He knows we're onto him and he definitely knows we'll be here talking to the two of you. Of course, if you hear from and/or see him, please give us a call as soon as possible. Try not to beat him up." Presley said with a slight smile.

"Will do."

The detectives got up and made their way to the front door as John followed them.

"Thanks for everything," John said as he extended his hand to the officers.

"No problem, just be good to each other. Something weird is going on here; don't throw in the towel just yet."

"Yes sir."

The detectives got in their car and drove off. John walked back inside and shut the door. Annika still sat on the couch hugging a throw pillow tightly. John walked over and sat beside her again, "We need to talk."

The word confused was an understatement. Connor was beside himself. How could Annika be having his baby? That was impossible, of course, yet John had sounded so sure about it in the hospital lobby. It had to be some kind of mistake, but Connor knew he would never get the chance to explain it. He would never see any of them ever again. His stay in Arizona was finished.

The last thing he'd clearly remembered was the collision that left the detectives incapacitated and immobile. Connor drove his car to an Amtrak station and left it there. It was risky to take a train, but he had no other choice. Hitchhiking only seemed to get other people in trouble, and he was tired of dragging others down with him.

Connor's new plan was fairly straight forward—take a train ride back to Baltimore, see his precious Kelly again, and then turn himself in. What other options were there? She'd been right from the beginning; he should have never run in the first place. But he was scared and nervous, and knew that if he could simply buy himself some time alone, he could prove his innocence.

That didn't happen. Instead, he'd potentially ruined the lives of a great family and, according to John, might be the father of Annika's baby. All the while, he'd never moved one step closer to clearing his name.

His life was over.

Connor boarded the train and was somewhat surprised when he was allowed to buy a ticket. He'd almost expected a SWAT team to rappel down from the ceiling and arrest him. He was disappointed they didn't. He found his seat, and twenty minutes later the train pulled away. The journey would take a while, but he had no other place to be. He knew this would be his last train ride.

What if everyone was right? What if Connor had killed Jansen, what if he had impregnated Annika? Was there any way he could be guilty of both actions? Of course not, but at this point there was no other explanation. He was the common denominator.

With his eyes shut, Connor began to think about everything he would tell Kelly when he saw her. He'd written her a few short notes over the last six months, but soon he would see her gorgeous face. In his mind, he pictured himself kissing her fingers, her wrists, her forearm, her elbows, her shoulders, her neck, her chin. Then he got to her face, where he started in on her cheeks, her forehead, and her nose.

He pictured himself kissing her lips, only they were different. He kissed her earlobe, but something wasn't right. The texture, the smell of her skin—Connor opened his eyes and saw that he'd been kissing Annika!

His eyes popped open and suddenly he was aware that he was back in his seat aboard the fast moving train. His shirt was wet with sweat. What was happening? Connor didn't love Annika; he loved his wife, Kelly. His mind was his enemy. The thought struck a chord somewhere inside him, but his brain moved on to other things. He needed medication, or alcohol...or something to keep his thoughts functioning normally.

Of course those things wouldn't work, but the world looked black in his head, and he wanted it to look blue and green again.

His thoughts moved back to Kelly, and he focused hard to make sure only her face hung in his mind. No other relapses occurred; only Kelly's tan skin and beautiful eyes.

The train rumbled down the tracks. Connor's assigned seat happened to be one that faced backwards, so that even though the train moved forward, he was still facing what was behind him. Connor vowed to leave his past behind. He couldn't stand the thought of staring in the direction of Phoenix for the entire trip back east.

He turned and sat in an empty seat across from his, one that faced forward, so that he now faced the general direction of Baltimore. Then the thought occurred to him that there was nothing for him there either.

Only Kelly; and a prison cell.

* * *

John prepared dinner for his wife Annika. She was still taking things easy because of her nausea. The atmosphere in their home had been slightly warmer since the detectives had left; at least John wasn't in his truck on his way to a hotel.

So many things had changed in the last few hours that neither John nor Annika knew where to begin. Their friend Connor was wanted for murder. Annika was pregnant. John couldn't have kids. John thought Connor was the father. Annika denied it. Too much.

After the detectives had left, John and Annika sat and shared their feelings with one another. Normally, John hated conversations like that, but this time it was much needed. He still didn't fully trust his wife, but he tried to put himself in her shoes. If she was telling the truth, then he had treated her horribly. Annika, in turn, tried to put herself in John's shoes. If she were a man that physically could not have children, she would be suspicious if her spouse ended up pregnant. So she tried to be patient with John knowing she would probably have the same reaction if the tables were turned. After their talk, Annika went to their bedroom to take a nap while John did some research on the internet. Now the two sat at a small table. Annika remained silent while John dished out beef tips and rice.

"I found out some information today, I think it might be able to help." John said.

"What's that?"

"We can get a DNA test on the fetus in two weeks. Results would be back a few weeks after that. And if we pay more we can get them back quicker."

Annika tried to hold back her hurt. She wanted to ask, "and how would that help, to prove that I'm not cheating on you...that I'm telling the truth...that you're not married to a whore!" But she knew she couldn't respond like that. John was hurting too. He needed confirmation. He needed to see the test results.

"Okay, so we just have to wait a little while. How do they do it? Is it invasive or dangerous?"

"It's non-invasive. They would only take a sample of your blood."

"And your blood?"

"Well, no.   They   would   need   hair   or   saliva   samples from...from..."

"Just say it."

"They need hair or saliva samples from the alleged fathers. Chewing gum, shower hair, whatever."

"So you want to test yours and Connor's?"

"Annika, I'm sorry. This isn't easy for me. But yes, I want to test both of ours, and if it's neither, then we move on to others. You said it yourself—someday the truth will come out. I'm just trying to find it. If you have nothing to hide, please help me."

This was the worst hurt Annika had ever felt. The scene was surreal, like she was watching someone get tortured in a movie, but that someone was her.

"Alright. Whatever you want to do, I'm in."

"How do we get samples from Connor?" John asked.

110

"I think his toothbrush is still in the guestroom. There's probably hair in the drain too. But I'm going to let you gather the evidence. I'm going to bed for the night." She got up and left the table.

"Annika, please. I promise I believe you...at least I'm trying. I just want to tie up all the loose ends."

"I understand," Annika said submissively, "I'm not mad at you. I just need some sleep. I don't want to be awake anymore. I'm sick of today."

She walked out of the room and disappeared around the corner as John sat and looked at her untouched plate of beef tips and rice.

17

Kelly Bryce had a renewed hope; and a renewed dread. There had been confirmed sightings of Connor in Phoenix, Arizona. According to the news, he was heavily pursued by the police, only to elude them as he had in the past. Over the past few months, the story of her husband had died down considerably as it was replaced in the news cycle by fresher scandals and crimes. Now it would be front page news again, at least for a little while. Kelly, however, felt this time would be different. Connor couldn't run forever, and she knew deep down inside that his story would soon come to a close.

It had been six months since she'd walked out of Harps, leaving Trace Lasser with a red cheek and sore ego. She'd found out a lot of information that night. Jansen was a rapist; Lasser, an extortionist. Trace then blackmailed Jansen in order to get Connor's job. He knew the company's stock would take off when the new outdoor equipment products would soon launch. Connor was simply in the wrong place at the wrong time, working for the wrong man.

But besides that, there was no other information on Trace Lasser; at least nothing that led to him being a murderer. He did threaten her, saying he'd get what he wanted and that they'd see each other soon, but those were empty threats from a drunken man.

The assault charges in Lasser's past were worrisome, though. Kelly had been in contact with a few officers she'd grown close to over the last few months. She'd learned that the general hypothesis was that Lasser had paid his accusers to drop all the charges. There was no way to prove that, and the police's hands were tied otherwise. She tried not to worry, not to feel insecure or weak; she could handle Lasser if she needed to. She was strong enough.

Of more importance, she also learned from her friends on the force that Lasser did in fact have a solid alibi the night Jansen was killed. He had no motive, no opportunity. Kelly had to face the fact that Trace Lasser was not a killer.

And her husband—was? Wasn't? Of course he wasn't. She knew that; she'd lain beside him the entire night in question. But that meant there had to be a third suspect. If it wasn't Trace Lasser, and it wasn't Connor Bryce—then who?

This was the lone thought that dominated Kelly's last few months. Her flower shop was doing well despite the rough winter weather. Financially she was making ends meet. Apparently Connor had found a way to survive because he hadn't used a single debit or credit card since the day he'd left. She hadn't talked to him since that day either—her, in the back of a police car and him standing by a pay phone. Kelly had only received the occasional letter in the mail, each postmarked in obscure towns she'd never heard of.

She heard a shrill ringing for the last thirty seconds and realized it was the phone. She stretched across the couch and picked up the receiver.

"Hello."

"Hey babe."

She bolted up from the couch—too fast as her head began to spin.

"Connor? Connor is that you?'

"In the flesh. Well, in the voice, but yes it's me. How are you Kel?"

She paused for an eternity. That question had a lot of answers.

"I'm okay. I miss you so much. I can't believe I'm actually hearing your voice. Are you safe? I've heard so much lately."

"I'm safe. I've had a few close calls with our police friends, but I'm safe for now. I miss you so much. Tell me everything. How's the shop? How's Sammy?"

"Good. Everything is good, Connor. But that's not the question. How are you? What are you doing? Where are you going? How are we going to be together again? Connor, how are we going to end this?"

"I…I'm not sure yet. I was hoping Jansen's killer would have been found by now. There has to be a missing piece somewhere; he has to make a mistake."

"What if he doesn't?"

"Then I'll find out the truth. It's still out there waiting to be answered."

"When will I see you again?"

"I'm not sure babe. Soon I hope. Things didn't work in Phoenix like I thought they would. I'm going to Houston for a while. I can get lost in that city pretty quickly. I have to stay low and blend in. I'm so sorry, babe. Sorry I ever put you in this situation. Sorry I ran, sorry I haven't come back. Sorry for everything. I'm not sure what else I can say except that I love you more than I did the last time I saw your face. My stupid job wasn't important. Jansen wasn't important. You are all that is and ever will be important to me. Please stay with me a little longer. Say it."

"I will. I will Connor. Come back to me as soon as you can. I love you so much." She was crying now. "Please come back to me safely. I can't go another six months like this. I'm about to lose it."

She heard Connor sniffle on the other end, "I will Kel, I promise. I'll see you soon, okay?" he said in a weak voice.

"Okay. I love you."

"I love you too."

Silence. Dial tone.

Kelly walked into her bedroom and fell into her pillow. Her emotions boiled up inside of her now, and there was no reason for restraint. She sobbed uncontrollably for what seemed like a decade. She cried so long and hard that her throat became sore and swollen; each swallow of saliva was a challenge. At some point, the evening turned to night, leaving Kelly cold on her bed.

* * *

Examining and documenting recorded phone conversations was a tedious job. Some people would share every intimate detail of their entire life on the phone, leaving Sergeant Barbara Watkins to sort through the mess and determine what was helpful and what was not. Code words, tips, hints at future rendezvous points, addresses—it was all a game, a puzzle to solve, and Watkins, a fourteen-year veteran, was good at it. The call she'd recently overheard, however, was no puzzle. She had been assigned the Bryce file, and though there wasn't much activity on their phones, tonight she'd struck gold. Connor Bryce was going to Houston. The voice match recognition was ninety nine percent. It was him; he'd messed up.

Sergeant Watkins scurried from her office and ran down the hall to the captain's office.

"Sir," she said as she poked her head in. The captain looked up, displeased at the interruption.

"What?"

"It's Bryce. He's going to Houston. He called his wife a few hours ago."

The captain sat back and smiled, "Houston. Do you know where he is now?"

"No, he wasn't on long enough to nail down a trace. But if he's traveling into Houston from Phoenix, we know what direction he's coming in from. Plus I can examine the recording again, see if I can minimize his voice and bring up residual audio. Maybe we can place his location by the surrounding noise."

"Great. Get that tape ready. I want to hear it. I'm going to call Pres and Suarez and get them to Texas. I'll be there in a few minutes."

Watkins left the room as the captain dialed in Presley's number. The detective picked up after a few rings.

"Presley?"

"Speaking. How are you Cap?"

"Better now. Bryce called his wife. He's headed to Houston."

"Houston? What's in Houston?"

"Four million different faces in the crowd, that's what."

"And he told his wife this over the phone?" Presley asked.

"Well he didn't stop by for tea."

Presley paused, "It doesn't make sense, Cap."

"What doesn't?"

"Why he'd laid low for so long, no contact with the wife. He's guessed the phones are tapped, and now, all of the sudden he calls her and says he's going to Houston. He knows we're listening. He's throwing us off."

"No he's not. He almost got caught. We're closing in on him...his world is closing in all around him. He's confused and running; people mess up when they get desperate. Some criminals make mistakes hoping they get caught."

"Not this guy. Captain, I know this man. I've seen him, watched him. He's smart. He's not trying to get caught. He's not confused. And with all due respect, he's not going to Houston."

The captain was quiet for a few seconds. "Well, I'm sorry Pres, I say he is. And that means you two are also. Be on the next flight.

114

Let me know when you touch down. I'll have a plan in place by then."

"Captain I feel like…"

"I don't care what you feel like. It's not your job to feel. It's your job to follow orders. This is all we have to go on now. You and Suarez get on that plane and call me when you land. Got it?"

"Yes sir."

The captain hung up his phone and marched down the hall to Watkins' office.

"You got that tape ready?"

"Yes sir, ready now."

Sergeant Watkins sat behind a large mixing board in a side room attached to her office. She cued up the tape and played it once normally for the captain. Then she said, "Now I'm going to take his voice out and bring the atmosphere noise up." She played with her board, lowering switches while moving others up, then she hit play again and the two listened to the audio together. Static filled the speakers for the first few seconds. Watkins worked her magic on the board some more, fiddling with knobs, until a *thump-thump* sound came through the speakers, barely audible. A few seconds later it sounded again, *thump-thump*. Then about half way the conversation, a bell rang lightly in the background followed by a horn. Then the tape was over. Without a word, Watkins played the audio again.

When it was over she asked, "What do you make of it?"

"Not sure," the captain said. "Not the highway I don't think. Subway maybe?"

"What about a passenger train?"

"Like an Amtrak?"

"Why not?" Watkins said. "It's fast, cheap. And I don't think Phoenix has an underground subway anyway."

"You're right. It makes sense. Good work Sergeant. I'll get someone on the Amtrak lead."

Watkins sat in her chair and typed quickly on her keyboard. A few seconds later she read off of her computer screen, "Phoenix to Houston, Amtrak, leaves twice a day. Houston address is 902 Washington Avenue." She looked at the captain and smiled.

"You after my job?" he said with a faint grin.

"No thanks. I'm too smart for it."

* * *

The conversation was a miracle. Though it was brief, it gave new life to Connor. He'd heard the voice of the woman he loved; the woman he would die for. She'd sounded weak and vulnerable, and Connor knew she was doing everything in her power to stay strong on the phone for his sake. She was remarkable. He knew, even now, that she was probably bawling her eyes out, revealing her sadness to no one but herself.

The Amtrak sped on well into the night. Connor spent the hours reflecting on Kelly's voice. He pictured her face as she smiled; the way her throat moved as the vibrations from her muscles formed words. He pictured her jaw line and her cheeks and the way her lips moved oddly when she said words that started with the letter "R." She was perfect; at least for him.

He would see her soon. There was no way in the world he was going to Houston. But if the police thought he was going to Houston, and Kelly thought he was going to Houston, that would make his trip back to Baltimore slightly less hard than it was already going to be. Connor knew Kelly's phone conversations were being recorded by the police. His only hope was that his scheme of throwing them off wasn't too obvious. Hopefully they would take the bait.

As for his future with Kelly—it was both bright and bleak at the same time. He would see her soon; hold her, cherish her, love her. Then he would turn himself in and end this madness. His head hurt worse and worse with each passing day. His concept of reality was as muddy as a river. He was dangerous. That was the conclusion he'd come to. He belonged behind bars or belted up in a white jacket. Turning himself in was necessary for the safety of others.

Connor felt a hand brush against his. Startled, he turned and looked at the face in the passenger seat next to him. It was Annika Mims.

"Annika? What...what are you doing here?"

"I came after you. I couldn't let you leave me," she said sensually.

Connor looked her over in a split second. She was wearing the same bikini that she'd worn the first time he'd seen her at the cookout many months ago.

"Annika, you can't be on the train with me. I'm going to see my wife! And what about John? And why are you wearing a bathing suit?"

116

"John doesn't want me; he knows about us. And when you're wife finds out she won't want you either. As for the bathing suit…I wore this for you. That's when it first started right?"

"When what first started?"

She leaned over and whispered as her lips brushed his ear, "Your infatuation with me."

"Infatuation? I'm not infatuated with anyone but my wife. And Kelly will never know about "us" because there is no "us"."

Annika gave a sly smile, "Connor, we both know that's not true. Does she know about this?" Annika gave her belly a small little rub.

"What, your stomach?"

Annika leaned into his ear again, pressing him against the window, "Your baby."

Connor backed away from her as far as he could, "That's not my baby. You know that. I'm going to get security." He tried to stand but she grabbed his wrist and pulled him back down.

"This is your baby. Don't you remember? Wanting me, undressing me, doing things only my husband should do?"

Connor briefly recalled their dance, his runaway thoughts, the long night in his hotel picturing Annika lying by his side. But that was it. Innocent. The thoughts festered in his head, but he never acted upon them. Did she know his thoughts?

"I never touched you. That's John's baby."

"Do you want to touch me? Do you want this to be your baby?" She was whispering directly in his face now, nose to nose. Her breath smelled like hot cinnamon. The whispers never stopped.

Connor wanted to die; she was right. He did want to touch her. He'd spent his last few weeks thinking about it. She'd known all along. But how? And more importantly, what was he to do now?

How could he get out of this situation?

Annika caressed his hand.

He didn't move it.

"Let's start over. You and me," she whispered.

"What about Kelly?" His words shocked him; he was considering it.

"You're life with Kelly is over anyway. I'm offering you me, for the rest of your life. We can get lost together." Her soft breath smelled sweet.

She was right. His life with Kelly was over regardless. His current plan had him behind bars at week's end; to spend the rest of his life in

117

a concrete cell. She was offering him hope and freedom. Kelly wouldn't even have to know. He would simply disappear, with Annika on his arm.

"I...I can't. I can't leave Kelly like that. I love her. She deserves better."

"She deserved better when you gave me my baby too, but that didn't stop you then."

"I didn't give you a baby. You have a husband. It's his!"

"It's not his! He can't have children. He can't make my dreams come true. He's come to accept this. He knows I deserve better." She slowly kissed Connor on the lips, then pulled away temptingly, leaving him wanting more. "You've made my dreams come true. John couldn't. You and I deserve each other."

Connor sat and swam with the lingering effects of her kiss; the smell of wet cinnamon hung in the air like a shroud of guilt. The child was his. He knew it deep inside. But it couldn't be. It was impossible. His thoughts screamed curses at him from every direction. He wasn't prone to impulsive decisions, but the look in her eye said it all. His decision was made.

"Where do you want to go?" he said, his face inches from hers.

"Baltimore," she whispered.

"We can't go to Baltimore. I can't live in the same city as Kelly."

"We're not going there to live. We're going there to get rid of her. She'll spend the rest of her life looking for you; for us. We can't have that."

"Get rid of her? You don't mean...?"

"I want you to get rid of Kelly. Permanently."

"But I can't, she..."

"You must," Annika said as she kissed him furiously on the mouth.

The train horn went off and Connor snapped his head up. Drool connected his face to the window. He looked around in an attempt to gain his bearings. The seat next to his was empty. He stood up and looked around at the unfamiliar faces of the other sleeping passengers. Connor sat back down in his seat and shivered cold as he realized his shirt was saturated with sweat.

The whispers never stopped.

18

The sound of the train was his friend, the hum of the tracks his companion. Connor realized he would miss these sounds as they pulled into the Baltimore Amtrak station. It had been nearly four days since he'd left the warmth of Phoenix; now the cold northeast winter bit at his bones in an attempt to break his will. Just like everything else.

He was here. Home. A few short miles from Kelly; a few shorts miles away from prison. The frigid sun dipped slowly in the west. Connor walked from the Amtrak station to the nearest park. He needed to be alone for a few hours until the city fell asleep. He would see Kelly tonight, but he couldn't risk going into their neighborhood while people were coming home from work or going out to dinner. He'd wait until all lights were out, then sneak in and surprise her.

His dreams of Annika were growing in his head; no end was in sight. Maybe he simply missed female companionship. Perhaps once he held his lovely Kelly, all thoughts of other women would be obsolete. Surely that would be the case.

He sat on a park bench and watched his surroundings. Couples bundled up in their winter wear, walking along the river; vehicles driving by in every direction, always in a hurry as they honked their curses at other cars. He was freezing and alone—and that was on the inside. His heart ached for his wife. He got up and hailed a cab.

Connor got in as the cab driver said, "Where to?" never taking his eyes off the road.

He gave the cabbie an address of a house a few blocks from his in case the place was under surveillance. He still had to watch his back at every corner. The driver pulled away and headed toward Connor's neighborhood. The trek would take about twenty minutes, Connor guessed. This was it, his last night as a free man. He put his head against the window and looked up at the winter stars.

Not long afterward, the cabbie pulled up to the address, prompting Connor to get out and pay the man. The taxi drove off, leaving Connor alone in the dark street. He walked quickly in the direction of his own home. Then he saw it, his beautiful house, it's high peaked roof outlined against the sky. No lights were on; Kelly was sleeping. Exactly as he'd planned. Just to be safe, Connor walked around the back of a neighbor's house and snuck quietly into his own backyard, obscuring him from possible prying eyes in the front yard. He took a key from under a special rock beside his gas grill, then slowly entered his house.

He crept up the stairs and into his own bedroom. He went into the bathroom, changed into shorts and a T-shirt, then sat on the edge of the bed next to his bride. This was it. He lay back as his eyes began to fill with tears, which he quickly brushed away. He had to stay strong, at least for tonight. He had to savor every ounce of his moments with Kelly. Connor turned his head and watched her sleep. Her eyes darted back and forth under her eye lids. She was dreaming—of him, he'd hoped. The sky-light above the bed allowed a strange amber glow to fill the dark corners of her face. Glazed lines ran from her eyes down to her pillow, revealing tracks of tears. Kelly had cried herself to sleep. Connor knew he'd caused them; he knew there would be more to come.

* * *

Annika clung to the toilet and deposited her stomach contents for the third time that night. Pregnancy was making it difficult for her to keep food down. Her doctor had put her on bed rest for the next few days. It would be hard, he'd said, but added that she was lucky to have such a wonderful husband there to support her. True words.

The problems they faced were too strong; and they—too weak. Both wanted to make things work, but neither knew how. Annika wanted a baby…was going to have a baby. But not John's; they both knew it wasn't his. It was impossible. However, there were other impossible things going on in their lives as well. The word impossible held no meaning. Annika had not had an affair, not one moment of weakness with any other man. Yet she was pregnant. Impossible. John could not produce a baby, but his wife was pregnant. Even still, he found he loved her more now than he'd ever had before. Impossible.

A few days earlier, John had given the doctors the hair and saliva samples that he'd extracted from Connor's things in their guest bathroom. Annika had given her blood sample. The entire process was heart-wrenching for the both of them. Annika was crushed that her husband didn't trust her, yet she understood on some level his need for answers. John struggled to push his doubt aside. On the few moments he fully trusted his wife, the pain would bite his soul and he would draw distant once again. The test results would be back in a couple of weeks, yet neither one of them truly cared. What would be answered? That Annika wasn't having an affair? Would that solve the problem? Could John go to bed every night not knowing how his wife got pregnant? Could Annika raise a child with John if he wasn't the father? The questions hurt...the answers would hurt worse.

John came into the bathroom as Annika threw up once again. He sat at the edge of the bathtub next to her and laid a damp rag across her head. "Thought this might help some."

Annika wiped the spit from her chin, "Thank you."

"Is there anything else I can get for you? Crackers, medicine?"

"No...no thanks. I'll be fine."

"Annika, you hadn't had solid sleep in days."

It was true, she thought. The dark rings under her eyes were growing by the minute. When she tried to shut them every night, sleep was nowhere to be found. She was constantly tired; constantly awake.

"I know, you're right. I need to go back to the doctor. The nausea pills I'm taking now aren't working. There has to be something else he can do."

John sat and stroked the top of her head, "I hate seeing you like this."

"I hate you seeing me like this," she said as she forced a small smile.

"I'd switch places with you if I could."

"You want to be pregnant, or sick?"

"Sick, although pregnant might be fun."

"Fun?"

"Yes, fun. You get to carry a baby inside you, feed it life for nine months, and then give birth to a beautiful creation. You will always be a mommy. I imagine there's nothing better than that feeling."

Annika sat on the floor with the cold rag against her head. She didn't know what to say. She needed this man that sat by her more than she needed food, water, or air. He was her sustenance.

She looked up at him through pooled eyes.

"John, are we going to make it?"

He gently grabbed her hand. "Of course we are."

"Don't tell me things you don't know for a fact. Don't tell me something you think I want to hear. I want the truth, John, I *need* the truth. Do you love me?"

"Yes," John said without hesitation.

"Even if this baby isn't yours?"

John took both of her hands now and cradled them to his mouth, ignoring their vomit smell, "Even if the baby isn't mine. I want to be

121

the greatest dad that's ever lived. But more importantly, I want to be the greatest husband that's ever lived. I've failed you there already; too many times to count. But from now on, from this day forward, I want to love you until there's nothing left to love. I want to love your baby, our baby, until my last breath on this earth. I've been a fool lately; I haven't handled things well. And I can't explain what's happened to us. Maybe it's not for us to understand. We have to be okay with that. Maybe we'll never know the answers. I have to trust you, and if you trust me, then we'll die in our old age holding each other's hand."

Annika wiped a lone tear from her cheek. "John, I do trust you. I always have. I want you back. Not the distant you, but the real you. I don't understand what's happened to me, but I do know that you're my husband, the one that I've pledged my life to. The one I've been with on top of life's mountains...and God knows we've been through our share of valleys. But this is neither, John—neither mountain nor valley. This is bigger somehow. And I don't know the end result. Like you said, maybe I never will. But I have to have you loving me. It's the only way I can go on."

John bent down and kissed her putrid, beautiful lips. "I love you and I will never leave you. Of that I am certain."

PART THREE

19

The soft rattling at the door and faint sound of crashing glass had Connor sitting straight up in bed, eyes scanning from left to right like a lifeguard at the beach. Had they found him? How could they have found him? He got up, walked to the bedroom door, and looked around the corner and down the hall. The gray and yellow moonbeams that poured through the windows revealed an empty living room.

The noises came again. Quieter this time, further down the hallway. Connor glided gracefully across the hardwood floors, his socks acting like the ice skates of an Olympian. He flicked on the light in the hallway, knowing he would see the face of the intruder. But he saw nothing.

Again, a light rustling, this time from behind a closed door. This was Sammy's room. Sammy wasn't home now, thankfully. He was enjoying his sophomore year at Virginia Tech. Perhaps he was back now, up late and unable to sleep thanks to his X-Box. Maybe he was sneaking out of the house on his way to a party; or worse…sneaking a girl in.

Or it could be the FBI on their way to drag him out in cuffs—dazed and confused.

Connor held his breath for a split second and then bolted through the door. Nothing. The only thing staring back at him was Sammy's bed, neatly made. Even the windows were shut and locked.

Connor's mind was foggy. The last six months had certainly left him cloudy in the head, though one would argue he that wasn't all there to begin with. How could he have become a fugitive? He had everything. He had it all. He didn't even remember killing his boss. He was as confused about that night as he was right now.

The glass smashed louder this time, like it was dropped from a height. Whoever was in his house was no longer trying to be quiet. The sound, though, came from behind him. Connor spun around and left Sammy's room. Quietly he returned to the den. The light from the moon shone like a spotlight upon a figure standing in the middle of the room crying.

Kelly. Crying and bleeding. Dark black splotches oozed through her nightgown.

Connor stood there in disbelief. He flipped the switch on the wall, bringing color and detail into the room. Kelly stood there weeping, clutching her chest, the black splotches on her nightgown now an ever-growing dark crimson.

She fell to her knees, blood pooling around her bare feet. Kelly turned her head toward Connor, and through a gurgled voice whispered, "Why would you do this to me? Why did you do this to me?"

Connor looked down at his own hands, and they dripped red.

* * *

Connor floored the gas pedal as he sped down the interstate. Kelly laid flat in the back seat, both hands clutching the wound in her chest. Her constant moaning was the only siren Connor needed. He couldn't think straight. The lines on the road blurred his peripheral vision as his speed entered triple digits. His wife was bleeding in the back seat; bleeding to death. From his hands.

No, not from his hands; couldn't have been. But it was.

The thought that had been plaguing Connor in the back of his mind now manifested itself in reality. And that reality was deadly. Connor was a danger to society; a danger to any and everyone around him. His desires…his deepest cravings and darkest longings, birthed themselves into existence as they danced in his mind. He was a killer, a liar and an adulterer. His hate had killed Jansen—in his mind anyway; but he might as well have pulled the trigger.

Connor took the hospital exit once he reached downtown Baltimore. The car was alone as it flashed in and out of the street lights. He was half awake now, still lost somewhere between coherence and stupor. He remembered that night vividly—lying in bed, wishing for Jansen to die the bloody death of a tyrant; the hate he'd felt as it boiled to life inside of him…the scorn he'd wished upon his dictator. No, he didn't break into the Jansen home, didn't force feed Jansen the deadly concoction of pills. Not physically. But he'd killed him…in his mind, in his heart; in his black, hateful soul. The evidence that linked him to the crime—the shoe and fingerprints—however they came to be, could only mean one thing: he would have to be judged. The world would have to know he was a killer. Its one thing to hate someone in your mind…at least *those* ugly thoughts could remain hidden. But murder was public. Maybe hate should be public too. Connor was meant to be judged. In a small way, he longed for it.

Kelly moaned loudly in the backseat as Connor took a sharp corner.

And Annika. Wow. Was she really having his baby? Of course she was. They'd done everything needed to produce a baby in his mind, and John was incapable of the task. He'd wanted Annika in every way a man could want a woman. She'd built a nest in his head, and Connor had made no attempt to remove it. And the worst part was, Annika had done nothing to deserve any of this; this hell was Connor's doing. She was innocent. He'd fed his thoughts the lustful passions of the darkest nights. Connor knew, even in his semi-catatonic state, that he'd committed adultery with Annika a thousand times in his head. In his thoughts, he never pictured Annika with a baby, but pregnancy is a real-life consequence of many affairs. And like the death of Jansen, his thoughts knew no boundaries. He would be the father of the baby. Questioning the possibility of such things was a waste of time at this point. They were true.

All he ever wanted was Kelly. To hold her. To love her. To treat her like the princess she was; the princess he'd dreamed about as a young boy. Now his princess lay bleeding in the backseat from a stab wound to the chest. And Connor was responsible for that too, wasn't he? Of course he was. Kelly was keeping him from Annika. If Kelly were removed from the equation, he could enjoy the fruits of Annika for a million eternities. Kelly held him back. She had to be dealt with. Isn't that the dream he'd had on the train just a short while ago? Annika whispering in his ear the sweet temptation of their erotic future together…Connor wanting to take her physically right then and there on the train. His conversation with Annika proved to be a figment of his highly questionable imagination. But Connor's mind games had produced the same result; Princess Kelly now clung to life.

She cried out loudly in the backseat. Connor began to weep.

The hospital was only a few miles away now—the end was a few miles away. He wanted to speak, but his mouth was full of cotton. He began his apology but found his throat muscles tight and sore. What could he say? I'm sorry? I didn't mean it? But he did mean it. He'd meant everything. The fact that his thoughts really happened was simply an inconvenience. He'd wanted Jansen dead, sex with Annika, and Kelly out of the equation; at least for the briefest of moments. But what difference did it make now? His thoughts

125

became real—so what! Most people thought those things anyway. In a way, he was better than them—the ones that kept their desires secretly hidden in their mental closets. At least he wasn't a phony. Everyone else was just as dirty as him, yet he would be labeled a monster, and the label was just.

The hospital was in sight now. Not much longer.

Connor choked on his own spit as he slurred, "Kelly...Kelly. We're almost there. Kelly, can you hear me? Say something. Anything." She'd been eerily quiet the last few minutes.

Silence.

"Kelly!" Connor shouted frantically. "Kelly, stay with me. Kelly! Oh I'm so sorry. Please be okay. Kelly!" the sobs echoed inside the cold car. "How could I have done this? What...what have I done?"

"Hush little baby...don't say a word," a weak whisper from the back.

"What...Kelly?"

"Momma's gonna buy...you a...mockingbird."

She was singing. Whispering.

"Kelly? Kelly, talk to me. Hold on Kelly...hold on!"

"Song...my mother...sang to me...fell asleep." Her voice was barely audible. Her eyes were shut. The car was full of pain.

"Kelly! You're not going to sleep now. Don't go to sleep Kelly. Stay with me. I need you awake. I want you awake. Keep your eyes open. Sing Kelly. Sing me another song."

Silence.

"Keep singing Kelly, we're almost there."

Nothing.

"Kelly, I can't lose you! Jesus, don't let me lose her!"

Barely a whisper could be heard, "Jesus loves me, this I know..." her breathing grew heavy, "...for the Bible tells me so." Her voice slowly gurgled the words, "little ones to him belong..." deep breath in, deep breath out, "they are weak but...he...is..."

"Good Kelly, very good. Beautiful." Connor had to keep her talking. "Did your mom sing you that too?"

The only noise in the car was the running heater.

"Kelly?"

Connor glanced into the back seat. The blood was everywhere. Kelly's eyes were closed; her chest rapidly moved up and down as her lungs struggled to sustain. She had stopped singing.

Connor pulled up quickly to the emergency room doors. He honked furiously as he put the car in park and jumped out. Nurses scurried out as he moved around the car and picked Kelly up in his arms. She was so small. Her arms hung limp toward the concrete ground. Her head dangled back on an imaginary pillow.

"What happened?" a nurse in green scrubs said as Connor rushed inside.

"Car wreck," was the first lie Connor could think of.

He laid her on a hospital bed that another nurse had wheeled out. Everyone was in a hurry. "Get her back into surgery now, page Doctors Durant and Pierce." said another one of the green scrubs.

Connor followed them back as they wheeled his wife into the bowels of the ER. That odd smell of a hospital lashed at his nostrils. It was one of the few details he actually took notice of. The team reached a pair of double doors and a green scrub turned and said, "I'm sorry sir, this is as far as you can go."

"You don't understand," Connor said, "that's my wife."

"I do understand sir, but you have to let us do our job now. There's a small room right down the hall, you can wait there."

"I can't wait in another room. I have to be back there with her!"

The green scrub grew impatient, "Look sir, you're wasting my time when I could be back helping your wife fight for her life. Now either make your way to the waiting room or I will call security. You cannot come behind this door. That's just how it is. It's safer that way."

If you only knew, Connor thought.

20

Connor Bryce had never gotten off a train in Houston. In fact, there had been no sign of him at all. Presley and Suarez had been in the city for days now, sitting, waiting, tracking down tips that proved fruitless. Bryce had disappeared again. The guy was a magician. Presley had known early on that something wasn't right. Guys as smart as Bryce don't reveal their plans on phones they know are bugged.

Houston rarely has a winter; it gets hit with a huge ice storm about once every fifteen years, but generally the season is mild. This winter was hot; and it was only morning. Presley stood at a checkout counter of a small gas station and tried to cool himself off in front of a small fan. He couldn't remember the last time he'd been cold. Suarez had been in the bathroom for twenty minutes now, and Presley was losing patience. Not that they had anywhere to be; just not there.

Finally Suarez exited the men's room.

"You sure you don't need longer?" Presley said sarcastically.

"I've been done for ten minutes. Just enjoying my alone time away from you," Suarez said smiling back.

"I'm still surprised you can go all by yourself. I'm very proud of you."

"Will you still be proud of me with a black eye?"

"You'd better bring some friends if you wanna dance with me, boy," Presley said as he ducked into the driver seat of their car.

"You'd better bring some friends to hold me back," Suarez joked.

Its jousts like this that defined their relationship. Sarcastic quips, witty comebacks, both men acting like they could do without the other. Over the years, it had all led to one thing: loyalty. And there's no better quality to have in a partner than loyalty.

They'd followed up on a tip as soon as the sun had come up. A malpractice lawyer had spotted who she'd thought was Connor Bryce while she was working out at a YMCA downtown. Both Presley and Suarez knew that wasn't their man; Bryce would most certainly not be playing basketball or lifting weights at a YMCA. But they had nothing else to do at the moment except to chase an invisible Bryce around the city. As expected, the YMCA Connor Bryce turned out to be a twenty-four year old Latino everyone knew as Chico. He had absolutely nothing in common with the real Connor Bryce except that he was a male under the age of fifty.

That was an hour ago. Now they rode the downtown streets in some of the more rundown districts. If Bryce were trying to fit in and stay off the grid, blending in with the homeless population was the way to do it. Presley and Suarez had decided to drive around and scan faces, hoping with the slimmest of hopes that Bryce's face would stare back at them. Not likely, not even remotely probable, but it was better than sitting at a hotel flipping playing cards into a hat.

Presley's cell phone rang.

"This is Pres." Pause. "What? When did this happen?" Another pause. "What's her condition?" Presley pushed the speakerphone button. The voice on the other end blared loudly as Suarez recognized the captain's voice in mid-sentence.

"...condition is not good. She's sustained multiple stab wounds to her chest and stomach. Both her lungs are punctured, four broken ribs, all kinds of internal bleeding. Doctor says she has a fifty-fifty chance of making it. She'll be here for a while. No telling when she wakes up; if she ever does."

"And Bryce brought here in?" Presley asked.

"Yep. Nurses say he pulled in at approximately 2:50 this morning. Drove her to the hospital himself. She was in the back of the car."

"And nobody stopped him? No questions?"

"It was chaos. They had no idea who she was; and they certainly didn't know who he was. Their first priority was to get her into surgery. Two separate nurses told me that Bryce wanted to stay. They thought he was in the waiting room. When a nurse came out to give him an update after an hour or so, he was gone. We're reviewing video surveillance right now."

"Why would he want to stay? To make sure she was dead? Finish the job?"

"Don't know. They said he seemed pretty hysterical. Crying, calling out her name, mumbling about how much he loved her. Doesn't make sense."

"Crimes of passion rarely do." Presley said. "So you want us up there?"

"You got it. As soon as possible. She'll be here waiting on you."

"Let's hope Bryce is too."

"Doubtful, although I do think he'll stay close by. He won't leave Baltimore with his wife in a hospital bed."

"Maybe. Maybe not. I'm not sure what this guy will do anymore." Presley said.

"Just get up here."

Presley closed his phone and looked at his partner as he pulled off to the side of the road. The pair had had a rocky sort of relationship with Kelly Bryce. They were trying to nab her husband for murder, yet she was always cordial with them. She was a fighter, defiant at times, fragile at others, but never weak. They'd grown to appreciate her contagious personality over the last few months.

Suarez spoke first, "She can't die."

"Yes. She can."

"But she won't. We know her. If there's a fifty-fifty chance, she'll win that every time. I'd put money on it."

"You might lose it."

Presley pulled back onto the road. The two remained silent for the rest of the ride back to the motel, deep in thought. There was nothing more to say. They packed what little belongings they had and headed to the airport.

The flight seemed to take forever. Each passing second grew greater with anticipation, anxiety, dread. They were traveling faster than ever toward the man who they'd spent over six months chasing. Yet also, with each passing second, Kelly Bryce clung to life as a machine helped her breathe. Another innocent life affected by a madman.

Finally they touched down and retrieved their luggage. One phone call revealed that Kelly was still alive but unconscious. There was no telling when she would wake. Presley wasn't as optimistic as his partner. He'd seen people die before, it didn't matter if they were fighters or not. Fighters die too.

The captain was in the lobby of the hospital when Pres and Suarez walked in. It was almost midnight now. Days and nights ran together. The previous morning seemed months ago.

"How is she?" Pres asked.

"Sleeping beauty. Vital signs are slowly improving."

"Good, can we see her?"

"Just for a second. Then I want you two home getting some rest."

"We can rest when we get Bryce," Suarez said.

"You can't get Bryce if you never sleep," the captain said. "Look, just go home, recharge your batteries, get up fresh in the morning and nail this sucker. I need you two at your best."

Captain had a point, Presley realized. They hadn't slept for what felt like days; perks of the job. "You're right. I can hardly see straight. Suarez, what'ya think? Meet back here in the morning?"

"I don't like it, but I could sleep a few hours."

"Good. I'll drop you off. First I want to see Mrs. Bryce."

"Me too."

Presley, Suarez and the captain made a brief stop at the nurse's station, then took the elevator up to the fourth floor. Walking into Kelly's room was like walking into a dream. Monitors, cords, beeps and chirps in every direction. Kelly lay there motionless under a soft white sheet.

"She looks so peaceful," Suarez said.

"She should. It's the first time in half a year she hasn't felt pain. Think of what she's been through every day."

Presley reached out and put a hand on her foot. It felt cold through her socks. "I've seen enough. I have to get some sleep. Tomorrow, we find who did this."

130

The trio rode the elevator back down into the lobby. When they walked back into the parking lot, a camera met them in their faces. A small lady pushed a microphone in the tall black man's face and asked, "Is it true that Connor Bryce brought his wife here last night with wounds to the chest?"

The story had been leaked.

The captain stepped in front of the microphone, "No comment."

"Is this the fugitive's wife? Is there reason to believe he's still in the area?"

"Listen, I will say this once, and if you ask me one more question I'll arrest you for interfering with our investigation. This is an ongoing case; we will answer more when we know more. And not until then. If any member of the media so much as steps a foot inside this hospital, they will be arrested. I'll have a press conference in a day or two. Now if you don't get that thing out my face, I'll break it and mail it to your boss in pieces."

The lady turned back to her cameraman, "And there you have it, straight from the horse's mouth. This is Theresa Lynn, live from Channel Eight. Back to you." The spotlight mounted on the camera shut off and the pair disappeared as quickly as they had arrived.

"Great," Suarez said, "that's all we need."

"Don't worry about them," the Captain said, "I'll handle the media. That's my job. You two find Bryce."

He walked to his car and drove off.

Half an hour later, Pres dropped Suarez off at his apartment, and then headed back to his own dark prison.

* * *

The man stood across the street. The hospital was large and foot traffic was plenty, making the crowd easier to get lost in. From this distance, this vantage point, no one would ever know that the hospital was under his surveillance. Soon he would have to find a way to get into the massive building without being recognized. Once inside, he would lay low, scope out the floor plan, then memorize the habits of the doctors, nurses, receptionists and every other employee in the main building. Every detail was crucial; every person had to be accounted for.

No one would treat him like that and get away with it.

She'd tried though…lord knows she'd tried. He always found it fascinating when women would try to stand up for themselves; when

131

they would try to be strong and courageous in the face of danger. It was an act, he knew. Women were not strong, at least not more so than him. And when he saw that look in their eyes as he stared at them up close, nose to nose, he saw their true colors then. They were scared, afraid, devastated. He had complete control each and every time. That's what he loved about the game.

This was not his first time. Women had fought him off before; their brave and defiant acts only egging him on. He needed that—the fight, the resistance, the cat and mouse game of who will break first. He never broke first; they always did.

It took him a while to realize that when women said no, they typically meant yes. Once that fact was established, his actions grew easier. Sure he'd been close to being caught before, that actually increased the excitement; made things more dangerous, risky. But he would never actually get caught; he was way too smart for that.

Today was colder than normal. The wind bit the man right in the face, and it never stopped. He might have to move his operation inside the walls of the hospital before he'd intended. It wouldn't be the first time his plans had changed in the middle of an operation. In this hobby, you had to learn to be flexible.

The only thing stopping him from moving inside now were the two detectives, Presley and Suarez. They were the only ones who would recognize his face, and they were in and out of the hospital every ten minutes it seemed. If they saw him here, what would his answer be? That he was worried about Kelly Bryce? That he cared about her well being? No…those answers wouldn't fly.

He had to continue avoiding them, at least for now. So he sat and watched, recording in his notebook the names and times of each person leaving the building. He had to track their movements, know their routines. People were creatures of habit, and once those habits were documented, he would know the time and place of every individual in that hospital at any time of the day. The skill took patience, luckily he had it. The puzzle was worth working; the puzzle was fun.

He took a sip of his coffee and burned his upper lip. Still too hot.

He sat and recalled the last time he'd looked upon her face. Boy, she was gorgeous. Why that idiot husband of hers would try to kill her, he had no idea. Pretty things like that were meant to live. They were meant for him.

He took another sip of his coffee, this time relishing the hot sting as it swirled around his mouth. The pain felt good. He took a small bite of the pastry lying before him, but it had no taste. He ate it anyway.

The man sat there for hours until finally evening turned into dusk. He'd written four pages in his journal now, all with names and dates and times; all of people's movements and trends and walking patterns. It would take him most of the night to study his notes and diagram his plan out on paper. But he had time for that too; he rarely slept.

Finally, he saw the two detectives leave. He quickly jotted the time down in his notebook. They had left a few minutes earlier the night before, but not enough to ruin the plan forming in his mind. And there was a plan, make no mistake about it. Soon…very soon, he would have some alone time with Kelly Bryce.

* * *

John Mims sat at his desk and continued to look over his latest set of civil drawings. He was working on a special irrigation system that would lead to an underground retention pond for a new hotel out by the airport. Annika sat in the den writing a blog on catering for weddings. Her pregnancy sickness had subsided recently, and she'd been chomping at the bit to get back to work. It felt great to type about cooking again. The therapy was highly needed. Things had been much better between her and John since they'd talked it out a few nights ago. He was open and responsive, she was loving and patient.

Everything was perfect.

Except for the television in the background, the house was eerily quiet. Annika put her laptop to the side and got off of the couch. She walked over to John's desk and put her arms around him from behind, then leaned down and kissed his neck.

"What is this?" he said with a smile.

"Nothing. Just me."

He swiveled around in his chair, "Just you, huh? And just what exactly are you doing?"

"I didn't want to bother you too long. I just thought you might need a break," she said with a wry smile.

"Well, I was just thinking of a break myself." John said as he took his reading glasses off. "Would you like to join me in the hot tub, or shall we skip that part?"

"Ah, that hot tub sounds like a great idea. I'll pour us some sips."

John walked to the bedroom to change. Annika sauntered into the kitchen and retrieved a bottle of wine off of the rack. She poured John a glass of the magic elixir, pausing as she watched thousands of tiny bubbles weave their way up the golden-white froth. For her, she popped the top on an ice-cold Diet Coke. This was her most favorite thing in the world. Forget the vacations, the trips, the shopping sprees, the gourmet foods. Those were great, but not the best. Sitting at home, next to her husband, relaxing in a hot tub with a drink in hand…these were her favorite times. She took the drinks out and set them on the ground next to the hot tub steps. John came out wearing only a pair of shorts.

"You changing?"

"Of course," she said as she planted a kiss on his cheek, "but I'm only putting my feet in. Pregnant women aren't supposed to get in hot tubs."

"Is that true?"

"I don't know. I've heard it a ton though, and I don't want to take any chances."

"I agree. You wanna get in the pool instead? No rules against that right?"

Annika walked over and opened the patio door. The air was warm but allowed a crisp, light breeze to dance across her face. Her question was answered.

"The pool sounds great." She went inside and changed quickly, not wanting to miss one more second outside on such a glorious night. She'd almost felt giddy, recalling emotions she hadn't felt since they'd first started dating. It was silly, really. Yet in truth, she had been to hell and back recently. Every aspect of her life had been torn down and rebuilt more than once. But now she had her husband back, and he had her. These moments were more special now than they'd ever been in the past. She had to cherish these times; another breakdown was always one piece of bad news away.

Soon, Annika joined John in the shallow end of the pool. The healing waters washed over her as she put her head under and came back up again. Invigorating.

They enjoyed their time in the pool; not a worry in the world.

The night moved by quickly, and as they both started to get chilly, Annika said, "Let's move this party inside."

"You just read my mind."

They got out and moved inside. Annika walked into the kitchen to refill their drinks. She happened to glance up and look at the television.

The sound of shattering glass sent John sprinting into the room as naked as the day he was born; he'd been drying off. He looked at Annika's face and recognized a look of stupor he'd rarely seen before.

"What is it? Are you hurt?"

She remained silent; her gaze never leaving the television. He followed her stare and looked toward the screen.

Connor Bryce. Their friend. Their enemy.

Annika scrambled to find the remote. "We have to turn it up."

John grabbed a blanket off the back of the couch and fashioned it around his waist.

Connor's face was in a box in the top of the screen as the news anchor spoke. Annika found the clicker and turned up the volume. "...and is being searched for in Baltimore and surrounding areas. His wife, Kelly Bryce, is in critical condition at Mercy Hospital. Again, if you're just joining us, Connor Bryce, the Baltimore resident wanted in connection with the murder of his former boss, Gregory Jansen, has apparently struck again. The details we have are fuzzy, but we can confirm that Mr. Bryce brought his wife Kelly to the emergency room earlier this morning. An undisclosed source tells me she has multiple stab wounds to the chest and abdomen area. If you have any information on his whereabouts, please call the police immediately. He is to be considered armed and dangerous. In other news, there's been an increase in the number of food poisoning cases..."

Annika turned the channel—same story. Different channel—same story. Connor had made national news. Again. She turned the television off and sat dumbfounded on the couch.

Without a word, John joined her.

Then all he said was, "Poor woman."

Annika stared straight ahead. "I know. I mean, I feel like we know her, yet she's a complete stranger."

"Let's hope she makes it."

"You don't think he did it do you? I mean, stabbed her like that?"

"I don't know. The Connor I knew wouldn't hurt a fly, but I'm not sure I met the real Connor Bryce. If he wanted to kill her though, why take her to the hospital? I don't understand." John said as he struggled to make sense of things.

"I don't either. I could never see him killing anyone."

135

"Although let's keep in mind, he was only down here because he was running from another dead body. He's the missing link to both crimes."

"So he's either a psychopath or he's being framed?"

"Is there a third option?" John asked.

Annika sat there, thinking. John went into the bedroom to put some clothes on. He came back out a few minutes later in a pair of flannel pants and an ARMY t-shirt. He joined his wife again on the couch.

"What she would we do?" she asked.

"What can we do?"

"Should we call the detectives that we met with?"

"What would we tell them?"

"I don't know. I just feel like we need to talk to them. Maybe we have answers for them...or them for us?"

"I don't think so babe. We have nothing to do with this. Connor's put himself in some deep weeds, and he has to get himself out."

"Connor's not the one I want to talk to," Annika said as she began to sweep up her broken glass. "I want to talk to Kelly."

21

"What's the latest?" Suarez asked Presley.

"Nothing new. No tips, no signs. He's disappeared again; like he doesn't even exist," Presley responded. "He's gotta be in the downtown area. We have cops watching his house and under-covers at all of his favorite hang-outs. But he wouldn't be seen there anyway. He's laying low; basements, alleys, abandoned warehouses. He won't leave the city."

"I agree," Suarez said. "It's like he's sorry for this one."

"What do you mean?" Presley asked.

Suarez paused to figure out his wording. "I mean, after Jansen died, Bryce ran across America. Then we tracked him down in Phoenix, and he disappeared again. But now, since he's done something to Kelly, it's personal. I'm not sure what I'm getting at, but I don't think he wants her dead. It's like his head and his heart are telling him two different things."

"Go on," Presley said intrigued.

"I don't know if there's more to say. I'm just thinking out loud, but here it goes. Bryce kills Jansen and doesn't even stick around for the funeral. We can assume he wanted the guy dead—no remorse. Then we find out that in Phoenix, the one couple he'd become close with, John and Annika Mims, are staring at divorce; and Annika has a baby in her belly that John didn't put there. In fact, for some reason, they think its Bryce's baby. So, let's assume it is Bryce's child. That would mean that he wanted to sleep with Annika so bad that he found a way to make it happen; possibly without her knowing it. You follow me?"

"Yeah but what's your point?" Presley said.

"My point is that if Connor Bryce wants something bad enough, he finds a way to make it happen. But not this time. If he'd wanted Kelly dead, she'd be dead. I think somehow, for some reason, he resisted the urge to finish her off. Maybe his love for her was too strong; maybe he's fighting too many demons to realize what he's doing or who he is?"

"Or maybe he stabbed her repeatedly and missed her aorta by accident?"

"Possible, but I don't think so. He brought her to the hospital to save her life."

"Or to cover his tracks; make it look like he was trying to help. Score some brownie points."

"Whatever it is, he's the link that connects this entire mess we're in. Connor Bryce holds all the puzzle pieces."

Presley thought about that for a moment. His partner's theory was a little out there, but Suarez had a knack for seeing the un-seeable. The man could sniff out a trail better than anyone, and now the hound smelled blood.

"So he stabbed his wife but didn't want to kill her?"

"If I'm right, yes."

"Are we talking about insanity here?"

"I don't think he's insane, but I'm not a shrink. I'm not sure if he's aware of what he's doing. Some people murder in their sleep; others black out only to come back into reality to discover they've killed a loved one. All the more reason for us to find him. And soon."

"So he's not guilty for his actions?"

"I didn't say that. I think he is guilty. If a man kills, a man kills. But we both agree this case feels different. A wise man once told me that there's no such thing as Standard Operating Procedure," Suarez said with a smile. "I think you're right though; Bryce is close by. He'll keep tabs on his wife. He didn't want her dead, and like I said, I think he feels sorry."

"And I think you're right—we have to find him soon," Presley said.

A knock on the door, "Detective, permission to enter?" a young uniformed officer said.

"Permission to enter? Boy, tell me what you came to say." Presley said, his patience worn thin.

"Phone call sir, a doctor from Mercy. Line three." The young lad turned and left.

Pres hit the speakerphone button, then the flashing line three light. "This is Pres."

"Yes this is Doctor Durant. I wanted to update you on our patient, Mrs. Kelly Bryce."

"How is she?"

"Stable, but she just woke up."

"Can we see her?"

"She asked for you specifically," the doctor said. "You'll never guess what she just told me."

* * *

The ride to the hospital was quick. Kelly was conscious and coherent; and talking. She would be their first witness that could place Connor at the scene of any crime. Detective Suarez drove while Presley sat in the passenger seat, thinking. Suarez was right, Kelly was a fighter. She'd walked through a hellish nightmare, only to come out stronger on the other side. Presley turned to Suarez as the car came to rest in a parking spot, "Keep your ears open. Everything she says will be important, whether it makes sense or not. Sometimes jumbled speech is better than a complete sentence."

"I agree. I'm surprised she can remember anything. Just that fact alone speaks volumes; she won't give up."

The detectives walked into the hospital and again took the elevator to the fourth floor. Kelly Bryce was in room 419. The door stood ajar, so Presley gave a light knock and slowly stepped in the room, followed by Suarez.

Kelly looked ragged.

Her forehead was damp with perspiration and her hair a nest of tangles. She was laying upright in her bed, exposing a myriad of bloodied bandages that wrapped around her midsection. Somehow, she smiled at them when they came in.

"So, do I look as awful as I feel?" she asked jokingly.

"Worse," Presley said with a wink.

"Thanks for the encouragement. So…how are you two? It's been a while."

Even in her state she was asking about others. The pain on her face didn't mask the shine in her eyes. That never changed. She held a morphine pump in her right hand to be used as needed. She strained for a sip of water through a straw, then clicked the pump once as she put the small cup back on her side tray.

"We're here. And we're in one piece, which is more than I can say for you. Can I get you anything?" Presley asked.

"I'm good, but thanks," Kelly said. "So, where do you want me to start?"

"How about at the beginning? What's the first thing you remember?"

"Didn't the doctor already tell you?"

"He did, but we want to hear it from you."

"Well, I remember going to bed…last night, the night before, maybe a week ago, I'm not sure what night it was…"

"Were you by yourself?"

"Yes. Completely alone. I fell asleep sometime around midnight I think. The next thing I remember is a searing hot pain in my chest. I put my hand there and drew back blood. I tried to sit up but there was a weight on top of me. I couldn't see anything, but no matter how hard I tried I couldn't move an inch. I tried to push whatever it was off of me but my hands pushed through air. There was nothing there. Then I felt another punch in my stomach, only it wasn't a punch but more like a slicing flame across my gut. I tried to scream but my voice was afraid to come out."

Kelly paused to catch her breath and clicked the morphine pump once more. "The weight on top of me wouldn't move. My eyes had barely adjusted to the darkness of the room, but there was no one in there with me. Then I felt it again, another stab in my chest. I screamed silently again and prayed I would die quickly. I looked down at my chest and stomach and could see multiple rips in my pajama shirt. They'd been cut through. But even as I stared at it, I saw my shirt tear once more and felt the cold knife pierce my skin just

139

inches above my belly button. It's like I was being attacked by a ghost."

Presley and Suarez both glanced at each other, unsure of what to say. Never had they'd heard such a tale. In any other scenario both men would have immediately dismissed the story. Real detectives relied on evidence, and a woman claiming to be stabbed by a ghost didn't meet the definition. But Kelly was describing it so vividly, so entirely graphic, that both Presley and Suarez imagined themselves in the bedroom with her, watching her squirm and fight against an unknown and unseen assailant.

"The attack lasted minutes, but it felt like hours. My bed sheets were bloody and my room smelled foul. Finally the weight lifted off of me, and I was able to move. The attacks had stopped. I laid still for a few seconds, unsure of what to do and scared to leave my room. And then I heard movement outside my door. In excruciating pain, I rolled of the bed and found my feet. I remember the hot feel of blood dripping on my bare toes. Both my hands held tightly around my stomach as I walked toward the sound. It was a light shuffling, like soft footprints. Finally I turned the corner. That's when I saw him."

"Connor."

"Yes. Connor was standing there…looking at me. He looked so helpless. His face held confusion; he looked…lost. Then I saw his hands; they were saturated with blood. At that point I knew I wanted to die, so I closed my eyes. That's the last thing I remember."

"I'm not questioning you, but I want to make one hundred percent sure," Presley said, "the man you saw was your husband?"

"Yes. For the last half a year I've seen his face every single time I shut my eyes. I miss him. And when I saw his eyes the other night, for the briefest of moments, it's like things were back to normal; until I saw the blood," Kelly said as her voice trailed off, "But yes, Detective, the man I saw was my husband."

"And you don't remember him bringing you to the hospital at all? Nothing about the car ride?"

"Not much. I think I remember singing, but I could be imagining that. I don't know what's real anymore."

"Singing? Why did you sing? Whether it's your imagination or not, tell us what happened," Suarez asked.

"It was Connor, he told me to sing. I'm dreaming, and I'm crying, and with my eyes open I see the streetlights going past me upside down." Kelly had her eyes closed now as she described her thoughts.

"The streetlights whirled around my head. And Connor's crying too in the front seat; crying as he drives. I hear him. I sing a nursery rhyme I knew as a kid, then I stopped and shut my eyes. Connor tells me to sing…sing him another song. I don't want to. I want to shut my eyes and go to sleep. The backseat is sticky and wet with blood. The air is hot and heavy. My head feels dizzy. I don't sing. Connor begins sobbing and my pain increases. I hear him ask Jesus to save my life. It's a desperation move; that much I know. Jesus is always the first person people cry out to when they're faced with death. When I hear him say that, I know things must be bad with me. I try to sing another song, but I don't have the strength. Then my mind goes black. I'm not even sure he heard me. I just wanted to go to sleep."

Kelly opened her eyes, back in present time, "Then I woke up here."

Presley held the straw up to Kelly's lips as she took in a small sip of water.

"Mrs. Bryce, I have to be honest with you. I'm not sure what to make of everything," Presley said. "I've never seen anything like this before. Your husband is an intriguing man, but he's also a very dangerous man. I have to ask you this, do you have any idea where he might be?"

Kelly shook her head. "Please don't hurt him."

"We don't want to, Mrs. Bryce. Believe me. But we have to find him. Detective Suarez and I think he's going to stay close by, possibly even in close proximity to the hospital. We think he wants updates on you, he'll want to make sure he didn't kill you."

Kelly thought that over for a second. "So what do you want me to do?"

"Nothing. Stay here and get well. You'll be here at least two or three more weeks; not out of the woods yet. Hang tight and get your strength back. We'll post some officers outside your door. You'll be safe."

"Detective…what's going on? Tell me what your gut says."

Suarez spoke up first, "My gut says your husband is conflicted, very unstable, and looking for answers."

"Is he a killer?" Kelly asked, "Your gut?"

"No. He's not a killer; not in the way we think of a killer. But he's not innocent either; he lies somewhere in between."

"And you," Kelly said as she nodded toward Presley.

"I think your husband needs help. And I don't know if he's a killer or not. Speaking freely, Mrs. Bryce, you didn't stab yourself."

"But he didn't stab me either. I was there."

"Maybe not with his own hand. But he's responsible. That's what my gut tells me. And when we find him, he can tell us his side of the story."

Kelly pushed the pain pump twice. She'd strained herself beyond the boundaries of a normal person. The detectives got up to leave, sensing it was time to go. There'd be plenty more questions to ask later.

"Mrs. Bryce, thank you so much for your time."

"Leaving so soon?" she asked as her eyes grew heavy from the morphine. Always the gracious host.

"We'll come back later if that's okay with you. You've been incredibly helpful today. More importantly, we're both glad you're alright."

"Thank you detectives."

"No problem, Mrs. Bryce. Goodbye."

Pres and Suarez found their car in the parking lot; neither said a word on their way back to the station.

22

The next week, John and Annika Mims were making their final preparations for travel. Annika had to move around some of her larger catering appointments, and John had a stack of blueprints to work through before he felt comfortable leaving for a few days. They'd spoke with Detective Presley on the phone, and he assured them that Kelly Bryce would still be in the hospital when they got there, although he wasn't sure a meeting was such a good idea, at this time particularly. Finally, Presley had relented.

"All right, I'm ready," John said as he zipped up his suitcase.

"Me too," Annika said as she sat at the foot of her bed. She took a deep breath and rubbed her stomach softly. She expected a call from her doctor at any moment with the results of the paternal DNA test. Why was she nervous? Oh yes, because the results of the test were a complete unknown and a possible weight that could drown her marriage into a deep, cold sea.

John was still playing the part of the loving, all-supportive husband; but would that role change if he was not the father? Naturally, Annika had her doubts.

The happy couple packed their car and headed for the airport.

The blues and whites seen from Annika's window seat should have been relaxing, but they weren't. Twenty thousand feet in the air and her anxiety was still enough to cause her hands to sweat. What was she doing? What did she hope to accomplish? Kelly Bryce was a stranger, a woman who'd just been assaulted and nearly killed by her husband. Yet, that was the answer to Annika's question. Connor Bryce. He was the reason she had to meet Kelly. Kelly was a complete stranger, a woman Annika knew nothing about. But even still, on some remote level, they were connected. Annika had to find out why.

The flight lasted a few hours, and when it landed the couple made their way to the hotel, a four star Doubletree not far from downtown. After unpacking their things, Annika turned to John and said, "So, what now?"

"Well, that's up to you really. It's getting late. I'm all for ordering some room service and firing up the hot tub. We can get some rest and then see about visiting Kelly in the morning. Or we can wake up and meet with the detectives tomorrow too; whatever you want to do really."

"Getting started tomorrow is a good idea, but why don't we order room service another night. I've never been to Baltimore, will probably never come back. Let's go out for dinner, see what the city has to offer. What do you think?"

"Sounds good to me," John said.

After quick showers, they both got ready for a night out. Annika retrieved the name of a great seafood place from the front desk that was within walking distance of the hotel. Always the learner, she loved visiting other places to see how they "did" food. Maryland was famous for many things, but nothing more so than crab cakes. Tonight she would dine on the best in the world. As a chef and caterer, nothing excited her more.

They left the hotel on foot and found the restaurant easy enough. Annika wore a delicate green dress that fell lazily across her hips. John wore a gray suit with a black dress shirt underneath. Sharp as a nail. Once they'd entered the restaurant, they both immediately knew they'd overdressed.

At the bar sat a group of guys pounding brews like there were no tomorrow. A full bucket of cold ones sat before them, sure to not last long. At a table to their right, a group of four rowdy elderly women were having a grand old time shucking oysters and sucking the rubbery meat from its shell. A juke box somewhere was blaring "Friends in Low Places." There were animal heads on the wall and fish frozen in form hanging from the ceiling.

"Maybe we have the wrong place," John shouted to Annika as he held her hand tightly. They were going to have to raise their voices if they were to communicate in this barn-party.

"I don't think so. The lady from the hotel said this place had the best seafood in Maryland. I should have asked about the dress code, but who cares. Let's have some fun."

They found an open table close to the back as a middle aged woman named J.R. took their drink orders. John took off his suit jacket and unbuttoned a few of his buttons; Annika put her hair up into a pony tail and kicked her heels off. They weren't exactly Tim and Faith, but they felt a little more comfortable.

Annika ordered the crab cakes and John the mahi-mahi. As an appetizer, lobster bisque and calamari. Annika tapped her bare feet to the tune of Travis Tritt as John read through a list of songs that could be performed during their karaoke hour that would start soon. Not much of the country listener, but he'd grown close to a few tunes from his childhood days.

The appetizers came and were done away with in no time; easily the best calamari and bisque they'd had ever had. Soon the main course was placed before them, and it immediately became clear the lady from the front desk wasn't in the habit of lying. Mahi-mahi that was as succulent as a steak; crab cakes that were worth going to war over. John and Annika ate like freed prisoners. The food and drink never stopped. As time passed, the atmosphere became louder; a country throw-down was brewing.

"Well," Annika said, "you ready to go?"

"Not quite yet," John said with a grin, "I want to sing a song first."

"Sing a song? Here?"

"Do you have a problem with that? I'm going to show these Maryland folk how we sing country in the southwest. You just sit there and let me surprise you." He stood up and went to the man wearing a cowboy hat that operated the karaoke machine. His Fu Manchu should have had a name. In a few minutes, John was on stage with a microphone in his hand. He looked as out of place as the largemouth bass hanging from the ceiling.

The music came in from a pair of cheap speakers by the small stage. "This song goes out to my lovely bride, the cute little lady in the green dress," John said as he pointed toward Annika. Hoops, hollers and whistles went up all around. The song was familiar, even to some non-country music fans—Deeper than the Holler by Randy Travis. Beautiful. Annika sat back and watched her husband stumble over words, never once hitting the right note. He'd even borrowed the karaoke operator's cowboy hat for the performance. The place was going wild for the gray-suited cowboy.

Annika reached in her purse for her cell phone, wanting to take a picture of Cowboy John. She'd missed three calls in the last hour. It was her doctor.

Anxiety swept over her face. She stood up and made her way outside the front doors. Talking inside would prove fruitless. Annika immediately dialed the number back; she could still hear John singing on stage over the phone ringing on the other end.

A voice answered, "Hello?"

"Um...yes. Doctor, this is Annika Mims, I'm sorry for calling so late. I just saw that I missed your call about an hour ago."

"Don't be sorry," the doctor said, "I knew this news was important to you and wanted to let you know as soon as your results were faxed to me."

"Yes sir, thanks so much. What's the verdict?"

"Well, Mrs. Mims, there's no easy way to say this but straight forward. According to the results, the father of your child is Connor Bryce. I'm sorry, Annika."

She was silent. Stunned. What was she supposed to say? Are you sure? I don't believe you! That's impossible! No. The test was what it was. Her child was Connor's, not her husband's. If only John were able to have kids, then neither one of them would have ever suspected that her baby was another man's. But the circumstances were different. She'd never slept with Connor, of that she was positive, but who would believe her? Would John?

"Annika...Mrs. Mims, are you still there?"

"Yes doctor," she said softly.

"Do you have any questions for me? We can do the test again if you like?"

"I don't think that's necessary, but thanks."

145

"Mrs. Mims, please know how sorry I am to deliver this news. I hope things work out with you and your husband. If I can be of any future assistance, please call me."

"Thank you, doctor. I have to go now." Annika hung up on the verge of tears. Her life was over, and no one knew it but her. She should leave. Run now and let John start his life over with someone else; someone he could trust. As soon as the thought crossed her mind, she felt two arms grab her from behind.

"Hello there pretty lady, would you like to dance?"

John spun Annika around so that they were face to face. Her tears betrayed her smile.

"What's wrong babe? Didn't like my singing?"

Annika put her head into her hands and openly wept. She sat on the curb of the parking lot shaking from the cold. There was no other way to say it...the moment of truth. "John, the baby...its Connor's."

John remained silent while his wife cried in the background. Then he took off his jacket, wrapped it around Annika's cold shoulders, and sat by her on the curb.

* * *

The bar was empty, but he didn't care. In fact, he preferred it that way; less people he could hurt. Connor threw back a shot of whiskey and motioned for another one.

"I think you've had enough for the night," the bartender said.

"I think you should pour me another drink when I ask for one," Connor replied.

The bartender slid him another shot and watched the man bury it in his throat. It tasted like water now.

"That's the last one," the bartender said. "And I mean it. I don't want to be responsible for you getting hurt."

"Responsible? What do you know about the word *responsible?*" Connor slurred. He wanted another drink already. His insides needed warmth. The bartender paid him no mind as Connor swayed lazily back and forth on his bar stool.

He'd been in Baltimore for what...days, weeks, months? He had no idea. His life ended the night he took Kelly to the hospital, bleeding and dying by his own hand. He'd left the hospital shortly after, not because he was worried about being caught, but because he was worried about hurting anyone his mind turned against. Prison bars wouldn't hold him, his thoughts would slip through. A straight jacket would prove useless; his mind could kill at will.

146

He had a power, a disease that no army, judge or jury could stop—his thoughts. Connor knew what was happening to him. It was impossible, but what is the word "impossible" anyway? Simply something that has never been done before; something so crazy that society says it can't happen? Well, this was happening, and it was possible.

Connor had hated—someone died. Connor had lusted—someone was pregnant. Connor had seen his wife as a barrier to another woman—she lay clinging to her life. His selfishness and malice toward others was dangerous. And there was no way for it to stop. No way, in his own power, that he could do away with his own selfish thoughts and desires. It was truly impossible for him to control his mind; it was a lion, and it devoured the lambs.

Connor tried to stand up and make his way to the rest room. His knees were nowhere to be found as the room spun. He fell face first into the bar railing, cutting his forehead and wounding what little pride he had left. Drunk people never have balance, but they always have pride. Another patron helped Connor to his feet.

"Can I call you a cab?" the bartender asked. Apparently Connor had worn out his welcome.

"I'll walk."

"You sure?"

Connor didn't respond. Instead he walked out the doors and into the cold night. He'd been sleeping at an abandoned warehouse down by the Patapsco River. It wasn't much, but it was warm and quiet. Right now it was his heaven.

He walked in through one of the broken loading dock doors and quietly stumbled his way over to his little corner of the world. This was such a fitting place for him to end up, Connor thought; a cold warehouse that smelled like a petting zoo. Sirens blared outside, then faded just as quickly, justice roaming the streets...protecting the innocent. But who could protect the innocent from Connor? Was there a justice strong enough for that?

The warehouse had no lights, making it difficult for Connor to find his way around. He still ate well; he had plenty of cash for food. He'd simply taken the homeless lifestyle by choice, not by necessity. Even still, deep down, Connor knew that no matter how far he stayed away from human contact, no matter how much distance he put between himself and others, his mind could still unleash chaos whenever it wanted. Distance was no obstacle…solitude meant nothing. So what was the answer?

There wasn't one.

Connor was cold except for his insides which had been warmed by the bottle the last few nights. A yellow haze came through the window from the street lights outside. Connor made his way to his small pile of personal belongings; all that he had to his name.

He'd grown use to sleeping on newspapers and torn clothing; an old boat tarp was plenty to keep him warm. Connor had no choice but to sit there, day in and day out, and wait. He called the hospital every few days to ask about the condition of his wife Kelly. He could never see her again, that much he knew. It was for her own safety; but he had to make sure that she would live and fully recover. The last report he'd gotten, she was still unconscious. He would try again tomorrow, and a few days after that, and a few days after that. He had to know, before he ended his own life, that she would live.

Once he knew that for sure, he would rid the world of Connor Bryce.

23

Kelly Bryce had been up and conscience for a few days now. She'd slept for three straight days after the first visit by the detectives. Her wounds were healing nicely, and luckily she would need no further surgeries. Her doctor said she would need at least one more week in the hospital bed, but would be released after that barring any setbacks. The morning had started out differently already. She woke up to a phone call from Detective Presley asking her if he could drop by sometime this morning with some visitors. Fine by her. He didn't say who the new comers were, only that she didn't know them. No matter, any new faces now were a welcome surprise. Lying alone in a hospital bed all day grew monotonous.

A nurse came in and set a breakfast tray in front of Kelly. "Any news from the detectives yet?" Kelly asked.

"No hun, not today."

They hadn't found Connor yet; no sign of him anywhere.

Kelly picked at her breakfast—instant grits, toast, and some assorted fruit. She needed to eat to regain her strength, yet hospital food probably wasn't the best way to entice her appetite. She watched television for an hour or so, but she hated daytime television; too much gossip on talk shows and bad lighting on soap operas. At some point between breakfast and lunch her nurse came in and said, "Mrs. Bryce, the detectives are here to see you if you feel up to it."

Kelly sat up in bed as best as she could, "Great, send them in please."

Seconds later Detectives Presley and Suarez walked through the door. "Good morning, Kelly, how are you?" They were on first name basis now. Well, she didn't know their first names, but dropped the "detective" and called them Pres and Rez.

"Much better today. Ready to get out of here. And you two?"

"We're good," Pres said as he dropped the morning paper in front of her, something he did every morning for the last week.

"And you Rez?"

"Doing fine little lady."

"I hear you brought some visitors for me today?"

"I did, they're waiting in the hallway."

"Well? Who are they? Bring them in."

Pres sat back in a small chair by Kelly's bed. "I don't know if it's as easy as that. These folks flew up here from Phoenix. They know Connor. This conversation is not going to be easy. In fact, it's going to be difficult, probably the hardest thing you've ever had to do. So what I want to know is…are you up for it? There's no shame in waiting until you get out. But this talk has to happen sooner or later, and since you're a grown up, I'll let you make the call."

She looked for signs of emotions of Pres' face but found none. "Pres, you're worrying me. Send them in; if things get too bad, they can leave."

He nodded his head and went out into the hallway. Presley already knew what the Mims came to share. Annika's baby was Connor's child. How in the world was she going to explain that? Pres and Suarez had met with the Mims earlier that morning and Annika had told both detectives the entire story—the test results, John's response, Annika's desire to speak with Kelly—everything. Pres had agreed to introduce the Mims to Kelly with the stipulation that Kelly ran the show. If she didn't want to see them, they were out of luck; if she grew tired or mad or in pain or whatever, then John and Annika would have to leave. They understood completely. They meant to cause her no harm; at least no further harm than the bombshell they were about to drop.

149

Presley came in a few seconds later followed by a beautiful woman and a striking man. Models in a magazine, beach volleyball players; they could have been either, or both.

"Kelly, this is Annika Mims and her husband John." Presley turned toward the Mims, "John, Annika, this is Kelly Bryce."

Kelly reached out her hand to the Mims. "Good to meet you Annika, John," she said as she shook both their hands.

"Mrs. Bryce, I…"

"Please, call me Kelly."

"Kelly, thank you so much for meeting with us today. We won't take up much of your time."

"Oh don't worry about that, I haven't seen people in forever. Would you like something to drink?"

"No thanks," Annika said.

"John?"

"No ma'am, but thank you."

"Well," Kelly said, "so you both know Connor?"

"Yes. We met him over the summer. He ran into my brother who ended up giving him a ride into Phoenix. We all went to a ball game together. Tony, my brother, went back to school in the fall, but Connor remained good friends with both of us."

"I'm guessing he didn't tell you why he was there?"

"No, and we never suspected anything either. Neither one of us had much time to watch the news, so I had no reason to question his story."

"I understand," Kelly said.

Presley and Suarez watched the conversation from just inside the doorway. So far, so good. Let's hope it stayed like that.

"How was he?" Kelly asked. "I mean, how did he seem? Happy, depressed? I haven't seen him in so long; I forget sometimes what his face looked like."

"Happy for the most part. Kind of withdrawn sometimes, but nothing that raised any flags with us. He and my husband got along particularly well."

"Really? How so?"

John spoke up, "We had a lot in common, I'm a designer of sorts, an engineer, and we both liked to come up with new designs for different things. He told me about an outdoor equipment campaign he was working on, and that kept us busy for a while."

"Ah, yes. The outdoor equipment," Kelly said. "Did you know that that's what started it all?"

150

"No," Annika answered.

"He'd come up with the idea for outdoor camping and hiking equipment that would be designed for people with physical handicaps; products easier for them to use so that they could still enjoy the outdoors. Long story, short…he got fired from his job, and the next morning his boss was found dead, murdered. A few pieces of evidence pointed to him, and he ran. Six months later he came back and stabbed me in my sleep."

"I'm so sorry about that Mrs. Bryce…Kelly. If this is going to be too difficult we can come back later or not at all. I just, for some reason, think it's important for us to get to know one another."

"I agree. You two probably know my husband better than I do at this point. It's not too difficult. If there's one thing I've found out about myself, it's that I'm tougher than I thought. Please, go on. Ask me any questions you want."

"I'm not sure I know how, I don't want to offend you at all."

"If you do, I'll let you know," Kelly said with a half smile.

Annika took a deep breath, then started, "Kelly, do you believe your husband killed his boss?"

Kelly thought for a moment, "Yes."

"Do you believe he meant to kill his boss?"

"No."

"Please explain."

"I can't," Kelly said. "I don't know how to explain it. But let me tell you what happened to me. My husband, from another room, stabbed me in the chest repeatedly. He did—I know he did. He knows he did. But I was awake during the attack and he was nowhere to be seen; it was like an invisible man tried to kill me. But it was Connor. I wouldn't believe the story if it hadn't of happened to me. But I think the same thing happened to his boss. I think somehow Connor killed him. In his head he wanted his boss dead. And then it happened. I know it sounds crazy, but I'm proof."

"It does sound crazy, but I believe you Kelly. My husband and I believe you. It's happened to us too."

Here we go, Presley thought. The fun begins.

"What do you mean it's happened to you? Did he hurt you? Oh God I hope not."

"No, he didn't hurt us. He…I'm…" Annika paused to catch her breath. Suddenly the air in the room grew thick.

Kelly reached out and took Annika's hand, "Please dear, whatever it is, I'm sorry he hurt you. You can tell me."

Annika somewhat regained her composure. She kept her hand in Kelly's. "John and I have been trying to start a family. Because of some medical problems he had as a child, he is unable now to have children. We've tried every different doctor we could think of, and no one could help us. We we're both incredibly heartbroken about it. Then we met Connor this summer. We all got along great, and we had him over our house all of the time for parties and stuff. Connor and I, personally, had a completely platonic relationship. We had little interaction with one another on personal levels; it was he and John that became such good friends. I was always in the background. I'm not sure what happened, Kelly, but Connor began acting strange around us. I figured he was just stressed out from work or whatever, we all go through it. Well, we invited him to John's birthday party. Everyone had a great time, Connor and I danced, nothing intimate at all. Please understand that; no lines were crossed. Anyway, he left after that, and though I didn't think anything about it at the time, looking back I believe it happened then."

"What happened then?" Kelly asked.

Bombshell. "Kelly, I'm pregnant. Connor is the father." Boom.

Kelly released the grip on Annika's hand and stared at the floor. "And...you're sure it's Connor's?" her voice came out scratchy and hoarse.

"Positive. We tested DNA from his hair sample. I got the call from my doctor last night. It's Connor's. The test is accurate. I don't know what else to say. My husband and I have been through nightmares with each other the last few weeks. Even now I'm scared he doesn't believe me; that he mistrusts me. But listening to your own story helped all of us I think."

"He wanted you pregnant? I find that hard to believe. Why would he want to have a baby with you?" Kelly asked.

"Honestly, I don't think he did. I believe he was lonely. I think he missed you terribly. I think he was lost and afraid. But I also think he was weak. People covet what they see every day, and he was at our house a lot. I believe, in his mind, we were together the way two lovers were together. I think he wanted me strictly for sex...for pleasure, and I think those thoughts built a castle in his head. Kelly, it sounds awful saying this, but he cheated on you in his mind. The same way he probably killed his boss, the same way he stabbed you. He didn't know I would get pregnant, but because we slept together so many times in his mind, it happened; a real consequence of his imagination. When people have affairs, sometimes the woman gets pregnant. It's a consequence, a ripple effect. Do you believe any of this? I'll leave if you want me to."

Kelly stared at the floor, motionless. Then she looked at John, "Do you believe your wife, sir? Do you believe that she never cheated on you with my husband? Do you trust her?"

"I do," John said firmly. "I had my doubts at first. Lots of them. But I think those were natural. This...thing with Connor...this is unnatural. I believe my wife. It's hard, knowing the child isn't mine, but only in blood. We will love our baby more than anyone has ever loved a child," he said as he grabbed Annika's hand. "God has given us a miracle. In the most unlikeliest of ways...yes. But a miracle nonetheless."

"And you, detectives, what do you two think?" Kelly asked.

"I think a lot of things," Presley said. "Right now, I think we have two witnesses that have proof of positive interaction with Connor Bryce in specific instances in which he's never touched them. You, Kelly, with the stabbing, and you, Mrs. Mims, with your pregnancy."

"You think that will help?"

"I do. But it doesn't matter what I think; it matters what a jury will think. Even still, I believe we have enough to create some kind of reasonable doubt. Might be enough to hang the jury. I don't know, really. Those are all questions for the district attorney. But leave that to us, all three of you need to continue to heal."

"This is so hard for me to believe. Adultery? Pregnancy? What's going on? And why does my heart hurt so badly?" Kelly asked as she shut her eyes.

Annika grabbed her hand again, "I'm so sorry."

Kelly took a few deep breaths and then asked calmly, "What's the best case scenario for my husband."

"That he gets help as soon as possible. It's not too late for that."

"And the worst?"

"That he continues to hurt people either on purpose or by accident. Then we have to stop him however we can."

* * *

The visit from the Mims was interesting. It would have been easy for Kelly to loathe Annika. The westerner was having her husband's baby. But something had changed inside of Kelly in the last few

153

weeks since the stabbing. Her perspective. Her husband was a sick man. But how much sicker was he than everyone else? The difference between Connor and the rest of society was the fact that Connor's deepest thoughts had become real. No one would want their desires and fantasies to manifest themselves in reality; yet for some reason, that's what was happening to Connor Bryce. Did it hurt that Connor had spent countless hours inside his head dining on the lustful appetites of another woman? Absolutely. Was it excruciatingly painful knowing his seed was growing to life inside someone else's womb? More than words could say.

But her perspective told her that her own thoughts, at times, were just as evil. Her own mind was an enemy to itself. She'd hated before, she'd lied before, she'd lusted before…and to what result? Nothing—on the outside. But those thought's had eaten at her senses and tainted her heart. Her hate came out in her words towards others. Her lust had disrespected her own husband without him even knowing it. Her lies had killed more people than she'd cared to admit. And that thought, this realization, was the key to it all. It's not one's physical actions that will be judged one day, but the actions of the heart and mind. Dwelling on evil temptations is just as bad as plunging the knife. Hating is pulling the trigger. Lusting is committing adultery. Envy is robbing a bank.

Connor was no different than she was; no different than every single person that had ever been born. We're all killers; some on the outside, but all on the inside.

So what could be done about it? Kelly had had plenty of time alone with her thoughts recently. She'd searched each tiny corner of her brain trying to figure out how to stop her endless pursuit of evil selfishness. Her thoughts controlled her actions; they were a cancer to her body.

And what about God? John Mims had said that God had given them a miracle. Had he really? What was God's agenda in all of this? Certainly everything with Connor had happened for a reason, but what? And that was yet another change in Kelly's perspective. The old Kelly would be the first to admit—things don't happen for a reason, they just happen. Not every decision had to affect something. Not every domino that falls has to push down another one. Her struggle was in knowing or not knowing the reason behind each domino.

If things happened for a reason, wouldn't it make sense to believe that we, as humans, should know and understand what that reason is?

If we don't know the reason behind everything, then why should we care about the things that we don't understand? Why should Kelly care about her thoughts; things that will never see the light of day? Why should Connor care about his desires when he knows that they're locked in his brain? Because, as Kelly had recently discovered, thoughts are real; there's a reason they happened in the first place, a symptom of a deeper problem within the heart. Her heart. Connor's heart.

This all led her back to God's agenda. Was he a puppet master playing games? No, that wouldn't make sense. She knew little about God, by choice, but had heard people say that God is the ultimate definition of love. A loving God would not pull strings to wage war, would not make his minions dance for amusement. A loving God would try...would never stop trying, to passionately pursue his creation. A loving God would work in—what John Mims had called—the most unlikeliest of ways...to turn every eye of every person back toward him.

That was it—the cure for selfishness. God had not caused the evil inside of them, he'd exposed what was already there.

If only she could get to Connor before it was too late. She was stuck here, inside her prison, while Connor was who-knows-where firing live bullets from a loaded mind. She shut her eyes and slowly attempted a silent prayer.

The door to her room opened and closed. "Lunchtime," a voice called out.

Kelly continued her inner cries for help. Peace quietly began to wash over her body from the inside out. Not a tingling feeling, not euphoria, not a lightning bolt to the senses, but a quiet peace. A whisper, a soft song. Her heart was so dreadfully sinful that it literally hurt. But even that sting had slowly begun to fade as her prayer continued.

When she was finished, she opened her misty eyes to a new world. A peaceful world.

She also opened her eyes to the back of a man wearing blue scrubs. "Ah, I'm starving," Kelly said as she gave her arms a long stretch. "Did you say lunch was here?"

"I did," the man said as he turned around. "You hungry?"

Kelly looked into the eyes of Trace Lasser.

24

He was on her before she could scream, taping her mouth shut with a single motion of his wrist. Whether it was reality or the haziness from her drugs, Lasser seemed to be moving faster than sound. In her mind, Kelly was screaming and kicking, biting and flailing, anything to ward off her attacker. In reality, her reactions were slow and her speech pathetic. Her muscles, cold from weeks of non-use, refused to fire at her command. Yet even as fast as the scene played out before her, it still seemed like slow motion.

Trace Lasser leaned over and whispered in her ear, "I told you that you hadn't seen the last of me. I just hope you missed me as much as I missed you."

Kelly tried to speak through the tape but her words were muffled. Lasser held a syringe full of a clear liquid up to her neck, "Now don't scream, or I'll have to put you to sleep. Do you understand?"

Kelly nodded. He ripped the tape from her mouth, keeping the needlepoint inches from her jugular. "How did you get in here?" she whispered through burned lips.

"That was the easy part. The guards outside your door have been going to lunch the same time every day for the last week. I know— I've been watching. They leave one rookie to stand guard; he looks like he's twelve. Do you think he's going to question every single person that looks like a doctor? I can tell you that he doesn't. People are creatures of habit. Once you have them pegged, the rest is simple. In fact, right now Rookie Cop is halfway down the hall at the nurse's desk flirting with his flavor of the day. Same thing he's done every day this week. I had to be patient and plan ahead. That's something else I've learned while watching things from afar. You see…there's always an opportunity. You just have to wait for it."

"But why here? The detectives just left; they might even be in the building still. It seems like a risky move to me."

"Batman and Robin are gone. I saw them leave minutes ago. And besides, they're here to protect you from your husband, not from me. No one knows I'm here. And the risk just makes it that much more exciting. I could have had my way with you a million times over the last few months; all alone in your house—but where would the fun in that have been?"

"I know you didn't kill Jansen," Kelly said, trying to buy time.

"Of course I didn't, I already told you that."

"So why are you here…there's no need to keep me quiet, I have nothing on you."

Lasser smiled as he walked to the foot of the bed and picked up a black bag. "You have nothing on me…that much is true. But you still have something *for* me, and I always get what I want. You asked me out to dinner months ago, dangled your looks in front of me, then tried to trap me with a murder that *your* husband committed. Then you slapped me and walked out! That's playing hard-to-get if I've ever seen it. I knew then, watching you leave, that you wanted me; you just didn't know it yet. I've seen that look in other women; they all want me, they just need some convincing."

Lasser reached into the black bag and withdrew a clear liquid bag. He walked over to the Kelly's IV bag and stopped the drip. In seconds, he took off the old bag and replaced it with his own. It took Kelly a few seconds to realize what was happening. Trace Lasser had his own medicine, Lasser's magical concoction, and he was about to snake the poison through her veins. Whatever it was, she knew she would never wake up from it. In fact, knowing what he'd do to her once she was unconscious, Kelly prayed that this would be her last taste of life.

She tried to move again; her muscles refused. Her fate was as good as sealed, but she still had to fight. Not for her life, but for everyone else's. Lasser had to be stopped. Her hand, still under the sheets, grazed the remote control by her right hip. Kelly slowly moved her fingers around the remote, her only lifeline to the outside world. Her fingers fumbled around the buttons; she had to find the call button for the nurses. If her memory was correct, and at this point who knew, her lifeline was a large red button at the bottom of the remote. She needed more time.

"What's that you're giving me?" she asked as Lasser was almost done hooking up his new brew.

"I call it *Elation*. It completely paralyzes all of your muscles while heightening your senses. That means you'll feel everything I do to you and you'll have no choice but to lay there. I figure I have another twenty minutes or so before we have another visitor; plenty of time. I'll be long gone by then; but something tells me you'll still be thinking about me," he said with a wink. He stood back to examine his handiwork. "Done," he said.

Her senses drained, Kelly could barely feel the buttons of the remote. She tried to maintain eye contact with Lasser as best as

157

possible. If only she could risk a quick peek under the sheets...but that was impossible. Her fingers continued their blind search for anything that felt like a button. Her fingertips were hard and cold, making recognition even more difficult.

Lasser readjusted the medicine bag one final time as he connected it to Kelly's IV on her left hand. Finally, he opened the drip. Kelly felt the world grow cold as the icy liquid pulsed through her arm. *Drip, drip, drip.* Her fingers grew numb and fuzzy. On the remote hand, her index finger grazed a large, raised button at the bottom of the controller. This had to be it—the emergency call button. Kelly tried to push the button, but her fingers wouldn't move. She strained to force her muscles to fire this one last time. Nothing happened. The cold, poisoned medicine dripped steadily into her veins. *Drip, drip, drip.* Surely it hadn't taken effect that quickly.

Kelly barely wiggled her fingers; they felt tingly and numb. That was good. When they stopped feeling...that would be bad. The medicine had yet to take full effect. She felt for the button again, this time with her thumb; hopefully it would be more powerful. Kelly lined the meaty part of her thumb directly over the button and told her brain to tell her thumb to push with all its might. She got nothing. *Drip, drip, drip.*

Then it happened. Her body became completely relaxed; too relaxed. Only her eyelids moved as they tried to blink away her hellish reality. Kelly could no longer feel the remote in her hands. Her fingers lost their wiggle. She tried to make a sound through her voice, but her muscles lay dormant. She couldn't even produce a moan. In the silent hospital room, her life slipped away; yet she was still alive. Death would be a present. Kelly had no choice but to look straight ahead and mourn the fact that she had never pushed the call button. Help was right there in her fingertips, then her fingertips had died. Now her only movement came from her eyes; she quickly wished that the drugs would have taken that from her as well.

Trace Lasser walked into her field of view. Apparently full muscle paralysis only took a half minute or so. He'd been waiting patiently at the side of the bed. "Can you move?" he said, already knowing the answer. "No, no of course you can't. You can't even answer me," he said with a smile. "But...we can still communicate. You can still *feel* things, right?" he asked as he pulled a knife out from his black bag. He slid the knife gently across her forearm as he looked into her eyes. As the blade delicately cut through the top layers of her skin, her eyes grew wide with terror and pain.

"Yes...it looks as though you're still with me," he said as he put the knife back into his bag. "But I didn't come here to kill you. There are so many other things to do first," he grinned. "First, I'll give you the pleasure of the full Lasser experience. You'll kick yourself for not accepting me months ago. Then I'll pump you full of so many medications that you'll be lucky to remember your own name. You won't remember an ounce of this, which is a crying shame. I hope that means we can still be friends. Now...I hate to keep my guest waiting."

Lasser sat comfortably at the side of Kelly's bed and gently touched her arm. She stared back at him through lifeless eyes. Her body couldn't move, but her mind could. And as she consciously blocked out the rest of her world, she shut her eyes and cursed herself for not punching that button.

* * *

"That went about as well as could be expected," John said to Annika.

The two were at a coffee shop just across the street from the hospital. After leaving Kelly Bryce in her bed and the detectives in the parking lot, John and Annika decided that they'd needed to sit for a few moments to reflect on their conversation. Betty's Java Café was the perfect place.

"It went better than expected," Annika responded. "It's hard for me to believe her story—Connor stabbed her from another room through some kind of mind power? That seems so impossible. And yet, here I sit with a baby in my belly that was put there by a man I've never touched. That's impossible too. If the media ever gets a hold of this we'll all be committed to a psych ward."

"Maybe we belong there." John said.

"Maybe. I just feel so bad for Kelly. She has done nothing to deserve any of this. She has a son. How is she going to live the rest of her life with this hanging over her? How is her son supposed to live a normal adult life under this cloud?"

"I'm not sure," John said. "But they'll find a way. Kelly seems like one tough cookie. And she was smart enough to think this through and put things together way before anyone else did. Her son will draw strength and wisdom from her."

"So where does that leave us?" Annika asked.

John smiled. "It leaves us as a father and mother of a soon-to-be beautiful baby. Our child," John said as he leaned across the table and kissed his bride.

"I can't believe this is actually happening," Annika said as she held John's hand. "I'm going to be a mother. You're going to be a father. John, thank you." She squeezed his hand. "Thank you for not leaving me, for believing me, and for loving me."

John returned her squeeze. "Of course." John sat back in his chair and sipped his coffee. "Now the only question is…what are we going to name him?"

"Him? How are you so sure?"

"Wishful thinking," John said with a smirk. "All guys want a son. It's one hundred percent certain this situation won't happen again, so a boy would be a dream come true. Having said that, a little girl would turn my world upside down. In all honesty, I truly don't care. I still can't wrap my head around the fact that we are actually going to have a baby. I've been dying to tell my parents."

"Me too," Annika said. They'd decided to put off telling their parents for a while until the whole situation became a little clearer— and a little clearer it had just become. There would still be a million questions, and most of those questions had no answers. People were going to have to be okay with that.

"But as for the names, I like Haley if it's a girl and Jonathan if it's a boy," Annika said.

John thought about that, "John junior? Just promise me we won't call him Junior, or J.J."

"I like Johnny, after you."

"Johnny Mims," John repeated. "I like that. And Haley. Princess Haley Mims. Almost takes my breath away. I say we call our folks."

"I agree. Just remember, stick to the basics for now, but let's tell the truth. A miracle has happened, and somehow, beyond our knowledge, we became pregnant. My parents won't know the difference anyway; they have no idea about your medical past," Annika said.

"True. And I can handle my parents. They'll be so shocked I hope they don't pass out," John said as he searched his jacket pocket for his phone.

"Babe, have you seen my cell phone?"

Annika already had hers out and was in the process of dialing her parents. "No, I haven't seen it since you turned it off inside the hospital."

"I bet it fell out when I took my jacket off. Can you try to call it?"

"I can try, but it won't do any good if you turned it off," she said with a smile. "Just run back over there real quick, I'll be right here waiting for you. I think I'm going to try one of their raspberry scones."

"Okay. Be right back," John said as he zipped his jacket up to his chin.

He left the coffee shop and jogged across the street to the hospitals main entrance. The elevator ride to the fourth floor was surprisingly quick. As he approached the nurse's station, John found the nurse and a police officer in a conversation. His first thought was that something might have happened to Kelly. Then he saw the nurse laugh while she reached out to touch the officer's elbow. This was a personal conversation, not a business one. John didn't mind interrupting. "Excuse me," he said as the nurse looked up at him. "I'm sorry to interrupt, I was just here just a little while ago; I came to see Kelly Bryce. I believe I left my cell phone in her room. Is it possible for me to run in and grab it real quick?"

"Visiting hours are over," the young policeman said.

"Then can you or a nurse go look for me?"

The officer gave the nurse an exasperated look as he shook his head. "Sure, Sir, I don't mind at all," he said sarcastically.

The officer walked down the hall and went into Kelly's room. John stood at the nurse's station awkwardly as he waited for the cop to return. Suddenly John heard a loud thud come from the direction of Kelly's room, followed by a yell. John looked at the nurse as her eyes grew large. Without thought, he rushed to the door and pushed it open. The young officer laid face down on the cold tile, asleep to the world. A doctor stood over him while he tried to catch his breath. He was bleeding from the nose. He looked up at John, John looked over at Kelly. She was lying completely motionless, yet her eyes darted back and forth between the doctor and the police officer. Her eyes were two round circles of fear. Something was terribly wrong. John knew all of this in a matter of seconds.

John looked back at the man in scrubs in just enough time to duck under a fist coming from his left side. What was happening? The doctor came again with a jab that connected to John's nose. His head snapped back and warm blood ran down his lips and into his mouth. John took a step back to regain his thoughts. The doctor reached for a syringe on the table and held it in his hands like a chisel. Before

John was ready, the doctor came at him from the side. John blocked the doctor's hand as the syringe stopped inches from his neck. The doctor was short, but country strong. John mustered the energy to bring a knee up into the doctor's ribs. The connection forced the man to stumble backwards as he tried to catch his breath.

For the briefest of seconds, John stole a glimpse in Kelly's direction. Her eyes harbored terror and despair. The man grabbed a knife from a black bag, then came at him again. John was ready. He'd already beat up one man in a hospital in the last few months, he was about to make it two.

The doctor tried a swiping motion with the knife. John dodged it and then threw a jab of his own on the rebound. It connected with the man's mouth. John felt something break at the end of his knuckles. In confirmation, the doctor spit out a mouth full of blood and two teeth. John smiled.

"I hope you have more than a knife in that bag. You're gonna need it."

The doctor wiped the blood from his bottom lip, then charged again. Enough was enough. The doctor threw his arm in a long arc as the blade sliced through the air. John stepped back at the last possible moment as the knife tore through his shirt. The doctor had overexerted his strength, and upon missing his target, briefly lost his balance. That was all John needed. As the doctor leaned one way, John threw a haymaker from the opposite side, putting all of his weight behind it. The sound was sickening. John's right hand hit the doctor square in the jaw, and as he followed through with the punch, he felt the man's jaw tear loose and wobble back and forth as it hung lazily from the doctors head. He'd broken it.

The doctor hit the floor with a thud. John stood over him for a full minute to make sure the man didn't move an inch. Once he was certain that he wouldn't, he kicked the knife and syringe to the opposite side of the room. Then he went over and stood beside Kelly. The entire fight lasted only a minute or two. They always seemed longer when you're in the midst of one.

Two police officers burst through the door, followed by the nurse that had been standing with John just a few minutes earlier. She had gone for help. It was a good thing too, because from the initial looks of it, John was standing next to two bodies on the floor, one police officer and one doctor. At least the nurse knew the first part of the story. Kelly would be able answer to answer the rest. Hopefully.

162

25

The winds of despair blew cold through a broken pane of glass by Connor's head. He'd passed out hours ago, only to wake up with the fangs of winter stabbing his face. Perhaps he was still dreaming? God, he hoped not. His dreams, if you could call them that, were a whirlwind of screams and sirens, high-pitched squeals and low-toned vibrations. He tried stuffing little balls of newspaper in his ears days ago to no avail. The screams were coming from inside, not out. The noises never stopped—eyes open, eyes shut; it didn't matter.

Connor rolled over on his side for two reasons, one to get the cutting wind out of his face, and two, to hurl. What was once a peaceful little abandoned warehouse now reeked of booze and vomit. He'd been asleep two days, maybe three. Why wake? It could have been Tuesday or Friday. He'd tried and succeeded at having as little human contact as possible, for their safety and his. There was the gentleman at the liquor store he'd talked to a few times, but so far the guy was still alive.

He used a steam pole by the wall to help him to his feet. The ground spun like a coin on a table—moving side to side one way while spinning delicately another way. Good. Maybe if his mind stayed sauced then it wouldn't hurt anyone. But no. That's not the way it worked. Even in his drunken state, Connor knew that much.

Drops of rain pinged loudly off the tin roof. The vibration in his head grew so loud his jaws clinched involuntarily. He was going crazy. Wrong. Not *going*...was. He had completely lost all sense of time, perspective and reality.

He only knew one thing—that he was a killer and a danger to society. All society, every society. No prison could hold him, no jacket strong enough to trap the thoughts out of his brain.

He actually knew two things. He knew he had to take his mind out of the equation; he was the only person who could stop himself. No one else would understand. In the interest of society and the human race, he had to take one for the team. It was a welcoming thought.

It was the only way.

Connor slowly found the strength to put one leg in front of the other, and surprisingly without falling, made his way to the unlocked cargo doors. One look outside revealed a wall of gray rain sweeping across the river headed his way. Fitting.

He stood at the doorway in true contemplation. What would be his next plan of action? How could he terminate his existence in the easiest and most painless way possible? He'd never thought about suicide before, not in his past life. But now, ever since he'd stabbed his wife Kelly, he'd...KELLY!

He now knew three things; and the third was the most pressing. Kelly Bryce, his precious wife, was recovering from multiple wounds *he* had inflicted. He had to check her status. He'd been calling every few days from a pay phone across the street, and every time he called he got the same response—she was stable but unconscious. But that was what, three, four days ago? More? Connor cursed himself for allowing things to have gotten so far out of control.

Here he was, drinking himself into oblivion, while his wife fought for her life. This was why he had to die—his selfishness. Even in times like this, he'd only been thinking of himself. Poor Connor, killer Connor, why-is-this-happening-to-me Connor. His world, as dark and ugly as it was, still revolved around him. This wouldn't change the fact that he had to die, that was as good as done. But it did mean he had to make sure Kelly would live before he proceeded with his plans.

Hail now joined the rain as it fell harder, the pings on the metal roof popped like firecrackers. Baltimore could get frigid in the winter, but when you're all by yourself, it's downright nasty.

Connor made his way to the corner where he'd kept his few belongings. Bending down slowly, he found enough change in his backpack to place a call to the hospital. He walked back to the cargo door, threw his jacket hood up over his head, and marched to the pay phone across the street.

This one was different; he could feel it. This call would bring him good news. Kelly would be alright. Years from now, she'd be remarried to someone that couldn't hurt her, someone that would be a good husband to her, the man she'd deserved from the beginning. As he slid each coin down into the belly of the black box, he knew his wife would be okay. After a deep breath, he punched the number to the hospital.

A lady answered on the third ring. "Mercy Hospital, how may I direct your call?"

"Fourth floor please." Connor responded.

"Hold sir."

Music. Music. Music. Then ringing. "Fourth floor, how may I help you?"

164

"Yes, I'm Doctor Thomas Miller from the medical institute..."
Well, he couldn't very well say he was Connor Bryce now could he,
"...I'm calling to get an updated status on the condition of a Mrs.
Kelly Bryce."

"I'm sorry sir; I can't give you any information on a patient without
approval."

"May I speak to her personal doctor, or will I have to get
permission directly from her? I just want to know if she's woken up
yet. The last time I talked to her doctor he informed me that she'd
been asleep for days on end."

"Her doctor isn't available right now, sir."

"How about Mrs. Bryce then, I just tried to call her room but no
one answered?"

There was a long pause on the other end.

"Mrs. Bryce cannot speak either sir; she's busy talking to
detectives. Now please, I'll let her doctor know that you called, or feel
free to try back later. I'm sorry, but I can't help you..."

Dial tone. Connor had hung up.

When he'd heard those magic words, *she's busy talking*...his heart
almost burst. Kelly had recovered. She was talking to the detectives
at this very moment. He hadn't killed her! Every ounce of sadness
and remorse he'd felt over the last week had now, at least temporarily,
vanished. Kelly would live. She was talking. The nurse, in that one
sentence, had given Connor all he'd needed to hear.

All of the sudden he wanted to run into her hospital room and
throw his arms around her, let her know how immensely sorry he was.
He wanted to beg her for forgiveness, beg her for another chance. He
would promise her that he'd get help; he'd swear he would change.
No more selfishness, no more hatred, no more lusting after other
women. He had his woman. Or at least he used to. And he could
again, if she would just give him another chance.

Stop it! What was he thinking? The risk was far greater than the
reward. This was no time to talk himself out of his original plan. If
he ever saw Kelly again, how could he guarantee he wouldn't hurt
her? He couldn't. That's a promise he wasn't sure he could keep.
No. For Kelly's sake, for her happiness, he had to kill himself. The
decision was made. That was the only light at the end of his tunnel.
It was in fact, a train, and soon it would hit him dead on.

All he had ever hoped for in the last few weeks had come true. Kelly was alive—would be alive for the foreseeable future. That meant only one thing.

Connor briefly considered packing his things to take with him. Then he realized—where he was going, things were useless. He staggered out of the warehouse door and headed toward the bridge. The water of the Patapsco River would be frigid this time of year; if a jump off the bridge didn't kill him, the freezing waters soon would. Rain came at him from all directions and small bullets of hail stung his face. Still, Connor made his way toward the bridge.

This was his fate; so be it. He'd accept it with his head held high. He deserved judgment; he deserved his punishment. No complaints from Connor Bryce. He'd taken a life, ruined countless others for generations to come. And all because of his inability to reign in and extinguish his selfish desires before the small flames had turned into wild fires.

Connor walked out onto the middle of the bridge. Cars passed him right and left, none paying any attention to the homeless drunk man by the railing. He put his hands down on the cold metal beams and looked over the side. The river thrashed angrily down below. Just as well, he wanted no gentleness from it anyway.

Slowly, only because that's the only speed he could move while drunk, Connor began to climb the side beam of the bridge. A car honked.

After a few steps, his feet found the horizontal side beam, the guardrail that separated car from river. One step forward and he was a goner. Connor stood there for a few seconds without a thought. More cars began to honk now as the man on the side rail gained attention. Voices began to shout. Connor heard nothing. Suddenly his mind went to his wife. With a last whisper, he muttered, "God, be with Kelly; have no mercy for me."

And as the hail smacked down all around him, he opened his arms, leaned forward, and fell through the air.

* * *

Trace Lasser was carted out of the hospital room on a stretcher. His head and neck were strapped firmly to the backboard, his jaw bandaged tightly in place over his ears and around the top of his head. He was escorted by four of Baltimore's finest to another part of the hospital. Detectives Presley and Suarez showed up a half hour later.

"How you feeling?" Presley said as he and Suarez entered Kelly's room.

"Fffnnn…ffiiinne," Kelly mumbled out. Her muscle paralysis was slowly wearing off. The doctor said it would take at least six hours for the drugs to fully leave her system. Speech was the first motor skill to return, but the going would be slow.

"Well, don't exhaust yourself. Just lay here and rest. I know your doctor has talked to you. Looks like you'll be here a few more days. We'll have some questions about any interactions you've had in the past to Mr. Lasser, but this looks pretty cut and dry. In the meantime, I don't want you talking. It'll be a while before you're fully operational. I just want to know one thing," Presley said, "did he hurt you?" Just nod yes or no.

Kelly shook her head side to side.

Presley smiled slightly, then squinted his eyes. "Kelly, we let you down. The people responsible will pay, but I told you I'd keep you safe, and I didn't. I'm truly sorry. It won't happen again."

Kelly tried to smile but it proved difficult. Her mouth felt like she had just left the dentist's office after a root canal. If she were to take a gulp of water she was sure it would have dribbled down her chin and neck. She thought about giving the thumbs-up sign, but that too was impossible at the moment. In her best effort at non-verbal, non-muscular communication, she put on a half smile and looked back and forth using only her eyes from the detectives to the door, detectives to the door.

Presley smile back, "Alright, call me if you need anything," he said as a joke. Pres and Suarez left the room and found John and Annika in the lobby where they'd been asked to wait. After John's earlier altercation with Lasser, he'd actually found his cell phone, which he then used to call his wife who had been waiting for him at the coffee shop across the street. She'd rushed over immediately.

Pres and Suarez sat across from the Mims.

"So," Presley said, "That was interesting."

John gave a coy smile as he nursed his busted nose, "What do you want me to say?"

"Start from the beginning."

"I'd lost my cell phone, thought it might be somewhere in Kelly's room, came back, wasn't allowed in, an officer went in to look for it, a nurse and I heard a thud and a shout. I went in and took care of business. That's all there was to it."

167

"Yeah, that's the report I'd gotten too. She was lucky you came back. You seem to have a knack for getting into fights at hospitals."

"It's a gift," John said. "So, is the officer I found on the floor going to be alright?"

"He'll be fine," Suarez said, "His punishment from the police department will be worse than the beat down he just received."

"And tell us again that Kelly will be fine," Annika said.

"She'll be just fine. Lasser hadn't started whatever it was he'd had planned yet. I believe if you're husband hadn't intervened when he did, we would be telling a different story."

"Well, what now?" John asked.

"With Trace Lasser in custody and Kelly back on the road to recovery, we go back to an all-out search for Connor Bryce."

One of the police officers responsible for guarding Trace Lasser poked her head in the lobby door, Presley and Suarez looked her direction.

"May I speak with you," she asked.

The detectives excused themselves and walked outside into the hallway.

She jumped right in, "You need to come hear what Lasser is saying."

"I didn't think he's "saying" anything; not with a broken jaw," Suarez said.

"Well, he's not, but he's writing down his account. He just told us that Connor Bryce put him up to the whole thing; paid him money to finish off Kelly."

"Does he have proof?" Presley asked suspiciously.

"I don't think so, but he'd be careful not to leave a paper trial. I'm not sure what to make of it, but wanted to let you know immediately."

"Thank you, officer."

She turned and headed back down the hallway. Suarez turned to Presley and said, "I don't believe it for a second. Lasser's trying to use Bryce as a scapegoat; trying to cast doubt on his own guilt."

"I agree. We have to follow up on it because that's our job, but I don't buy it either. Actually, let's ask the captain to put someone else on the Lasser case. We need to stay focused on Bryce."

They walked back in and sat back across from John and Annika.

"Sorry for the interruption," Presley said, "Where were we?"

A rapid knock on the side wall diverted their attention yet again.

"Detectives?" another officer called from the doorway.

Presley waved him over. The officer hurried across the room, obviously in a hurry.

"Well, go on, what is it?"

"Just received three different calls of a jumper down by the Patapsco. Witness descriptions of the individual match closely to your man Bryce. Same height, same build. Paramedics are on the way now. Whoever it is, we'll be lucky to find him in this weather."

Presley and Suarez both stood, "Thanks. We're on our way." The officer turned quick on his heels and scurried off again.

John and Annika had overheard everything, "We'll keep in touch," Suarez said.

"Go," Annika said. "We'll be fine. I hope you find him."

"I'm not sure what we'll find," Presley said. "We've been chasing ghosts for six months."

26

The storm had finally pushed through as Presley and Suarez drove up to the boat ramp half a mile down the river from the bridge. The current moved swifter now than it had before the downpour; the waters swirled a murky chocolate brown. Presley took control of the situation immediately.

He barked orders to a group of younger uniforms, police boat operators, and rescue divers. "Find out how far a man Bryce's size can float in waters moving this fast. Then add another mile. We'll start our search that many miles downriver and work our way back up to the bridge. I want to make sure there's no way he floated past our beginning search point. And get me as many eye witnesses that saw him before he jumped as you can find. I know the conditions are awful and the waters freezing, but this is what we get paid to do, so let's do it."

Pres turned to a boat captain, "We're coming with you," he said as he motioned Suarez to step onto the boat deck after him. "Alright," he yelled to the group from the side of the boat, "I want two other units with us and the other four units downriver. We work our way towards each other. Check the banks, piers, boat docks—any and everything, you know the drill. Paramedics are standing by. You find anything, breathing or not, get on the horn immediately. We don't leave until we find him. Any questions?"

None.

The search was painstakingly detailed as the minutes ticked by. Another small round of showers moved in, then moved out just as quickly. Minutes turned into hours. One boat had found a large suitcase by a sewer inlet. When opened, it was full of Hawaiian shirts and cargo pants. Another boat happened upon the carcass of a recently deceased dog. And the grand prize of the day went to a rescue diver who'd stumbled across a sunken minivan that was full of stuffed animals.

No Connor. No anybody.

The day was drawing to a close. Whoever jumped off that bridge had now been in the water for over three hours. This was no longer a rescue, it was a recovery.

"We can't do much once this sun goes down," Suarez said. He was exhausted from hours of scanning the banks. The shadows were beginning to play tricks on his eyes.

"You're right; we'll have to pick up tomorrow morning. We'll move our search grid further down river. If he's dead, he'll sink until he gets gassy; then he'll pop up like a cork. If he's alive, he'll soon *be* dead so it really doesn't matter." Pres stared out over the flowing river, "If the rains hold off this water level will drop some overnight; might make things a little easier."

"True," Suarez said. He turned and pounded his fist on the boats outer railing. "I was just hoping to find him alive. It didn't have to come to this. I wanted to talk to him; get inside of his thoughts. Why wouldn't he let us help him? What's he so scared of?"

"Himself," Pres said.

Presley's two-way phone chirped from his side for the thousandth time that day. Presley un-holstered it and motioned Suarez closer to him.

"Go ahead."

"Presley, this is Wheaton. We got something down here." Presley motioned for the boat captain to head immediately down river. Detective Wheaton was in one of the units working their way back towards the bridge.

"Go on."

"A body. Looks like our man. No I.D. but I've seen his picture a million times. It's him; doesn't look good. He's got a weak pulse, blue face and lips. Already called the EMT's, they'll be here in two minutes."

"Good work Detective. Headed your way now."

The boat flew down the river. This was the moment they'd been waiting for the last six months; the moment of truth—capturing Connor Bryce.

Presley saw the red flashing lights on the bank from a hundred yards off; the paramedics were quick. The captain throttled down the engine and let the boat coast the rest of the way to the shallow bank. Once they were close enough, Presley and Suarez both hopped off the side of the boat and onto shore.

Detective Wheaton met them at the top of the hill.

"They just pulled him out. Follow me." Wheaton led the gentlemen around a guardrail to the back of the ambulance. There he was, Connor Bryce. He had EMT's on every side of him—cutting off his cold clothing, starting an IV, checking his poor excuse for vital signs.

Presley studied the man's blue face. It was unrecognizable from the face they'd seen at the diner months ago. It even looked different than when they'd seen him at the hospital in Phoenix. What was it that had changed? What did he look like now? Presley kept the answer in his head: Death. Connor had given up.

"We gotta get him out of here," yelled a paramedic. "One of you want to ride with us?"

"You got room?" Presley asked.

"I wouldn't ask if we didn't." He wasn't rude, just in a hurry.

Presley looked at Suarez who gave him a nod in return. "Follow us Rez," Presley said as he jumped in the back of the van.

"Right on your heels," Suarez returned.

He had to borrow a black and white from one of his colleagues as their car was many miles upriver. Suarez followed the ambulance as a knot formed in his stomach. This was wrong…all wrong.

Presley couldn't take his eyes off of Bryce. Monitors and machines beeped and buzzed all around him. But there Connor was, sleeping silently. The man that had killed without being physically present, that had stabbed from another room. No one would ever believe this. One of the most powerful minds in recent memory was also one the most dangerous. Yet here Bryce was, laying helpless just a few inches in front of him. Silently, and completely out of character, Presley sent up a small prayer for the life of Connor Bryce.

That's when he heard the steady hum of a flat line.

* * *

Dashes of light danced around him like kids waving sparklers on the fourth of July. Silver and gold streams of ribbon flashed across his vision. The air was electric yet slightly chilled. Connor was lying flat on his back. He lifted his head and stared down at his feet. He saw nothing. He held his hands up in front of his face but couldn't make them out through all the lights.

He wasn't even sure his eyes were open. He heard voices, faint and distant, but their words were a mumbled mystery. Suddenly he was standing up. He couldn't see his feet, but they were steadfast underneath him. Connor walked through a room decorated with purple and gold lights, the strands blinking at different intervals and in no particular pattern. All of the sudden the lights changed—red and silver. A slight fog hung in the air as he tried to focus his eyes on anything of familiarity. For all intents and purposes, he was a blind man walking.

He tried to recall the last thing he remembered…the last place he was. Yes—the bridge. He remembered floating through the air. He remembered the chunks of hail as they smacked the back of his head on the way down. He remembered the water rushing up toward him. He remembered the open arms of the nasty river as it welcomed him in head first.

Splash.

Then he remembered cold. Dark. Empty. Black. He remembered searing pain from his head to his feet; he remembered screaming loudly underneath the water as his back arched in agony. He remembered doubling over and heaving under the roof of the river as he swallowed mouthfuls of water while he tried to breathe. He remembered crying in the darkness, not knowing if the cold liquid on his face were his tears or the bottom of the river in which he now called home. He remembered being so cold that his body involuntarily convulsed with the hopes of warming itself. Then he had quit shaking; his apathetic body floating limply in the water, too cold to go on.

He heard a drum beat, faint and distant from behind him.

Connor walked in the direction of the noise; his feet keeping pace with the rhythmic thumping. He walked for miles through an empty black room as the noise grew louder and louder. At some point, he approached a large hole in the ground. The drum beat was banging heavily from within the crater. He had to get down there. He walked the top rim of the large hole looking for access into its depths. Soon he came upon a ladder that extended down into the bowels of the black abyss. Slowly, Connor began his descent.

The drumming in his ears grew so loud it was almost painful. The darkness gave way to blurry hues of red and purple lights, barely visible deep below. As Connor's eyes slowly adjusted to his surroundings, he noticed majestic stalactites the size of skyscrapers hanging from the roof of the cave. A metallic smell began to fill his nostrils the further down he went; not pleasant, yet not repulsive. And the beat went on.

The pain began in Connor's shoulders, then spread quickly down to his thighs and calves. He'd been climbing for hours; his muscles quivered in spasms. His fingers cramped so badly that he was now stopping every few minutes to stretch them as best as he could. His parched throat thirsted for any liquid. He'd believed himself to be at the halfway point when the stalactites met the stalagmites hours ago. Now the large trunks of the stalagmites grew as round as football fields. Surely they would meet flat ground soon.

The lights intensified as he descended, casting shades of deep crimson red and a purple so dark it was almost black. His muscles ached so badly that he almost let go of the ladder a few times by accident. He'd thought he had a good grip of the rungs, but sometimes his muscles revolted and wouldn't support his own weight. Only his sharp reflexes and a quick recovery had saved him from falling to his death below.

Finally after hours of climbing, his feet felt solid ground beneath them. Connor could feel the vibration of the drum beat inside of his ears. He could picture the tiny hairs of his inner ear standing to attention with each thump. This was it; this was where the loud beat was originating from.

Connor stood at the bottom of the ladder to digest his new environment and rest his weary muscles. Along a side wall a little ways off, Connor noticed what looked like picture frames hanging from the wall; thousands of them. With piqued interest, he slowly walked toward the monument of photographs. The air in this room was thick; nothing held any color outside of red and purple. Connor examined the first picture and stopped cold in his tracks. It was a picture of him as a baby—little red and purple Connor Bryce.

Why would his picture be up in this room; and a baby picture no less? The next still shot was a gold framed photograph of his parents right after he was born. Then a picture of baby Bryce crawling across

173

a green shag rug; then at t-ball years later; then playing basketball; at a park; eating mashed potatoes; feeding carrots to a dog underneath a table; at school; behind the wheel of his first car; graduation—the pictures never stopped. Every motion and memory of Connor's life was on that wall; some he remembered clearly, others he did not.

Thump-thump, thump-thump.

Connor walked slowly down the line of pictures, smiling at some, shaking his head at others. Who had done this? And what was its meaning? The giant wall was devoted to him, to his whole life, to his entire being. It was a running timeline of his thoughts, his loves, his priorities. It was an upscale model of who he was; the wall *was* Connor Bryce.

And then, just like that, it hit him: pictures of him everywhere, the metallic smell in the room, the red and purple lights, the thumping of the drum—Connor was standing inside the walls of his own heart.

He hit knees immediately and cried out in anguish. He knew this could only mean one thing—he was dead. How else could someone stand inside their own heart? Having the sense of mind to know you're dead, yet still having conscious thought was a sickening, eerie feeling.

The beating of the drum grew louder and faster.

Suddenly Connor jumped to his feet. The thumping beat was racing now. His heartbeat! If he could hear his own heartbeat, he couldn't be dead. He was alive; had to be!

He was alive and still somehow walking the floors of his own battery.

Connor raced back toward the pictures hanging on the enormous wall. If the timeline held true, then Connor could see what was in his heart immediately before he'd found himself in this...place.

He ran down the side of the wall as fast as he could. Thousands and thousands of pictures flashed by him as he raced passed them without hesitation. Minutes stretched into miles as the rapid thumping pushed faster.

The end was now in sight; not much further.

Connor slowed his sprint down into a trot, then a fast walk. He was nearing the end of his pictures. These were the ones he'd wanted to see. He stopped just short of the frames and began looking at the photographs. The first one he saw brought tears to his eyes—Kelly, his precious wife. They were both frozen in midair, hand in hand as they jumped from a rock ledge into a lake. That had just taken place this past summer, a few weeks before...before...before what?

Connor quickly scanned the next few pictures, all of Kelly. This was good, great in fact, but for some reason not exactly what Connor was looking for. Something was still missing. The frames were nearing an end; picture time was almost up.

Connor walked further down the wall, looking, scanning. A picture of him at work caught his attention. He was talking to his boss, Mr. Jansen. Floods of thought washed over him in an instant. Connor's boss Jansen; he'd been killed by…by…

By him. By Connor Bryce. Through wounded eyes he looked at the next picture. It was cast in shades of dark purple and black. The picture frame was splintered metal. Connor Bryce stood at the foot of Gregory Jansen's bed. The old man had just been murdered, his wife lay snoring by his side. Connor had killed him. He wasn't there, in physical form, on that ugly night. But this was a picture of his heart…from his heart, and it clearly showed what Connor already somehow knew to be true. He'd killed the old man.

Connor sunk to his knees and buried his head in his hands. He knew this was what he'd find, yet still hoped for something…cleaner. But no, this was the dirtiness that was Connor Bryce. This was the ugliness of his heart, and the power of the heart was much more powerful than any physical action. In the heart, there were no physical actions, only desires that—if left to fester—became reality.

No one wants to see what they truly look like. The result is never pretty. Connor would never be pretty again. He stood up clumsily and fumbled toward the next set of pictures. Pictures of…wait, that couldn't be right…Annika Mims? What was she doing hanging on his walls? She meant nothing to him! She didn't belong there!

Annika's face smiled back at him through the framed glass. In an eruption, Connor slammed his fist into the face of the frame, shattering the glass into a million pieces and cutting his knuckles to shreds. Her face still smiled.

"Stop it!" he screamed, the sound of his voice fading instantly. There were no echoes in the heart. The *thump-thump* of his drumbeat now sounded like a car engine. Connor scanned the next few pictures of Annika; only she wasn't alone. Connor was with her in the deep red walls of a hotel room. They were together.

Glass flew as Connor ripped the frames off of the wall. How could he have been so stupid, so selfish? She did not belong there, not in his personal sanctuary. But the heart doesn't lie, does it? In truth, Annika had never been with Connor in any of those places or positions shown in the pictures. But in Connor's heart, she had. She'd earned her way onto that wall of his; he'd hung the frame personally.

Lost. Broken. What kind of man was he? He didn't know; he never wanted to know. Yet more pictures begged his attention; the last set of photographs on the walls of Connor Bryce's heart. And they belonged to Kelly.

Shattered.

They'd been smashed already! Had someone else been there? Connor would have never smashed Kelly's picture to pieces. But who else would have access to Connor's heart? No one. And so it was. The final picture frame on the wall—his lovely wife Kelly, lying in bed sleeping...broken to pieces. No sense in arguing with himself anymore. Connor knew the truth. He'd smashed this picture long ago. With his thoughts, his actions, his selfish desires. He knew what kind of man he was, selfish and small.

He took the broken frame off the wall and slid again to the ground. There was nothing left to look at. He was evil. His thoughts, yes; but more than that. Matters of the mind can be good or bad, yet even the bad ones can be cured before any virus spreads and breeds. But once evil desires spread, they leave the brain and build their black castles in the heart. That's where man's true nature is exposed. That's where the things most important to him are photographed and framed.

Connor hadn't killed or fornicated *only* in his mind, but he'd let those thoughts form an empire in his heart. Then someone had died, families were broken. His heart was responsible...and he was responsible for his heart.

Connor lay flat on his back, clutched Kelly's broken picture to his chest, and began to cry. Deep purple and crimson red lights drifted around the room. The deeds were done. There was no changing anything that had taken place. These were wrongs that couldn't be righted.

Connor was at the end of himself. He deserved judgment; the worst. He put his head back on the cold ground and remembered the last words he'd prayed before he'd jumped into the icy river, *God, be with Kelly; have no mercy for me.* Yet even before he'd prayed it, God had answered that prayer. And was he, God, in the pictures of Connor's life? Where was he on the wall? Didn't he care; wasn't he concerned about his own creation? How could he be so blatantly absent? Connor knew the answer before the questions fully formed in his mind. Connor was in control of what pictures went where; he controlled everything about his heart, including what was allowed in. He'd decided to keep God out.

Millions of times.

His heart beat faster than it ever had before. The drumming in his ears was now accompanied by a high-pitched hum. Connor heard a thunder-clap boom in the distance. The wheels were falling off.

A loud crash announced itself fifty yards from where Connor laid. One of the stalactites had broken loose and fallen to the ground. A hundred yards away in the other direction another one followed. The ground produced a low rumble as it started to shake back and forth gently first, then violently. Connor shut his eyes as he realized what was happening; his heart was caving in on itself.

Pictures fell off of the wall above him, red and purple drops of rain now fell down from the black storm above. Thickness filled the air as a fast moving fog began to fill up the room. Still Connor did not move.

Why would he? This was his home. This was his judgment.

As rocks of his own heart continued to crash all around him, as the ground shook and cracked open to his right and left, Connor lay motionless, gently weeping.

He looked up as he softly whispered, "Thank you for being with Kelly. If you can find mercy for me, I beg for it now."

Then he heard an explosion. The drum had lost its beat.

His heart had collapsed.

* * *

Dashes of light danced around him like kids waving sparklers on the fourth of July. Silver and gold streams of ribbon flashed across his vision. The air was electric yet slightly chilled. Connor was lying flat on his back. Loud thunderclaps vibrated off the walls of his brain as enormous amounts of heat and warmth spread through his body.

Voices trailed off in the distance. Or were they closer? His eyes refused to open as the thunderstorm moved directly over him now. Bolts of lightning flashed all around him; with each one his body convulsed. A hot air spread across his mind as his fingers and toes began to tingle. He wanted desperately to open his eyes but still could not find the strength. Specks of cold air hit his face like raindrops, yet there was no liquid.

Another lightning bolt flew down from the sky and struck him squarely in the chest. Connor arched his back in immense pain. The bolt sucked every ounce of air out of his lungs, and as a reflex he sat up and burned for more. He drank a deep breath; the air was cold and different. It tasted fresh, crisp.

The voices grew louder. He knew he was dead. Connor was suddenly aware of someone's hand on his forehead and another hand on his chest. Slowly, he tried to open his eyes. The light that entered sizzled his retinas and forced him to close his eyes immediately and lie back down. Over the next few minutes he opened the tiny slits and slowly let his eyes grow used to the burning white light.

Finally his gaze held focus as things started to take shape. The first thing Connor remembered seeing, lying on his back, was the upside down face of a black man with long sideburns. This must be what God looks like, he thought.

27

Tyrone Presley and Miguel Rodrigo Suarez both sat at the end of the bed. Neither had slept in days. Their captain had told both of them to go home and get some sleep hours ago; that they'd be notified when Bryce woke up. Obviously neither had followed those orders. They sat patiently and talked little at the foot of the hospital bed, each man lost in his own thoughts.

Presley was done; with everything. This case was simply too much. How was he supposed to track down and arrest a man for not actually "doing" anything, even when that man still bore complete responsibility and was a danger to society? He was no longer chasing criminals; he was chasing bad desires and malicious thoughts. How was he expected to testify at Bryce's trial? Okay, sure they had evidence against him, but nothing was more effective than the testimony of two very believable and level headed eye witnesses in Kelly Bryce and Annika Mims; and when the paternity tests of Annika's unborn baby were included, more than enough reasonable doubt would have to creep in the jury's mind. Maybe. Who knew with juries these days? This was far from an open and shut case. It wasn't even anywhere in the middle; it was truly a case that stood alone. When it was all said and done, whether Bryce was guilty or innocent, Presley would turn in his badge. He was through with this nonsense.

Suarez wasn't done with police work, but he was long overdue for a vacation. He pictured himself down in the Gulf fishing for red snapper, kingfish and grouper. He could feel the Florida sun on his face and the smell of salt in the air. How long would he have to wait until the trial was over? Months? Years? There would be a media circus every step of the way. And though he would probably never say it publicly, he wasn't even sure Connor Bryce should stand trial for his crimes. Was he responsible for the death of Gregory Jansen and the attempted murder of his own wife Kelly? Yes, he was. But if everyone who had ever hated literally killed, we'd all be on trial, Suarez concluded. What was the precedent for a case like this? There wasn't one; hopefully there'd never be another. But even still, Connor Bryce, a man just like Suarez himself, would be in jail—possibly on death row—for a murder he honestly didn't do. Suarez still couldn't wrap his brain around it. Florida couldn't come soon enough.

No one else had been allowed in the room except for the two detectives and their captain. Ironically, Kelly Bryce was still recovering just a few doors down the hall. She'd been informed that her husband had been apprehended, was currently in custody, and was recovering from an accident in a nearby hospital. Presley thought it wise to let the truth come out naturally in its own time. Obviously Connor and Kelly had a lot to catch up on; there were wounds that might never fully heal. On the other hand, there would be plenty of time for talking. For the moment, neither needed to know that the other was a few short steps down the hallway.

Presley watched the man's face at the head of the bed. Cuts and bruises surrounded his forehead, dark circles framed his eyes. As if on cue, they opened. Presley was looking directly into the eyes of Connor Bryce.

"You're not God," was the first thing Bryce said.

Presley audibly chuckled, "What gave it away?"

Connor brought his hand up to rub his eyes only to find both of them chained to each side of the bed rail. He gave Pres an inquisitive look.

"Had to be done," Presley said. "You seem to know how to slip out of them anyway. How you feeling?"

Connor thought about it for a moment, "Rested."

"Not the answer I was expecting but it'll do.

"I've been awake and on the run for over six months now. Not once have I slept in peace. I'm not sure how long I've been here, but I'm in no hurry to leave."

"Do you feel like talking or should we save it for later?"

"Might as well do it now. Do I need a lawyer?" Connor asked.

179

"Do you want one?"

"Not really. They wouldn't believe me."

"Probably not. This will all be off the record. You have a lot more interrogations coming; I just want to talk man-to-man now. The rest can wait."

"Okay," Connor said.

"Well," Presley said leaning forward in his chair, "what do you remember?"

"Everything," Connor said. "I remember everything more vividly than I thought I would. Running from you before you broke down my door, hitchhiking across country, escaping out the backdoor of the diner, Phoenix, John and Annika, Kelly...everything. I remember everything. I wish I didn't, but I do," he said in apparent pain.

"Connor, did you kill your boss, Gregory Jansen?"

"Yes," Connor said unblinking.

"Did you physically kill your boss, Gregory Jansen?

"No."

"And did you sleep with Annika Mims?"

"No."

"Did you impregnate Annika Mims?"

"Yes," he said, as badly as it hurt.

"Did you stab your wife, Kelly Bryce?"

"Yes."

"Did you literally stab her with a knife in her chest and stomach?"

"No."

Detective Presley sat back in his chair and looked at the ground. This was unbelievable. Bryce was telling the truth. It was in his eyes. Suarez looked at Presley, who gave him a slight nod.

"How do you explain this?" Suarez asked.

"I can't. Not in terms that make sense," Connor replied.

"Explain it however you can, Mr. Bryce."

Connor was silent for a half a minute; his eyes searched the ceiling, thinking. "Have you ever gotten caught up in hate, detective? Have you ever loathed someone, wished them ill-intent? Have you ever hoped bad things would happen to a person that you truly despised?"

"I have," Suarez said out loud.

"And have you ever met a woman and let your desires for her run wild? Have you ever been unable or unwilling to control your thoughts about that person? Have you let unbridled passion and desire turn into a passion that you, in your own control, found impossible to stop?"

"Yes."

"And lastly, have you ever seen your significant other as a barrier to some of your impure fantasies and thoughts? Have you ever said to yourself, "If I weren't tied down to this person or that person, I could be with whoever I wanted...do whatever I wanted?" Have you ever had those thoughts?"

"Yes," Suarez said again.

"Well, I have too. Only mine came true. That's how I explain it, detective. I'm responsible for the hurt that I've caused others. Whether I physically did anything or not, in my world, the actions of my heart *are* my reality."

"Is it still like that now?" Suarez asked as Presley jotted down a few notes.

"Yes. It will always be like that. It should be like that. My entire life, I've been fake with people. I've hid things in my heart, dark things that shouldn't be there, but on the outside I've tried to stay clean and pretty for everyone. I want to look a certain way or be viewed in certain lights by certain people. But that's not me. My heart is me, and it should be what people see first."

"So how do you plan to control your thoughts in the future? How can you make sure this won't happen again?"

Connor Bryce tried to sit up a little higher, but found it difficult with his hands in cuffs. "I can't," he said. "I can't make sure my hatred doesn't harm others; that my lustful cravings don't get out of control. Not by myself."

"You gonna see a shrink?"

Connor managed a small smile, "No. Not a shrink. But I am going to try something else. And if you think I've talked crazy so far, you haven't heard anything yet. Believe me, it sounds insane to me too, and I'm not sure I can explain it well, but here it goes. I've seen, detectives, the inside of who I am; as a person, as a human. I've literally seen my priorities. I've stood inside my own heart." Connor looked at both of them for a reaction and got none, so he went on.

"My priorities—things I hold dear; my desires—things I want to achieve or accomplish. Some of those things are ugly; they're ugly and selfish and all about me, me, me. Well, I've tried to do things on my own and I've failed. Miserably. And worse than that, my decisions have rippled into tsunamis that have demolished other families. And it's because I want control. And that, detectives, is what I have to give up. I've searched my heart, and the only god that

181

lives there is me. I have to change that…I need the real thing. That's my only answer."

Suarez stood up and looked out the window. Presley stayed seated, still staring at the fake tile flooring.

"I sound crazy, right?" Connor asked. "Don't answer that, it doesn't really matter. I deserve whatever is coming my way. I asked God to take care of Kelly, he did. I asked him to show me mercy; and for some reason he did. What do I have to complain about? Crazy or not, my perspective has changed. The only question is: what happens to me now?"

Presley stood up and joined Suarez by the window. "Now," he said, "you'll go on trial. It'll probably start in a month or two, might finish up a few months after that. Usually high profile cases like this get pushed through the system quicker than others. That's your good news."

"And the bad?"

"The bad is this: you're probably looking at Murder One, maybe Manslaughter if you're lucky, plus the attempted murder of your wife. I'm not sure about any charges in regards to Annika Mims. I can't think of any laws that you technically broke. But that's for your attorney to figure out. What I'm saying is this…you're looking at a good bit of jail time."

Connor considered that for a moment. "I deserve jail time."

"Well then I'm glad we're on the same page."

Presley walked to the side of Connor's bed and without saying a word, unlocked the cuffs and small chain around his bed frame. Connor sat up and rubbed the sore spots on his wrists. "Thanks."

"Don't mention it. Just don't tell my captain. He'll be here in a few hours. I'll put them back on you later. Until then, Suarez and I will make ourselves at home."

"Detective?"

"Yes?"

"My wife…how is she? She's in this hospital somewhere. I know it. Do you think, if at all possible, I could see her?"

"How do you know she's here?"

"This is where I left her bleeding and dying on that awful night. Then I called here every few days to check on her."

"Connor, why do you think you didn't kill your wife?" Presley asked. "In every other situation, reality followed through with your thoughts exactly. But in this one, it seems you subconsciously wanted her out of the way...dead, but somehow you didn't harm her enough to kill her?"

Connor shut his eyes as Presley finished his question. He'd thought about that same thing a hundred times; each time, he faced the same conclusion. "I think somehow her love for me overshadowed the filthiness of my own desires. When I attacked her, her love fought back. Her love was strong enough for the both of us; that's what saved her, and in turn...me."

Presley stood by the doorway and leaned against a wall, "Look, I would love to let you see her, but you know I can't do that. Not now. She's going to need lawyers, you're going to need lawyers, and if justice is going to be done then we have to follow protocol. Allowing you to see her now would get all three of us thrown in the slammer, and even though I feel different about you now than I did six months ago, I don't want to be your cellmate."

"I understand," Connor said as he looked out the window from his bed, "Could you at least give her a message for me?"

Presley walked from the doorway over to the window and sat in a chair in the corner. "I'm officially telling you that I cannot pass along any messages from you to your wife. However," he said as he looked Connor in the eyes, "what would you say to her if she were here now?"

"I'd tell her that I love her, that I'm sorry, and that I'm a changed man whether she can find it in her heart to forgive me or not. I'd beg her to love me back; I'd thank her for saving my life."

"Is that it?"

"No, I'd tell her that she's the only woman that I ever want to be with. I'd make her believe me. I'm an ugly man on the inside. Parts of that are gone, but I'm more committed now to fixing the parts that aren't than I've ever been before. She needs to know that, detective."

Presley moved away from the window, whispered something to Suarez, and then moved to the door leading out into the hallway.

"Where you going?" Connor asked.

"I need to check on some other patients," Pres said with a wink.

28

"Ladies and gentlemen of the jury, have you reached a verdict?"

"We have your honor. We, the jury, on the charges of voluntary manslaughter, find the defendant, Connor Wesley Bryce..."

Connor was beside himself. The last eight months were just as much a blur as his six months on the run before that. He hadn't been allowed to lay eyes on Kelly until the first day of his trial a few weeks earlier. He remembered when she'd first walked into the courtroom. Time seemed to stop. His heart exploded inside his chest as he'd resisted every urge and temptation to run and scoop her up in his arms. Instead he just looked at her...for something, anything...desperate for some sign of emotions from her eyes. Then they'd met—hers and his. She looked...joyful? No, that couldn't be it. But it was. She looked peaceful; her eyes looked happy. If anyone's eyes could actually smile, Kelly's could.

But why did they glow? Was she happy to see him? Surely not. Was she glad the trial was underway so that her murdering, adulterous husband could finally pay for his heinous crimes? Probably. They still could not speak to each other. Connor wasn't sure if they ever would. Even still, he'd refused to complain. He was joyful that God had answered his prayers months ago. Kelly was alive. That's all that mattered. She didn't deserve him anyway; she deserved better. And heaven knows that he didn't deserve her, but worse.

Connor remembered staring as another pair walked in the courtroom—John and Annika Mims. She was very pregnant now and looked to be due at any moment. And the child was his. Immediately Connor looked to the ground as shame and humiliation slithered through his chest and across his face. He'd refuse to make eye contact with either of them. In fact, he refused sight all together as he shut his eyes and put his head in his hands. Had he asked for and been handed forgiveness for his sin? Yes. But he still struggled with forgiving himself, as most people do. He'd ruined lives; some possibly could be healed, others never would. What would Annika tell her child about his or her father? The truth? God, he hoped not.

And John—how in the world John didn't leap over tables and chairs to strangle Connor, he'd never know. But he didn't. He'd walked hand-in-hand with his wife, ready for the truth to come out at trial. And what did the Mims hope to get out of the proceedings? Did they wish the death penalty on their old friend? Were they there to demand child support for the next eighteen years?

Still in his memory, Connor remembered seeing another odd couple walk through the courtroom doors: Detective Presley and Detective Suarez. Both men looked a little more rested than when Connor first saw them after they'd shocked his heart back to life months earlier. No doubt they were happy this case would be wrapping up one way or another. It took its toll on everyone, yes, but specifically the two badges. And what outcome had they wished for him?

In fact, what did Connor want his own verdict to be? He had shocked the world when, against the counsel of his lawyers, he entered a plea of guilty on all charges. But, as he'd explained, he *was* guilty on all charges, everything that had happened—happened because of him. Why lie and say "not guilty?"

It was widely known building up to the trial that this was a set of circumstances never before seen in any murder case. In fact, there seemed to be mitigating circumstances oozing out of each piece of evidence and every testimony of witnesses. Concrete evidence linked Connor to the murder and attempted murder scenes, yet witnesses—primarily Kelly Bryce—knew the physical location of her husband in both circumstances.

In the case of Gregory Jansen, she knew beyond a shadow of a doubt that her husband Connor Bryce was with her the entire night. In the case of her own attempted murder, she knew that Connor had not physically stabbed her with a knife. He was responsible for the wounds, yes, but he hadn't literally stabbed her. Did those facts make a difference? Who knew? But they seemed important enough to share. Even Kelly's polygraph test was entered into evidence, and the results backed up what she had been adamantly saying for months; that her husband was with her both times, and neither time had he literally committed any crimes.

Wow…what a cluster.

The prosecution new that Murder One charges would never stick, nor would Attempted Murder. So they decided to charge Connor Bryce with Voluntary Manslaughter, a charge that carried less weight than murder. Connor disagreed with the watered-down charge . He'd murdered someone—he wanted to be held accountable for that murder. But unlike his own defense team, the prosecution did not have to listen to his wishes; it was their job to press charges against him that they felt they could win. So Voluntary Manslaughter it was.

Yet nothing shocked Connor as much as the witness that his defense team called on one of the last days of the trial—Mrs. Eleanor Jansen, his boss's wife. In reality, it was fine by him. Let her testify; let her sadness show to every man and woman of the jury. Let her tears fall as she talked about the wretched man that killed her husband. Connor didn't care; he'd actually preferred it. Again, he wanted full judgment for his crimes.

But if that was the intention, to bury Connor with the testimony of a grieving widow, why had his defense called her to testify and not the prosecution? Immediately he was curious. She climbed the stand, swore her oath, and the questions and answers had begun. She'd explained that she remembered nothing about the night her husband had died. She'd recalled her emotions when her poor husband was removed from his home in a body bag, then laid to rest a few days later.

Connor had worked for her husband for years, and she knew him very well. Company outings, award dinners, Christmas parties— Connor had always been very nice and cordial with her. She testified that her husband Gregory spoke highly of Connor. One time she even recalled her husband expressing interest in Connor taking over the company upon his retirement. Mrs. Jansen, through her husband's own praise for his young employee, thought the world of Connor Bryce.

Then she'd found out Connor was the leading suspect in her husband's death. Eleanor told of the anguish and emptiness she'd felt. She couldn't believe it; wouldn't believe it. And though evidence such as the shoe and fingerprints of Connor Bryce were found at her home, she still felt uneasy about casting a stone his direction. She kept repeating the same phrase over and over again throughout the trial, "There's no way that Connor Bryce killed my husband."

"I'm sorry, Mrs. Jansen," Connor said from his chair behind his table, "but I did. I was furious at him, and for one night at least, I hated him. I wished him dead. I'm so sorry, that's shallow I know, but it's all I can say."

The courtroom had erupted in chatter. The judged pounded his hammer and shouted for order. The defense lawyers hung their heads in defeat. They'd made an obvious decision to not put Connor on the stand and allow him to testify—for that very reason.

Mrs. Jansen left the stand in tears. Connor was reprimanded and warned to keep his mouth shut unless he wanted to spend the night in solitary confinement. Confinement didn't bother him, Connor thought to himself, he'd been though worse recently.

Finally the testimonies were over. Every face in the room held a look of confusion and mystery. The faces of the jurors looked exhausted. They'd spent six hours in deliberation, obviously lost in the complexities of this most unusual case. Then Connor and his team of lawyers were summoned back to the courtroom. It was time.

"Ladies and gentlemen of the jury, have you reached a verdict?"

"We have your honor. We, the jury, on the charges of Voluntary Manslaughter, find the defendant, Connor Wesley Bryce..." her voice was nervous as the piece of paper in her hand shook, "guilty as charged."

The courtroom erupted again as the verdict sank in. Connor didn't feel...anything. No surprise, no frustration, and sadly, no relief. He was numb. Kelly sat by the Mims; all three immediately hung their heads and closed their eyes. This was not the way things were supposed to work out. Connor was supposed to be innocent, reunite with Kelly, and live happily ever after. John and Annika were supposed to tell their child that his/her real father was not a killer, had never been in jail, and was simply a very confused individual. Those were now dreams...they'd always been dreams.

Neither Presley nor Suarez said a word. Instead they simply looked at each other and shook their heads. What had they truly expected? A hung jury? An innocent verdict? If there was anything Connor Bryce was, it wasn't innocent. But what would his punishment be? How long would jail be his home?

As the murmur in the courtroom settled down, the judge announced that sentencing would take place in one week. He thanks the ladies and gentlemen of the jury for their time, banged his gavel, stood and walked out. Just like that, one of the most intriguing and perplexing cases of the last century was over. Connor Bryce, guilty of manslaughter, would have to wait one week for his sentence.

* * *

It was raining outside. Storming. Connor sat in the backseat of the police car as he rode to the courthouse. Today was the day he'd find out his punishment. Fifteen years...twenty years...more? He tried not to think of the things he would miss over the next two decades: his son's graduation, his wedding; Kelly's smile, her mere presence. Those thoughts alone were punishment enough, though he doubted the judge would see it that way.

The courtroom was full again. Connor had been on television more in the last few months than most athletes are throughout the course of their careers. But soon, once those metals bars lock closed around him, the world will move onto someone else, another media attraction.

Connor recognized some of the same faces. Kelly was there, of course, her face as beautiful as ever. They still had not been allowed to speak, although Connor's lawyers told him they could have a few moments after the sentence was read. Detectives Presley and Suarez sat in the back, both soaked to the bone from the downpour outside. Mrs. Jansen was sitting one row in front of them, looking neither sad nor mad, but sympathetic. There was still someone missing…the Mims.

And just like that, the doors in the back of the courthouse opened up and in walked John and Annika Mims. And a baby. She must have given birth in Baltimore.

Annika held a small human tightly to her chest as she swayed it gently back and forth while walking beside her husband. Connor blinked his eyes as he suddenly felt lightheaded. This was his child, a child that he had made; a child that didn't belong to him, yet *was* his; a child that would never know its true father.

Connor's lawyer leaned over and whispered in his ear, "I'm so sorry, I forgot to tell you. I just got the call myself a few minutes ago. Annika had her baby a week ago today, right after trial let out last week. The judge called me and told me she'd be coming today, there's really no legal reason to keep her out. I'm sure this must be difficult. I wonder wha…"

Connor blocked out everything else the lawyer had to say; it wasn't important. His child, his flesh and blood, his baby, was there. Yet simply by being there, by the child's own existence, it reminded Connor of his awful sins of lust and selfishness. He watched John and Annika as they took their seats a few rows behind Kelly. John's face was beaming as he stared intently on the face of his little child. In truth, that's who the child belonged to…its rightful father was John. John was the one that loved it, that loved its mother Annika; that would provide and keep it safe for the entirety of its life.

Was it a boy or a girl, Connor wondered as his thoughts kept referring to it as…*it?* What was its name? Did it favor him or Annika or neither? Did it have hair? If so, what color? How much did it weigh at birth, what color eyes did it have? The excitement of a newborn was unlike any other experience. And no couple deserved it more than John and Annika. Their faces shone with joy in the miracle they were holding. And that's exactly what it was, Connor realized. Instead of looking at the child and being reminded of his sinful past, he should look at the child as a miracle from God. It was an awkward thought, no doubt. And yes... the circumstances surrounding the child were non-traditional by every definition, but miracles have no tradition. They just are.

The Mims were happy. Kelly was alive. His son Sammy was unharmed and would have a full and fruitful future—life was good for Connor Bryce. Then the side door opened and the judge walked out. Immediately a knot formed in Connor's stomach. He wanted justice, but he was still nervous. The judge held the attention of the entire court as he sat behind his throne.

Connor's lawyer looked at him and nodded. Connor stood up, feeling suddenly vulnerable and naked. His mouth was dry as a bone.

"Mr. Bryce," the judge said, "you have been found guilty of Voluntary Manslaughter. Today the court will decide your sentence. Before I make my ruling, do you have anything you would like to say to the court?"

His voice was incapable of sound. Frantically he cleared his throat and took a sip of water. "Yes...yes, your honor. I do."

Connor turned and looked at Mrs. Jansen. "Ma'am, I have nothing to say to you that will ease your pain. My actions are inexcusable. I ask that somehow, you find it in your heart to forgive me. If you cannot, I understand that too. Please know that I never meant for things to be like this. I'm truly and utterly sorry."

Connor took another sip of water, then turned his attention to John and Annika Mims. "John, you have every right to hate me. This goes without saying, but I need to say it anyway. You are ten times the man that I will ever be, and I have no doubt you will be the best father your child could ever ask for." A tear fell down John's cheek as Connor continued. "It's hard for me to find the words to express my sorrow and remorse for my thoughts toward you and your wife. You both took me in and treated me as part of your family, and I betrayed that trust. I can't apologize enough. Will you allow me to speak a few words to your wife?"

John nodded his head as he wiped his eyes.

"Annika, I'm a weak, weak man. I think the world of you and John, and I wish nothing but the best for the both of you. I deeply apologize from the bottom of my heart. My heart…Annika, my heart is dirty and black. I'm trying to clean that up, but it will take some time. I don't know how to explain to you what happened other than saying this. That child you're holding, regardless of how it happened, is a miracle from God. I don't know if you believe that or not, but it's true. That doesn't mean my thoughts were acceptable or justified, I promise you they were not. But if there's anything I've learned, it's that God can take a bad situation and make it good, he can bring peace out of a storm. He's in the process of doing that to me. I hope you'll allow him to do that to you." Annika began to weep.

He moved his attention to the back row. "Detectives, you put up a good chase. Thanks for staying on my tail and never giving up. Your persistence has saved more lives than you know. I'm sorry for your exhausting days and sleepless nights. I hope you can forgive me. And lastly, thanks for finding me in that river."

Connor took three large gulps of water as he turned his body to the work of art sitting on the front row directly across from him. Kelly already had tears and snot running helplessly down her face. She'd been crying from the beginning.

"I remember our wedding day. I stood at the front of the church with my hands clasped in front of me. The back doors swung open and out you stepped. Your white dress, your face, your smile. My world was over; I was dead. You owned every part of me from that moment on. Kelly, my flower. Shakespeare doesn't have the words to describe what you mean to me. I have no explanation as to why I ran. I ran because I was scared; not of the police, not of jail…I was scared of myself. Then I got lost…so lost, Kelly. Lost without you…lost inside myself. I hurt one person after the other. I couldn't be stopped. I was drowning and suffocating at the same time. That doesn't make sense, I'm sure, yet that's how I felt. But Kelly, if you don't believe anything else I say, please believe this. I will never stop loving you. My actions…my thoughts in the past, I can't take those back. But I also refuse to let my future be a slave to the mistakes of my past. I want you in my future. Now, always, and forever. I love you and always will."

It took everything in his will power to break off eye contact with his wife. But Connor wasn't done; he had one more person to talk to. The judge.

Connor took a deep breath. "Your honor, thank you for allowing me a few minutes of the court's time. I stand here before you a guilty man. There's no doubt in my mind about that. I deserve whatever sentence you give me. Justice must be served and I must be held responsible for my actions. I deserve a lot of things, and mercy is not one of them. I prayed for mercy once, from another Judge, and for some reason, I received it. I won't ask it of you. I'm guilty of a thousand things...I'm guilty of a selfish heart. I've hurt countless people; my decisions were costly. I've committed a lot of evil, and if I've done any good whatsoever, I can't find it. Thank you for listening to me, and I accept your decision."

With that, Connor sat down.

The only noises in the room were the heartbeats of a hundred people. The judge sat back in his chair, took his glasses off, rubbed his temples with his fingers, and then put his glasses back on. He looked around the courtroom, then directly at Connor.

"Connor Bryce, please stand." Connor stood.

"You are guilty sir. Both in your own eyes, and the eyes of the jury of the state of Maryland. That much we agree on. Your case, your actions, your decisions, I've never quite seen anything like it, and I'm not sure how everything worked out the way it did. You yourself claim your guilt in the crimes, yet apparently you physically had no part in them. Evidence links you to the scene that can't possibly be true. Yet you remain adamant about your involvement. Again, your guilt has already been established; it's my job to sentence you based on the law. But I find myself in a predicament. I can't very well sentence you to the full extent allowed by the law. In my opinion, I would not be doing justice to you, myself, or the court. I also don't want to give you a slap on the wrist. I must be cautious. How am I to know that your history won't repeat itself? You seem like a changed man, but if I had a nickel for every time a man stood in front of me claiming he'd found religion, I'd be richer than I am today. Yet this seems different. You, sir, seem different. Therefore, I sentence you, Connor Wesley Bryce, to no less than three and a half and no more than eight years in federal prison. Based on your behavior, you will have the opportunity for parole at a date to be determined in three and a half years. Your length of time, sir, is up to you. I wish you the best."

The gavel struck hard as the sound of wood echoed off the walls.

The courtroom began its mumbles and whispers as Connor sat, dissecting his sentence. Three and half years...eight years. Both seemed like an eternity, yet one was leaps and bounds shorter than the other. There was no way around it—the judge had been lenient in his ruling. Connor knew that—considering what he'd done—mercy had been extended yet again. He could possibly be a free man in three and half years. He had accepted his sentence; his judgment. He'd accepted mercy. Did he deserve it? No. Did everyone that admitted their guilt get shown mercy? No. Not in the world's justice system anyway. Yet Connor had found mercy in two places, both inwardly and outwardly. Mercy from two judges. Relief washed over him. He wouldn't spend the rest of his life in prison.

The courtroom cleared, leaving Connor and his lawyers in the empty room. They were busy describing the sentence as a victory when a police officer walked up and, as Connor stood, cuffed his hands behind his back. "There's one thing left for you to do before they take you away," Connor's lawyer said. "Your wife…I talked to the judge before your sentence. He agreed to let you see her for a few minutes, with police in the room of course, but it was the best I could do. I suggest you take advantage."

"Thank you…for everything," Connor said.

"Don't mention it," his lawyer said as he gave a firm handshake. "I'll see you soon; hopefully as a free man in a few years."

"Count on it."

The police officer led Connor out of the main courtroom through a side door, down a small hallway, and then opened the door into another small room. Connor walked in and saw Kelly. His heart beat so hard he could feel it in his temples. He didn't know what to say. He had absolutely no idea what her feelings were toward him right now. It could be anything from love to hate, from revenge to redemption. She could be giving him divorce papers to sign before the cops took him away. The thought broke his heart.

"Hey you," he said as he smiled through tears.

Kelly Bryce raced toward him, threw her arms around his shoulders, buried her head in his neck, and sobbed uncontrollably. "I love you," she whispered.

29

Four Years Later

The boxes tumbled down all around them. John Mims found himself tangled up in sheets like a mummy. A scream came from the bottom of the pile; then a hysterical laugh. Annika came running in from another room.

"John, what happened?"

"Our fort came down," he said as he scooped up a body from the floor.

"Is Wes alright?"

"Of course he is; kid's tough as nails, but I know his weak spots," John said as he raked his fingers back and forth over the little boy's ribs.

Little Wes squirmed back and forth as he tried to work his way out of his father's grasp. "No daddy," he squealed in between laughs. John put down his son who quickly scurried back to the collapsed fort. The boy had grown like a weed since the day he was born. Since then, John and Annika both spent most of their time at home. They were both incredibly fortunate that their careers allowed such a privilege.

And the name: Wesley—Connor's middle name. Odd? Perhaps. But then, the story behind the life of their little blessing was also odd. In fact, it was John's idea to name his son Wesley. He'd approached Annika with the idea a few days before she'd gone into labor. They'd been toying around with baby names of both sexes for the last few months, and finally at Connor's trial, it came to him. Wesley Mims. Annika had had her reservations at first, for obvious reasons. "Do we want to name our son after a man like Connor? Why don't we name him John, after you?"

John knew what her reaction would be, but explained his thinking anyway. "Connor, regardless of his past mistakes, was, is, and always will be a huge part of our lives. We can't act as if he never existed; I wouldn't want to if I could. If there's anything we learned from Connor's story, it's that we are all responsible for what lies in our hearts, not just the actions we perform. One thing is as important, if not more, than the other. Connor admitted his guilt like a man, asked for our forgiveness, and will serve jail time for his crimes. I can't say he and I are that different. I can't say he and *anybody* are that different. I forgive him. I'm our child's father, that will never change, but if it weren't for Connor we wouldn't be having a child. If you truly don't like the name Wesley, we won't use it. Just think about it."

Annika had thought about it, and it grew on her. Then when she'd finally given birth and was told it was a boy, she knew his name was Wesley. That was four years ago.

193

Now the little one was a hundred miles an hour nonstop. Forts, trucks, cowboys, tire ropes, and scrapped knees. All boy.

"When will they be here?" John asked his bride.

"Anytime. I was hoping you'd have this room cleaned up for our guests."

"And disrupt fort time? If we leave our flanks unguarded then we leave ourselves open to attack. Now, you're either with us or with the enemy," John said as he held a Nerf gun to her stomach, "maybe we should just take you hostage now?" he said with a smile. "What do you say Wes?"

"Jail her, daddy," came the voice from deep within the fort.

"Can't argue with that," John said.

Annika smiled and dropped to her knees to crawl inside the tangled mess of sheets and boxes. Soon, the doorbell rang. "It's them," she said as she squirmed back into reality.

Why was she so nervous? Easy. Connor Bryce had just been paroled from prison; three and half years for good behavior. Kelly and Annika had kept in touch over the years, and Annika was happy to learn that there had been no further episodes involving Connor with crimes involving his heart or mind or whatever. She still didn't fully understand his condition. Regardless, when Annika had learned that Connor would be released, she and John thought it would be a good idea to invite the Bryce's to Phoenix for a few days. Souls were still in the process of mending, but the time together—without the circus— would be cleansing. At least they'd hoped.

Annika walked to the front door as John and Wes made their way out of the fort. After one deep breath, Annika opened the door.

Connor Bryce.

"Mrs. Mims, how do you do?" were Connor's first words.

"Good sir, and you?" she said as she extended her hand.

"Better than I've ever been," he said with a smile. He looked better, that much was true. The tired face, the ragged eyes, the disheveled hair...it was all gone. He looked healthier than the Connor she remembered years ago. A little grayer, a few more wrinkles, but still healthier. Kelly came right behind and immediately gave Annika a hug. "Annika, I can't tell you how good it is to see you. Thank you so much for inviting us down here. Really. I don't know what to say. You and John, your hospitality...it's just so thoughtful."

"No, no problem at all," Annika said as she returned the hug. "We have a lot to catch up on. And this must be Sammy?" she said as she shook the hand of the man standing behind Kelly.

"Yes ma'am," he said as he shook Annika's hand. "Pleasure to meet you."

"Is it Sammy or Sam?"

"Sam please," he said politely.

"Well please, come in, come in, make yourselves at home. My two boys are running around playing fort. They'll be here shortly."

"We're not playing fort," said John from down the hallway, "we're protecting our queen," he said with a smile. John hugged Kelly and shook Sam's hand; then he saw, standing in the back of the pack, Connor.

John walked over to him, smiled, and shook his hand. "Connor, good to see you, I mean that." Connor hugged John and opened his mouth to speak, but John cut him off. "Would you walk with me please?"

Connor nodded. He was already anxious enough about seeing John and Annika again. How could you look someone in the eye after doing the things he'd done to them? How could they even stand his presence? Connor was changed, yes, but that didn't mean he deserved a second chance.

The two men walked silently down a hallway, through a pair of double doors, and then onto the porch by the swimming pool. The backyard brought a thousand memories back into Connor's mind. The last time he was here, he'd danced with Annika at John's birthday party as his mind spun from her intoxicating allure. He shook the thoughts out of his head. Those thoughts weren't important anymore, they had no control over him; but it was still weird being in the backyard.

Connor, anxious from the silence, began to speak, "John...I'm so..."

John held up his hand. "Don't. No need to. That's not why I called you out here. You've apologized a million times. You've been alone with your thoughts for years in prison. You've worked out your problems and, from what I hear, have changed your thinking. No, there's no need to apologize. I forgive you...did a long time ago. All I wanted to say to you is this. Thank you. Thank you for your honesty, your openness, and for your leadership. You have a family to lead now...to lead differently than the way you've lead them before. I'm still trying to figure out how to lead mine, but I know this much...I can't do it by myself. My decisions aren't always the best, and my selfishness gets in the way. And I never would have known that if it hadn't been for you. I don't care about the circumstances that brought our paths together. This plan we're in the middle of…it's bigger than us. You showed me that. Please know that you're forgiven, by me and by God. Now I'm going to need help from both of you as Annika and I raise this boy. I want you to be willing to help me."

Connor shook John's extended hand, "Of course I'm willing to help. But only if you help me in return. Keep me accountable."

"You know I will," John said, "or I'll punch you in the face again," he said as he mimicked a half punch toward Connor's nose.

"Yeah that was a good one, I can still feel it," Connor said, touching the bridge of his nose. "What's that incredible smell?"

"That would be dinner, I think it's ready," John said as he looked at Connor, "We good?"

"We're good," Connor said. "By the way, I'm truly humbled that you named your son Wesley; Kelly told me. I'm glad things have worked out for you two. You're the greatest couple I've ever met. And now, the greatest family I've ever met. I don't know how you do it."

"I'm blessed," John said, "but so are you. Look at the two of us: we both have great wives, two beautiful sons, and two great jobs."

"How'd you know about that?" Connor asked.

"Kelly told Annika, Annika told me. There's nothing better than starting your own company, and with your brain, as imaginative as it is…" John smiled, "there's no stopping your success."

"I hope you're right."

"Of course I'm right. I'm also hungry," John said with a slap on the back.

The two men walked inside to a table full of food.

The rest of the party was already seated. Dinner was served and laughs were shared. Sitting back during dessert, Kelly asked, "So, what are our plans for the weekend?"

John and Annika looked at each other. "Well," Annika said, "the Diamondbacks are in town, we thought we might go to a game?"

Connor looked up from his pecan pie and without missing a beat said, "That sounds like fun; I've always been a huge fan."

Anyone who hates a brother or sister is a murderer, and you know that no murderer has eternal life residing in him.

1 John 3:15

Each person is tempted when they are dragged away by their own evil desire and enticed. Then, after desire has conceived, it gives birth to sin; and sin, when it is full-grown, gives birth to death.

James 1:14

"You have heard that it was said, 'You shall not commit adultery.' But I tell you that anyone who looks at a woman lustfully has already committed adultery with her in his heart."- Jesus

Matthew 5:27-28